Praise for

THE PEOPLE OF PAPER

A *Los Angeles Times* Bestseller
A *Los Angeles Times* Favorite Book of 2005
A *San Francisco Chronicle* Best Book of 2005

"Salvador Plascencia weaves together the daily life details of this world and the big ideas surrounding them to a stirring end effect. *The People of Paper* is a terrifically original debut."
—Aimee Bender

"García Márquez and Calvino might come to mind upon reading *The People of Paper,* but that's not the half of it. Add the beatific mundanity of life in Ben Katchor's comic strip *Julius Knipl, Real Estate Photographer,* pile on the dispassionate presentation of fantastic circumstances in Cabeza de Vaca's 16th-century travel diaries, and toss in the Museum of Jurassic Technology's cat-and-mouse game with truth—imagine all that and you're almost there." —*Minneapolis Star Tribune*

"An anarchic literary feat, Plascencia's debut is a wild evocation of the powers of writing, one sure to give readers new respect for the fragile and dangerous uses of paper."
—*Time Out New York*

"In this debut, Salvador Plascencia artfully constructs a mythical present, populated by infant prognosticators, mechanical tortoises, disintegrating villages, saints forgoing canonization in favor of *lucha libre,* and yes, people made of paper. . . . Plascencia articulates his characters' longing with such acute detail that it is impossible not to speculate how much of their sorrow might be his own. This conjecture doesn't last long before the author exposes the beams of his story and renders the novel self-conscious in a manner reminiscent of Calvino or Pirandello."

—*The Austin Chronicle*

"[The publishers] should have equipped [*The People of Paper*] with warning signs and seatbelts to protect those of us naive enough to get caught up in the fairy tale first pages, those of us who ignored for a moment that this is a book for mature adults, people with scars, people who should not expect a book about a childproof world. They might have dropped a few more hints, might have whispered: 'This book will lock you in a shed of tears.' They should have said the truth: This book is sublime."

—*The Mumpsimus*

"The author of this book is acclaimed, as he should be, as a new Latino voice. Born in Mexico, he immigrated to California, graduated from Whittier College and holds an MFA from Syracuse University. Being heir to the American dream, he has adopted a dreamy style of writing reminiscent of Borges and [García] Márquez."

—Curledup.com

"Moving . . . A mischievous mix of García Márquez magical realism and *Tristram Shandy* typographical tricks . . . Plascencia's virtuosic first novel is explosively unreal, but bares human truths with devastating accuracy."—*Publishers Weekly* (starred review)

●

THE PEOPLE OF PAPER

THE PEOPLE OF PAPER

by
SALVADOR PLASCENCIA

A Harvest Book • Harcourt, Inc.

Orlando   Austin   New York   San Diego   Toronto   London

Requests for permission to make copies of any part of the work should be submitted online
at www.harcourt.com/contact or mailed to the following address: Permissions Department,
Harcourt, Inc., 6277 Sea Harbor Drive, Orlando, Florida 32887-6777.

www.HarcourtBooks.com

Interior illustrations by Sarah Tillman.

First published by McSweeney's Books in 2005.

Library of Congress Cataloging-in-Publication Data
Plascencia, Salvador, 1976–
The people of paper/Salvador Plascencia.—1st Harvest ed.
    p.   cm.—(A Harvest book)
1. Lovesickness—Fiction.   2. Loss (Psychology)—Fiction.   3. Psychological fiction.
4. Experimental fiction.   I. Title.
PS3616.L37P46   2006
813'.54—dc22   2006015098
ISBN-13: 978-0-15-603211-7   ISBN-10: 0-15-603211-2

Text set in Garamond Three

Printed in the United States of America
First Harvest edition 2006
A C E G I K J H F D B

Para mi papa, mama, y hermana.

And to Liz, who taught me that we are all of paper.

TABLE OF CONTENTS

PROLOGUE   ●

CHAPTER   PART ONE

1   I I I
2   ●
3   ●●●
4   I I I
5   ●
6   ●●●
7   I I I

CHAPTER   PART TWO

8   ●
9   ●●●
10   I I
11   ●●●
12   ●
13   ●
14   ●

CHAPTER   PART THREE

15   I I I
16   ●●●
17   ●
18   ●
19   ●
20   I I I
21   ●
22   ●●●
23   ●
24   I I I
25   ●●●
26   ●
27   I I I

PROLOGUE

•

She was made after the time of ribs and mud. By papal decree there were to be no more people born of the ground or from the marrow of bones. All would be created from the propulsions and mounts performed underneath bedsheets—rare exception granted for immaculate conceptions. The mixing pits were sledged and the cutting tables, where ribs were extracted from pigs and goats, were sawed in half. Although the monks were devout and obedient to the thunder of Rome, the wool of their robes was soaked not only by the salt of sweat but also by that of tears. The monks rolled down their heavy sleeves, hid their slaughter knives in the burlap of their scrips, and wiped the hoes clean. They closed the factory down, chained the doors with Vatican-crested locks, and marched off in holy formation. Three lines, their faces staring down in humility, closing their eyes when walking over puddles, avoiding their unshaven reflections.

The march was to proceed until the monks forgot the location of the factory—an impossible task for a tribe that had been trained to memorize not only scripture but also the subtle curvature of every cathedral archway they encountered. And so they walked south to the Argentine land of fire and back north to the glacial cliffs of Alaska, cataloging birds and wingspans. The monks lifted the penguins' flippers and stretched measuring tape, silently reciting the data, trying to displace the coordinates of the abandoned factory. After scribbling the figures onto their scrolled parchment, they rejoined their marching formation and counted off in their assigned order, skipping the fifty-third number, an unaccounted monk who had been lost miles before in the desert's basin.

And though she was born inside the factory, she was not a daughter of monks. She had been created without Vatican sanction by a man whose hands were ravaged by paper cuts. His name was Antonio, and like all stories of creators who bring life from the dead, his story began with a struggling butcher, who chased a gray cat, caught it, took off its studded collar, and slit its throat. The fur and organs were scraped from the cutting board into the trash bin and the warm meat was placed in the refrigerated display case with a skewer and flag that read "FELINE 3.15/LB."

Antonio was only a boy, still wearing his grammar school uniform, when he saw his Figgaro split open and naked. At the counter, without crying, he pulled six bills from his pockets and ordered three pounds of feline.

Antonio received Figgaro wrapped in the white of butcher paper, and while there was sadness and the urge to change from his grammar school uniform to one of mourning, he resisted, instead walking to the stationery shop, buying the Sunday edition and a roll of hand-pressed construction paper.

Locked in his room for three days, he folded and tore away at the paper. On the second day and after thirty-three paper cuts, all minor except for one that cut deep into the meat of his hands, there were thirteen perfect origami organs and ropes of wound capillaries and veins made from tissue paper.

When he unwrapped Figgaro from the butcher paper, there was still warmth in the cat's body, despite the gutting and the hours of refrigeration. The paper heart went in first, followed by the main veins and then the smaller capillaries. Antonio connected liver and lungs, the stomach and newsprint digestive tract, patching the belly with college-ruled sheets, and before the last layer of crumpled paper could be flattened Figgaro was playing with his tail.

It was through this experience with the marvels of paper and his pet cat that Antonio discovered his calling. After five years of medical school and lab experiments with series of radial pleats and reversed folds, Antonio became the first origami surgeon. Medical journals tried to discredit the merits of paper: they said the velocity of the circulating blood would punch holes through the compressed wood pulp, supporting their claims with hand-drawn charts of exploding hearts. But Antonio's hearts never leaked or burst, and as a tribute to his doubters, he shaped the cardiovascular walls using the index pages of the journals. His only failure was a liver that broke down into cellulose fibers, after which microscopic chunks of paper were found in the blood stream of a San Isidro woman. But she drank so much Irish whisky it was a wonder she had even lived past menopause.

But it was not his detractors that ended his career as an origami surgeon. Antonio's medical art was made obsolete by the innovations of Swedes. Bioengineering replaced paper and forced Antonio's scarred knuckles and hands into retirement. He bought a folding table and moved from streetcorner to streetcorner, laying out his paper hearts and kidneys and yards of capillaries. Falling from the prestige and sterility of a surgeon to the dust and anonymity of a street vendor, Antonio found no one wanted paper organs anymore. So he unfolded the hearts into turtles and the kidneys into swans, and he tied the braided capillaries around the necks of the tiny paper animals like leashes. And soon a crowd like the one that gathered around the wicker basket of corn and tequesquite bread began to encircle Antonio's table.

The crowd shouted the names of animals and Antonio folded on cue; they loved the creatures he created. Even men who carried sickles and whose hands and souls were worn and splintered, men who were callous not only to the feel of silk but also to the beauty of landscapes because all they ever saw was terrain and toil—even they, after sliding their sickles into their belt loops, pulled at the tails of paper swans and watched the flapping wings.

And impatient lawyers and city clerks, who had never in their lives felt the grip of a hoe or sickle, but had tasted the silver of salad forks and steak knives, waited behind women and grandchildren to witness Antonio's foldings. These men, who admired the precision of paper beaks and the excellent architecture of the Pegasus's wings, had forgotten that they themselves had once laid on Antonio's operating table and that their own hearts had been replaced by paper.

It was in these times that Antonio's fame approached that of other great craftsmen: Senillo the rope weaver and the late Señor Casique, whose ladders had long ago stopped being used for climbing and now adorned the inside of the Guadalajara cathedral. Yet despite the respect and celebrity that origami animals brought, Antonio suddenly abandoned what had become a coveted vending post, leaving behind the folding table and two neat rows of animals. He retired his sideshow of paper animals and went in search of a nobler purpose, looking for the factory.

When it was obvious that Antonio would not return to his post, his origami was appraised by the clergy, and those who felt a debt in their conscience offered the folded paper as penance. The swans and unicorns began appearing along with the Eucharist on altar shelves.

Even later, when Antonio defied papal authority and trespassed on what was classified Vatican property, the church held that his origami creations were commissioned by the hand of God and fit within the guidelines of sacred art described in the strictures of Vatican II. And though Antonio's excommunication papers were filed, the figurines were allowed to remain on the altars.

Antonio followed church rumors that had passed from cardinals to priests and then down to rectory altar boys. He visited every one of the cities they mentioned, asking for the whereabouts of the factory.

Those who did not ignore him simply shrugged or pointed to a skyline of smokestacks. Had it not been for a disgruntled monk who spoke defiantly against a life of constant walking and bird-watching, Antonio would never have come upon the doors of the factory. The monk handed Antonio a scrap of parchment. Written on it were caliper measurements and detailed illustrations of feathers, ordinary details found in any field guide, but the underside of the paper revealed the never-before-disclosed coordinates of the factory. At the bottom of the page, in the same handwriting, the monk signed in careful cursive, using not his Christian name but his assigned position in line: fifty-three.

Antonio followed the scribbled directions. He stole a wheelbarrow from the corrals of the old butcher and filled it with cardboard, towers of books, placemats, napkins, and every other sheet he could find, not caring if the finishes were matte or glossy. He oiled the bearings of the lone wheel and then left, pulling a plastic poncho over his own head and a tarp over the mound of papers.

On a Tuesday, when the windy world was soaked and covered in gray clouds, Antonio found the factory. It took his wrinkled arms and liver-spotted hands four hours to saw through the reinforced platina of the

Vatican-crested locks. Once inside, Antonio repaired the broken cutting tables, converting them into workbenches and then spilling paper and cardboard onto them.

Antonio split the spines of books, spilling leaves of Austen and Cervantes, sheets from Leviticus and Judges, all mixing with the pages of *The Book of Incandescent Light*. Then Antonio unrolled the wrapping paper and construction paper and began to cut at the cardboard and then fold.

She was the first to be created: cardboard legs, cellophane appendix, and paper breasts. Created not from the rib of a man but from paper scraps. There was no all-powerful god who could part the rivers of Pison and Gihon, but instead a twice-retired old man with cuts across his fingers.

Antonio was passed out on the floor, flakes of paper stuck to the sweat of his face and arms, unable to hear the sound of expanding paper as she rose. His hands were bloody, pooling the ink of his body on the floor, staining his pants. She stepped over her creator, spreading his blood across the polished floor, and then walked out of the factory and into the storm. The print of her arms smeared; her soaked feet tattered as they scrapped against wet pavement and turned her toes to pulp.

PART ONE

El Monte Flores

CHAPTER
ONE
III

Federico de la Fe discovered a cure for remorse. A remorse that started by the river of Las Tortugas.

Every Tuesday Federico de la Fe and Merced carried their conjugal mattress past the citrus orchard and laid it down at the edge of the river. Federico de la Fe would take out his sickle and split open the mattress at the seams while Merced sucked on the limes she plucked from the orchard.

Merced sent Federico de la Fe across the river to cut fresh straw and mint leaves while she pulled straw, wet with urine, from the open mattress.

For the first five years of their marriage Merced felt no shame in having a husband who wet his bed. She got used to the smell of piss and mint in the morning. And she could not imagine making love without the fermenting stench of wet hay underneath her.

When Little Merced was born, Merced joked about Federico de la Fe giving up his cotton underbriefs in exchange for cloth diapers like the ones their daughter wore. But instead both child and husband slept in the nude, curled around Merced. The ratio of mint leaves to hay was increased; and although Merced feared chafing, she spread white sand on the bed to absorb the moisture.

But Merced grew impatient when Little Merced learned to use the chamber pot and Federico de la Fe's penis continued to drip on the sheets. "This is the last straw I'm putting into this mattress," she told Federico de la Fe at the river. "A wife can only take so many years of being pissed on."

Federico de la Fe went to the botanica to find a remedy, because he could not think of anything sadder than losing Merced. The curandero behind the counter gave him a green ointment to rub on his groin and two boiled turtle eggs to chew, a prescription designed to cure his enuresis.

As Federico de la Fe chewed on the shells and meat of the eggs and spread the salve, he felt the weight of a distant force looking down on him.

The medication failed. My mother got up from the bed and wiped the wet sand from her back. She left my father as he slept and I stared at her long and tangled hair.

When my father awoke and discovered that my mother was not in the house or in the river washing herself, his sadness began.

"Merced, it is just you and me," he said with a voice that was sore and full of sadness.

My mother was gone and my father chased goats and sheep to bring me milk. At night, instead of sleeping nestled between my mother's breasts, I slept next to my father and felt the wet warmth that had driven her away.

It was not until I turned eleven that my father discovered a cure for his decade of sadness, a cure that he never revealed to me. With his sadness the cure also took away his need for washed sheets and fresh straw and mint leaves.

"If only I had stopped when you were a little girl and your mother was still here," he said, but his sore voice had healed.

Two weeks after losing his sadness, my father told me to put my things in the pillowcases that my mother had stitched. He said that we were going to Los Angeles— where he could work in a dress factory and I could go to school and learn about a world that was built on cement and not mud.

Half an hour before the Guadalajara Tag Team title match began, I went into Satoru "Tiger Mask" Sayama's dressing room to review our strategy. His mask hung on the side of the mirror while he sat on the couch shuffling his flashcards.

"Burro," he read from one side of a flash card and then flipped it to read the hiragana writing. Satoru Sayama had mastered Brazilian jiujutsu, aikido, and kendo, and was now working on the ancient romantic art of Spanish.

I went over the setups for the flying cross chop and the diving plancha attack.

"Hai, hai," Satoru nodded and continued with his flash cards.

As I left Tiger Mask's dressing room I heard a voice coming from a crack in the brick hallway that had grown into a hole.

"Señor Santos?"

I looked through the hole and saw a man with a young girl behind him holding two pillowcases.

"We are going to Los Angeles, but before we go I want my daughter to see the last of the Mexican heroes." He lifted his daughter so I could see her and then put her down and walked away.

From the top rope, as Tiger Mask held down La Abeja Negra—so I could deliver my diving plancha—I saw the girl and her father eating roasted peanuts. I delivered the plancha and then tagged Tiger Mask, making him the legal man in. Tiger Mask executed his Japanese tirabuzon submission hold and the peanut shells fell from the girl's lap onto the adobe floor where her pillowcases rested.

I thought that perhaps I could follow the girl after the match. But she had come too late in my life; I was an old man and she was just a young girl with flowered underwear. Instead, I tagged, so someone else could watch over her.

SATURN

When Merced left, Federico de la Fe fell into a depression that was not cured until ten years later. An itch had developed on the back of Federico de la Fe's hand and no amount of scratching could relieve it. He resorted to hand-feeding opossums and sticking his bare fingers and fist into beehives. The bites from the opossums and the stings from the honeybees temporarily relieved the severe itching. But it was not until Federico de la Fe resolved to stick his hand into the wood stove—where Merced used to cook tortillas and boil goat's milk—that the itch completely disappeared.

Federico de la Fe put his hand in the embers until it hurt so much that he could not feel his sadness and instead smelled only his singed flesh. After he wrapped his hand with an old scarf and rubbed on the green ointment that the curandero had given him, he wrote down all the things the fire had cured:

1. itch
2. bed-wetting
3. sadness

Federico de la Fe's only regret was that he had not discovered fire ten years earlier. Every night, when the sun hid underneath the flat earth and Little Merced slept on the dry straw bed, Federico de la Fe went into the kitchen and lit the stove so his remorse would not return.

LITTLE MERCED

My father said that before we could go to Los Angeles we had to see the last of the Jaliscon wrestling heroes and partake in the long tradition of lotería.

I dragged the two pillowcases as I followed my father to Don Clemente's arena. I walked through the hallways, while blood from the morning's cockfights seeped into the cloth of the pillowcases.

I remember my father lifting me and making me look at a man who wore a silver sequined mask. Through his eyeholes I could tell that he was a very handsome man, but a sad one with a lonely life.

In the arena we watched the match from the third row. My father bought me a bag of roasted peanuts and I asked for limes to squeeze into the bag.

"Your mother used to eat limes all the time," my father said. "They started rotting her teeth." I promised not to eat too many. "Just this time," I said, and he conceded two limes from his brown travel bag.

I ate the roasted peanuts soaked in lime juice and watched Santos tag Tiger Mask and step out of the ring. Perhaps it was my imagination—or the stench of the dead roosters underneath the seats—but I felt Santos's sad eyes staring at me.

After Santos and Tiger Mask defeated the Abejas Negras, we left the arena and followed a group of old ladies to the lotería tables in the cobblestone park at the center of the city.

LOTERIA CALLER

At the beginning of the night, before the first game started, I had to announce the rules and pretend I had a ridiculous name. I said:

"I am Don Senilla de la Silla, your caller for tonight's lotería.

"Sixteen beans per card. No more, no less. You buy two cards, you get thirty-two beans, three cards forty-eight, four cards... you get the picture.

"I'll pull a card from this deck and then I'll announce the image. If the same image appears on your designated playing card, put a bean over that square. Once you fill the sixteen squares, call 'lotería.' I will then go to your table to confirm your card and award you the cash prize of eight hundred pesos and a porcelain statue of our savior the Virgin of Guadalupe."

There was nothing spectacular about the night Santos and Tiger Mask defeated the Abejas Negras. The same people who were at the table every night were there holding beans in hand—the only exceptions were a couple of gringos and a man and his daughter who I had never seen before. The young girl was pretty, but, like her father, had terrible luck when it came to lotería.

I started the game and the first card I drew was:

EL DIABLITO

SATURN

Federico de la Fe did not win a single game of lotería. He thought that perhaps an evil omen was at work. The only pictures he ever placed a bean over were those of the devil and the grim reaper:

Little Merced did not win a game either, but none of her cards pointed to any signs of evil or premature death—only benign images of watermelons and banjos.

Just before midnight they left the cobblestone bingo park and headed to the red-brick bus depot.

They boarded Bus Number 8 on its north route to the border city of Tijuana. Federico de la Fe led Little Merced by the hand into the last two seats at the back of the bus, next to the toilet stall. Little Merced shoved her pillowcases beneath her seat and fell asleep across the burgundy cushions that smelled of sugarcane.

Ten minutes after the bus pulled out of the brick bus depot, four miles into the trip, Federico de la Fe looked out the window and then down at his daughter. He felt a slight inkling of the old sadness and feared that if he fell asleep he would soak his seat.

Out of this fear, Federico de la Fe went into the toilet stall and pulled out his sickle and heated it with a bit of phosphorus until it burned red. He lifted his wool Sunday shirt and pressed the glowing red sickle into his stomach until the sadness receded.

I bought three limes from an old salt
Indian who sold fruits and blocks of sodium. I hid the limes in my pillowcases and
pushed them underneath my bus seat.

I fell asleep and did not wake until
four hours later as the bus meandered
around the curves of the Chapoltemec
canyon. My father, who could sleep
through almost anything, snored, but
I could hear a woman talking in a baby
voice. I looked over the seat and saw a
woman wearing a wool Indian poncho
with twigs tangled into the thread. On
her lap was a slobbering baby who moved
only his lower lip.

"He's meditating. He was born in a
meditative state," the woman said. "At
first I thought that he was brain dead; the
doctors said that he was as dumb as a
turnip." She explained that she had nearly
killed him. But, as she was buying rat
poison for her baby turnip, the curandero
behind the counter looked into the baby's
eyes. The curandero told her that the baby
was actually a very powerful soothsayer
who was meditating. "One day he will
break his trance and add to the parchment
texts of Nostradamus."

"I know it seems like he is dead inside
but just yesterday I looked in his eyes and
I saw the history of the world on the
inside of his retina. I saw us as jellyfish
and apes, and then the ships of Columbus.

"And it's not just this world. Sometimes I see Saturn and stars and planets
that telescopes have never been pointed
at. The universe whirls around in his
head, and one day he will be able to tell
us about it."

I wanted a glimpse of the future; I
thought that in the contained vastness of
the baby's head, maybe I could spot my
mother's black hair. I wiped the baby's slob-
ber with my sleeve and stared into his eyes.

SATURN

Bus Number 8 arrived in Tijuana five days after it left the city of Guadalajara.

During their five-day journey, they ate a bit of salted pork, which Federico de la Fe had instructed Little Merced to put in her pillowcase, and a few corn cakes that Federico de la Fe carried in a nylon bag. Three days into the trip, Federico de la Fe discovered lime shells underneath his seat, but didn't think much of them. He figured that they had probably slid under him as the bus climbed the mountains of Culiacan.

During that journey, Federico de la Fe thought about dress factories and the technology of a country that would learn to soak color into the gray celluloid world of Rita Hayworth.

"Baja California, Tijuana," the bus driver announced, and spat out a wad of chewed sugarcane. Federico de la Fe patted Little Merced's head to wake her up.

"We're here," he said, and Little Merced reached underneath her seat and grabbed her two pillowcases.

At the front of the aisle, a woman made of paper insisted on giving Little Merced a hug and a kiss before they stepped out of the bus. Federico de la Fe at first resisted the woman's affections toward his daughter, holding Little Merced by the shoulders. He released her only after she whispered to him that she knew the woman and then opened her arms to embrace her new paper friend.

LITTLE MERCED

After peering into the Baby Nostradamus's eyes, I moved toward the front
of the bus and sat next to a woman who
was made of paper. She said nothing was
left of her people, except for her and her
creator. And she had left him passed out
in an old factory with thousands of paper
cuts on his hands.

She seemed sad. I looked at her newsprint arms and at the green construction
paper wrapped around her ankles and
asked if I could touch her. She nodded.
I put my hand on her arm and gave it a
slight squeeze, expecting it to crumple and
collapse. It was warm and I could feel the
blood climbing up the veins, into her fingers, and then racing back into her heart.

I asked her what her name was, but
she did not have one.

"In the rush and havoc of my creation
I was never christened. I do not know
what a proper name should be," she said,
and asked me if I could name her.

I named her "Merced de Papel" after
my own name, which was given to me by
my mother. Merced de Papel asked me
where my father and I were going. I told
her that we were going to Los Angles so he
could work in a dress factory and I could
go to school and learn about a world built
on cement. Merced de Papel was going to
Los Angeles too, but for different reasons.
She had heard that Los Angeles was the
last refuge for those who had lost their
civilization and were afraid of the rain.

MERCED DE PAPEL

Once the rainstorm ended I walked around
puddles and soaked litter. I thought about
Antonio, my creator, passed out in the old
factory. His hands bloody, spilling onto
the cement floor.

In panic and loneliness, I set out for
the nearest city and ended up in Guadalajara. I found a man who wore spurs on
his boots and prodded steer through the
middle of intersections and I told him my
story. He bought me a bus ticket and told
me that I should head to Los Angeles.

On the bus, a young girl—who was
made entirely of meat and wore flowered
underwear—told me about the city I had
just left and told me not to look back or
I would turn into salt.

"You remind me of my mother,
though I haven't seen her in years," she
said, and laughed. She went on to christen
me "Merced de Papel." After feeling my
arms, she said that I was warm and not a
soggy roll of Sunday news as she had
expected.

She went back to her seat and fell
asleep next to her father. When we arrived
in Tijuana her father walked her down the
bus aisle but before she stepped out she
said goodbye and hugged me.

"A baby Nostradamus is at the back
of the bus," she whispered in my ear before
she left with her father. I looked to the
back and saw a proud mother holding a
retarded baby with dangling legs and a
dripping mouth.

SATURN

In Tijuana, Federico de la Fe exited Bus Number 8 and instantly felt a hovering force pressing down on him. He sensed that he was being constantly watched from above; at times eyes stared down at him from three different angles.

The bus pulled away, sending a billow of smoke from the exhaust pipe. Plastic bags floated in the breeze and scraps of paper hung in the sky. Federico de la Fe, who had lived on the river of Las Tortugas and walked along its banks, listening to the rush of the current and the plop of frogs and turtles as they dove from the rocks and into the water, was now in Tijuana. Instead of the splash of water, the grumbles of engines and mufflers scraping on asphalt rankled his ears.

Across the street, Federico de la Fe noticed a vestige from his old home trudging through the gutter. He saw the dome of a tortoise moving along the side of the road; he watched as the animal turned into a driveway and crawled past a chain link fence. Federico de la Fe followed the tortoise, catching up to it, observing its metallic gleam and hinged tail as it climbed the steps of an old repair shop where they worked on Japanese cars and mechanical tortoises. In the mechanics' yard, empty lead shells were readied, polished, and sanded smooth. Federico de la Fe introduced himself to one of the mechanics, asking him if he could look at one of the empty shells. The mechanic nodded, opening the gate and watching as Federico de la Fe crawled into the lead shell, safely sheltered under the density of a metal that not even the most powerful x-ray in the universe could penetrate.

LITTLE MERCED

I bent down to look into the lead shell.
My father was inside, huddled with his
arms wrapped around his knees.

"Merced, I know that I'm wrong, but
I feel as if you are one of the people that is
constantly looking at me," said Federico
de la Fe.

I told him that someone had to watch
over him and that there was nothing
wrong in that. But he refused to come out
of the shell. He gave me some money and
told me to leave the pillowcases with him.
He handed me a shopping list to which
I added in very faint writing: "limes."

I figured that the inside of the lead
shell was very cold and that explained why
my father wanted three quarts of petroleum and a box of phosphorus sticks.

I asked one of the mechanics, whose
hands were black and greasy, if he could
point me to the market.

He was reading an old cloth copy of
Nostradamus's *Centuries,* and though
Mexico was a country of Francophobes,
never forgiving Napoleon III's cavalry and
bayonet charge upon the city of Puebla,
the mechanic read a bit of the rhyming
quatrains to me in French and then drew
me a map to the market.

I followed the map to a market that
had given up on salted pork and beef.
They packed everything in ice, distilled
their petroleum into gasoline and naphtha,
and shined their limes with a layer of wax.

I bought a small box of salt, six
pounds of frozen pork, bread, a box of
matches, three quarts of gasoline, and a
small bag of limes—small enough to hide
in my blouse. When I returned to the
mechanic shop my father was still underneath the lead shell. Through the small
opening, where the robot turtle used to
poke its head, I gave my father the gasoline, the matches, and a pork sandwich.

MECHANIC

I was calibrating the sprockets of an old
tortoise when a man of southern features
and complexion entered the shop asking
to borrow one of the lead shells on the
yard. Cereno, who refused to work on the
tortoises, was working on a Japanese engine
block. He ignored the man and instead
focused on the young daughter's knees.

I used to crawl underneath the lead
shell to think about different mathematical configurations for improving the locomotion of the turtles. It was absurd, but
I feared some hovering entity that seemed
to know everything about me, even the
ideas I had yet to patent. In the shelter of
the shell I felt free to think, and free of
any infringement on my theories.

Naturally, I felt some sympathy for
the man, and I agreed to let him use the
shell. His daughter, who smelled of citrus,
was kind enough to humor me as I read
her silly rhyming quatrains from the erred
prophet Nostradamus.

"I've looked into Nostradamus's baby
eyes," she said and cracked a small smile.
I laughed and drew her a map that she
could follow to the supermarket.

While the daughter was away I saw
her father come out of the shell and look
up at the sky. After praying briefly he
crawled back inside.

SATURN

Federico de la Fe came out of the lead shell while
Little Merced was at the supermarket buying groceries
and the materials necessary for his remedy for sadness.

Federico de la Fe looked up at the sky. His black
eyes moved a little to the left, toward the direction of
Saturn. For years he had sensed something in the sky
mocking him as he peed in his bed and dreamed of
dress factories and of his lost Merced. And today,
as he stood outside a junkyard hundreds of miles
from his home, the force upon him felt heavier than
ever before.

He watched as two clouds slowly joined into one,
and then crawled back into the safety of the lead shell.

LITTLE MERCED

I laid out a salting bed, made out of the *News of the World* and a couple advertisements for transmission fluid and engine seals. I spread the salt on the newspapers and rolled the pork and then wrapped it in the newsprint and slid it to my father, who remained in the metal shell.

I unbuttoned my blouse while hiding behind a rusting truck and took out the bag of limes. After eating one and throwing the peel into the cabin of the truck, I noticed a tribe of Glue Sniffers walking toward the yard. I quickly put the limes away.

They were selling wallets and knapsacks made of glue and string that they wove through whatever chunks of leather they could find. My father had said that the Glue Sniffers were not like other Indian tribes. Some of them were not even Indians. It was a tribe of orphans and runaways. And when the world was poor and starving they became sad and stopped pounding and stitching leather and sniffed glue instead.

When they approached me with their tan purses I told them to wait while I went and got my father.

I poked my head into the shell and felt the fumes of gasoline and the stench of burned phosphorus in my nostrils. I told my father about the Glue Sniffers and he said to let them in.

A Glue Sniffer with fair skin and duct tape around his waist went into the shell, accompanied by a dark but tall Oaxacan Indian who had one eye lost in meditation like the Baby Nostradamus.

While they met with my father I sorted through all the different bags the Glue Sniffers had made and occasionally turned to look at the lead tent, but all I could see was a red glow that pushed three shadows out of the shell.

GLUE SNIFFER

The transition from rubber cement to fire began under the lead shell of a man who was taking refuge from an ominous force and had discovered a different cure for sadness. His name was Federico de la Fe.

I explained to Federico de la Fe that I had to wrap my stomach because I could no longer control it. Misueño, who used to be a Oaxacan Indian before he left and joined us, shaved the hair from my belly and wrapped my belly and lower back with gray tape.

Federico de la Fe nodded and told us that he used to be from a river called Las Tortugas where turtles were made of meat, not sprockets and coils, and that while he lived on that river he had once come across a Glue Sniffer who explained to him that the purpose of liquid adhesives was to dull sadness.

He said that there was a better way. His cure did not upset the stomach or cause nosebleeds, and it did not tear away at the body where one could not see.

I pulled my pants down and Misueño took off his shirt. Federico de la Fe rubbed gasoline on my thigh, and on Misueño's stomach, and then poured a puddle into the palm of his hand. He spread it on his chest and lit a phosphorus stick and the flames spread. After the flames faded and the black on my thighs began to turn pink, the sadness that I felt was replaced by blisters and pus.

After Misueño and I left the lead shell, I continued Federico de la Fe's treatment for a week and I regained control of my stomach. I wrapped my thighs with gauze and threw my jar of glue away.

SATURN

Saturn was aligned directly over Federico de la Fe,
following him wherever he went, budging a half a
space centimeter for every five hundred land miles de
la Fe and Little Merced traveled. But once Federico
de la Fe retreated into the lead shell, safely hiding
from view and refusing to reemerge until the weight
from the air was lifted, Saturn withdrew into his orbit
and faded into the blur of the chalky galaxy.

LITTLE MERCED

By the time my father left the lead shell,
he smelled like the old Japanese combustion engines that the mechanics worked
on. His face was fuzzy and he had developed an allergic reaction to the metal; his
neck was blistered and his palms seemed
to be peeling. He asked for a tin tub with
hot water and soap; but before he stepped
into the water he looked up at the sky
and said that the air felt lighter.
I agreed, but I could not explain why.

"We are going to Los Angeles," he
said when he was shaven and clean and no
longer smelled like a machine. We said
goodbye to the mechanics and one of them
quoted Nostradamus's verse for safe travel.
We went to the market and sat in the
middle of a roundabout, watching the cars
and salting pork.

We packed the pillowcases with meat
and guava juice and walked toward the
border. We passed a honey garden and factories where Chinese men shoved beef into
aluminum cans. There were a couple of
teenage Glue Sniffers who tried to sell us
tasseled purses and leather knife cases.
I said, "No, thank you," and continued
walking until there was only loose dirt
and chaparral.

When we came across a white chalk
line that ran from the Pacific shore to the
Rio Grande, my father looked around to
see if anybody was following us or watching through telescopes. When he felt that
we were alone we stepped over the chalk
line and walked toward a world built on
cement.

CHAPTER TWO

●

LITTLE MERCED

When we reached Los Angeles none of the dress factories wanted my father. They wanted people who carried laminated cards with the stamp of a bald eagle.

"It's okay. I don't have to work in a dress factory."

Instead of hunching over a sewing machine, pulling and ironing fabric under the glow of fluorescent bulbs, we settled in a small town fifteen miles east of Rita Hayworth's Hollywood mansion, a town of furrows and flowers, where my father would work by daylight. And instead of the prick of sewing needles and pinking shears, it was thorns that would pierce his skin.

The town was called El Monte, after the hills it did not have. But everything else was named after flowers. Las Flores Market, Las Flores Street, and a small street gang called El Monte Flores. The gang wrote tags on telephone poles and on the asphalt where Medina Court intersected Las Flores Street. Most of the gang tags looked like this:

It was the first street gang born of carnations. But for them there was no softness in petals and no aroma in flowers. They felt only the splinters and calluses from tilling the land and smelled only the stench of fertilizer and horse shit. Their shoes were wet and the cuffs of their work pants crusted with mud. At midday they took off their shirts, wringing the sweat and then tossing them over their shoulders. And always a cutting knife was in hand. It was from these blades and hands that bouquets and potpourri came.

The city gangs with their pressed zoot suits, Al Capone cars, and automatic guns knew better than to call EMF a gang of sissy flower pickers. But EMF was not like city gangs either. They did not loot fruit stores or steal car parts; they just drank mescal and worked in the furrows harvesting flowers, next to my father.

The plantation paid thirty cents for each pound of carnations and fifty for the thorny stems of roses. Most people picked in the early morning before the dew evaporated so the scales would register both the weight of stem and petals and the condensed water droplets. And at times, either by accident or cleverness, a rock found its way from the furrows to the picking basket and then to the weighing tarp. And unlike dress factories, which cut checks only twice a month, the plantation paid every day.

El Monte was one thousand four hundred forty-eight miles north of Las Tortugas and an even fifteen hundred miles from the city of Guadalajara, and while there were no cockfights or wrestling arenas, the curanderos' botanica shops, the menudo stands, and the bell towers of the Catholic churches had also pushed north, settling among the flowers and sprinkler systems.

The original settlers of El Monte, people who had come from the east using the path of Santa Fe and the paved route of 66, gradually moved from El Monte to the foothills of Arcadia and Pasadena, towns that did not have the foot traffic of flower pickers or the smell of oregano and lard bubbling from the boiling pots of menudo stands. The only time that the pioneers of El Monte returned was in December, when they bought flowers to decorate the motorized carts that floated down the avenues of their newly adopted towns.

* * *

My father and I lived in a stucco house with deep sinks, planked and nailed floors, and a small front yard shaded by two lime trees. My father warned me not to pick limes from the limbs or the ground and I was obedient while under his watch. But when he was away I peeled the limes and ate the rinds, first sucking the juice and then chewing the pulp and veins. I discarded the shells into the paved gutters and masked the smell by cooking beans and sweet camotes and brushing my teeth.

At school, while we learned about the boundaries of states, the content of Lincoln's top hat, and the spelling of words, I sucked on the rinds of limes, swallowing the pulp and letting the acidity numb my lips and tongue and tingle my teeth. My mother had left before I could speak, before I could really know her, but I knew that I had inherited not only her brown eyes and black hair but also her love for the sourness of fruit.

I carried the limes in my paper sack and folded the mouth of the bag, making sure to keep it from my classmates. And they, to claim their own secrecy, kept the contents of their pails and sacks hidden from me. At lunch, Miss Clark watched over us. Those of us with paper sacks sat around the plastic tables and the boys and girls with lunch pails sat on the grass, staining the knees of their pants and the seats of their dresses. I would watch them open their pails, and I thought of the hinges pivoting and the smooth and sterile cleanliness on the inside.

Once, as we sat eating our lunches, Miss Clark called me and asked me to bring my books and bags with me. I feared that I had been discovered, that the shells had fallen out of my desk or that meat from the limes had stuck to the side of my face, but she did not say anything about limes or citrus fruit. She simply pinned a mimeographed sheet to the front of my blouse and sent me home.

That night my father read the note and asked me to loosen my hair. While I undid the French from my braid, he plugged the sink and filled it with petroleum. He soaked his head in the sink and I held the towel so he could dry his hair. He stuffed my ears with cotton and diluted the petroleum with vinegar. He held me upside down and dipped me into the sink. After two minutes I toweled off my hair, and vinegar and petroleum dripped on the wooden floor as my father dumped my blankets, pillowcases, and all of my clothes into the sink. With a tiny comb he went through my hair and I felt his fingers tracing the paths on my scalp. For the rest of the week I went to school smelling like the old combustion engines at the mechanics' yard.

My father had always thought of my mother's departure in terms of his own loneliness, but now the film of petroleum on the sink and our hair and the gray carcasses in the teeth of the comb made him think of the effects of her absence on my upbringing.

"If your mother were here this would never have happened," he said, and then crumpled the mimeographed sheet. From that day on he wore a shower cap whenever he went to work or walked by the fields.

Once the shine from the petroleum faded and my clothes lost their scent, I was allowed to sit among the other students again. But the ones with latched and shiny pails moved further into the grass, away from the threats that we might have brought inside our lunch bags or carried tangled in our hair.

On Sundays, my father and I lined up at the menudo stands holding our bowls and cloth napkins. We ate the soup on the sidewalk, and when we were done we walked past Las Flores Market and into the Virgin of Guadalupe Church, where we used our bowls as collection plates and to carry holy water home. The members of EMF gathered at the entrance but never went inside; they listened to the church Latin while standing under the arches and beams of the San Juan, spitting chewed petals and stems into the tray of ash and incense and kneeling on the cement when the Eucharist was raised. And once church ended, they returned to the flower fields.

Not all of El Monte was flowerbeds. Some sembrarrios of carnations had been replaced by strawberry fields, but no street names or gangs had grown from them. It was in these weeded and watered meadows that EMF's initiation fights took place. Membership into EMF started with a brinca—six men against one for a minute.

The first brinca I saw was Froggy's, though I did not know his name at the time. My father was in the bathroom pulling rose thorns from his hands while I sat in the yard underneath the lime trees looking at the flower fields that sat across the street. EMF trucks pulled up on the prepared but unsown dirt; the members opened their doors and then gathered in front of a Chevy.

Froggy took off his shirt and walked away from the huddle, tapping his chest to signal he was ready. It was not a fight like the one I had seen in the Guadalajara arena, full of tumbling and chokeholds; this was only fists and kicks. At first it was Froggy who launched the punches, crouching and uncoiling but never fully connecting. But once encircled, his hands went from fists to shields that covered his face. They pushed his hands down and hit his jaw and blood and petals flew from his mouth. Once Froggy was on the ground, between furrows, I saw only the backs of the men, their legs lifting and kicking Froggy.

When it was over, the minute expired, Froggy lay out in the mud of the field. They lifted him on their shoulders, pouring mescal on his head. The alcohol cut through the mud, cleaning and healing the cuts and welts. The curandero's green ointment was massaged onto Froggy's chest and shaven head. They hugged him, congratulating him for his endurance and suffering, and sat him in the passenger side of a Chevy truck. Then they drove away, each truck following the lead. The EMF parade, a parade with no Rose Queen or benches of spectators. This was EMF's ceremonial procession, and as always their newest member sat at the head of the caravan, leaving behind only tooth fragments and drops of blood to fertilize the soil.

I saw Froggy again a week later as I passed the field to bring pork and tequesquite bread to my father. Froggy was picking carnations. His shirt was off and I could see the welts and bruises and the scabs that had started to form. He was young, seventeen, but he picked more carnations than the older braceros who had experience picking lettuce and carrots. Froggy picked with two baskets strapped around his neck and used a smaller but more agile blade that butterflied as it cut. He stepped out of the furrows and dumped the carnations onto a plastic tarp. My father offered him some pork. Froggy tore a piece of the meat using the tequesquite bread and put it inside his busted lips.

"This is my daughter Merced," my father said.

I shook his hand. His palm was rough and blistered and the knuckles glistened with dew.

He touched my head and gently butterflied his knife, cutting a single strand of hair from its root, and in the same motion he wrapped the knife shut with a bow and knot that he made from my hair. Secured, he let me hold the knife, but when I pulled at the knot Froggy took the knife and went back into the furrows with two empty flower baskets hanging around his neck.

After work, when the scales were locked up and the flower trucks had driven away, the EMF cholos took off their sun hats, uncuffed their Dickies, and sat around the dominoes table drinking mescal and chewing rose petals. My father joined them but refused to remove his shower cap.

The dominoes pots were mostly butterfly knives, switchblades, and shears—all tools that made the cutting of carnations and rose stems easier. But there were also pots of cigarettes and dollars. During these long bouts of dominoes, when my father was away, and before he returned home smelling of roses and alcohol, his fingernails blunted by the blocks of numbered ivory, I picked and ate limes. I sat by the window watching for my father's return and hid the seeds and shells in my socks. Later, I emptied the socks in neighboring fields while pretending to steal strawberries. And soon, from what had been my litter, sprang my own orchard of lime saplings nestled between strawberries.

After the dominoes game my father came home with new switchblades, sometimes with packs of cigarettes. And once, a day after the crop duster had flown over El Monte, leaving behind a mist that ate away the larvae of medflies and also the paint coats of unprotected cars, my father came home with a leather knapsack, stitched and glued like the old Glue Sniffers used to make, full of dollar coins and two-dollar bills.

My father sat me on his shoulders and walked to the menudo stand, where we paid a fee for forgetting our bowls and ate from ones made of paper. After getting our fill of tripe soup and oregano, we walked to the church and entered from the side corridor that led away from the altar and into the church's Papal Pawn & Loan.

The store was run by an old Oaxacan who only spoke English and his native tongue. I translated for my father while he inspected the planes and manual drills and bits. My father said I could pick something from the shop. I looked through the pawned photo albums, old geometry books that had yet to cite Isosceles's principles, and collections of stamps. One of the albums belonged to a white family; they took pictures in front of racetracks, sometimes hugging jockeys and horses. There were pictures of the family standing in front of the Papal Pawn & Loan and pictures of babies and weddings and of the father in the stands holding up race stubs.

There were also watches, radios, and cameras, all sitting on the shell of a broken mechanical tortoise. Its head was missing but its inside was stuffed with coils and sprockets. There was no way to enter the shell.

I thought about the tortoise but instead opted for a lunch pail. We walked out of the shop; I swung my lunch pail and my father carried his drill and wood planes.

When we got home, my father chopped down a mesquite tree that had sprung up on the margin of the flower fields across the street from our house. He made planks from its trunk and by the end of the day had converted the mesquite into a new dominoes table on the top of which he painted a chess grid that I could use to play checkers or bragiso.

I washed my lunch box. I poured in a bit of mescal to cut at the grease that had gathered in the corners.

"Maybe I should get one, too," my father said, and tried stuffing some pork and tequesquite bread into the box. He set the lunch box on top of the dominoes table, and we ate dinner and then played bragiso with the pork bones. I cornered my father into the black squares. As expected, he turned the trap against me and as a reward sucked the marrow out of the bones.

"Your mother was the best bragiso player I have ever seen. When the bragiso masters came to Las Tortugas, she was always two moves ahead of them. She would lose only for the sake of letting them keep their titles and to avoid the obligation of traveling their circuit." He recounted some of the traps my mother had pioneered, and the rings, bracelets, and dresses she had worn. He said he was not sad, just remembering a little. Still he longed for a bed without box springs, and goat milk rich and full, unthinned by pasteurization, and he wanted to be able to remember my mother without thinking about his enuresis or the urine-soaked sand that clung to her back.

"Something took your mother away. It wasn't just my pee."

The next morning I mixed cream and oregano into the milk and whipped it until it tasted and looked like fresh goat milk. I fried eggs with chorizo that I had bought from one of the curanderos. I put my sweetbread and sandwich in my new lunch box and waited for my father to come into the kitchen.

"It smells like Las Tortugas," he said, smiling, and then sipped at the milk and picked from the frying pan. I grabbed my lunch box, hugged him, and went out the door. Knowing that my father would be distracted by breakfast, I jumped and plucked a lime from the tree and ran to school swinging my lunch box.

That day we learned about Abraham Lincoln and the letters that he kept in his stovepipe hat: two love letters and a dentist's receipt, both discoveries made the day of his assassination, when both his hat and his presidency toppled. It was a hot day and half of my class had been sent home with ditto sheets stapled to their T-shirts and dresses, so there was no one to sit with at the lunch table. Instead of eating by myself, I walked onto the lawn and sat on the grass next to a girl with pink bows and blue eyes.

"You're going to sit with us?" she asked.

I nodded and opened my lunch box and took out my sandwich as the kids around me spread their paper napkins on their laps. I took out my cloth napkin and told her that I could sit with them, that I could sit on the grass, because I had a lunch box like they did.

They looked at each other as if to confirm something and then back at my lunch box. The girl with the pink bows and blue eyes said, "That's not a lunch box, it's a typewriter case."

And she was right. My box was two times the size of theirs, and instead of the smooth, silver finish, mine was grainy and made of plastic. I didn't know what to say. I got up and sat at the table by myself, angry at my father for not knowing what a typewriter case looked like. But I did not cry or walk home with my head down. Instead, I ate my lime, peel and all.

When I got home, Froggy and my father were on the front lawn playing dominoes. There was no shade; the lime trees had been cut down and shaved into planks and a pile of uprooted lime saplings lay underneath the dominoes table.

Before I could tell my father that he could have the typewriter case, and that his inability to imagine that a typewriter could be carried in such a container had caused me great humiliation, he grabbed me and shoved his fingers into my mouth. He smelled the citrus on my breath and touched my front teeth, feeling enamel rub off on his thumb.

He shook me and then, gently, said, "Merced, they are rotting your teeth."

CHAPTER THREE

● ● ●

FROGGY EL VETERANO

Many years after the Saturn War and in the unwritten afterword of this book, Froggy survived to be a very old man. But his status as a veteran of a war and a novel did nothing to help him escape the city codes and county jurisdiction.

As he snipped at his beard and the silver hairs fell into the sink, county trucks pulled up in front of Froggy's stucco house, and men clad in beige uniforms wielding bolt-cutters split open the chain-link fence that surrounded his yard.

Froggy's wife sat on the wicker chair watching an old Rita Hayworth movie, while the uniformed men entered the yard, posted a notice on the front door, and rounded up the goats and fowl with electric prods and nets. When Froggy came out of the house, his beard wet and uneven, only the droppings of the roosters and goats remained. Froggy tore the notice from the door, whisker clippings catching on his shirt and falling to the ground as he shook his head.

MARGARITA

Rita Hayworth was born Margarita Carmen Dolores Cansino in a coastal town in Jalisco, where at the age of six she sowed a plum orchard irrigated solely by salt water. When the sea was dry she resorted to onions and sad memories to water the black soil, and when she could not cry she used the sodium-rich urine of mules. Later in life, as she danced with Fred Astaire in *You Were Never Lovelier,* she remembered the smell of mule piss and the burn of salt and longed for the days of tending plum trees.

Margarita's plum trees never grew taller than potted houseplants, but they bore more fruit than the towering orchard trees. The saplings collapsed under the weight of the salty fruit and Margarita mended the broken trunks with gauze and tar. She grafted sugarcane to the roots and branches, hoping to counter the taste of sodium, but the slight trace of sweetness was not enough, and the townspeople who spent their lives pulling nets and gutting fish decided to call the new fruit "saladito."

She had created an inedible fruit that only oxen and donkeys would eat, but people did not hate Margarita for that. And two decades later, when her pinup shot was airbrushed to the first test bomb and dropped on the island of Bikini Atoll, no one hated her then either.

JULIETA

The eight adobes of El Derramadero sat on a mountain two miles north of Las Tortugas, the town where Federico de la Fe and his wife Merced had built their home from mud and stone. But while Las Tortugas lived up to its name through its increasing population of non-mechanical turtles, El Derramadero had yet to earn its own. It was not until Julieta crumbled a cube of chicken bouillon into a pot of boiling water that the disintegration began to spread.

First came a landslide, then the collapse of stone fences, followed by the sudden decomposition of barbed wire and steel plows. The alloy utensils in the kitchen drawers broke into carbon and iron rust. Julieta did not take El Derramadero's decay with the same calm as the rest of the town; to them it was no more than a hailstorm or drought—simply something to be endured. But when the marble eyes of Julieta's cloth doll turned into brown dirt, Julieta told her mother:

"Everything is becoming dust."

Her mother simply shrugged and began to carve new spoons from the thick bark of mesquites.

FROGGY EL VETERANO

After the county trucks had taken the fighting cocks, laying chickens, and milk goats, Froggy wiped the splatters of rooster blood from the outside walls of his house. He gathered the eggs from the dirt and leaf nests, and then went inside and poured the curdling goat milk into cheesecloth. Despite his wife's requests, some of Federico de la Fe's battle plans still hung on the kitchen wall. A martial longing and hope for the return of Federico de la Fe kept Froggy from removing the schematics that diagrammed the progression against Saturn. Froggy remembered the day when Federico de la Fe had pinned the diagram to the wall. His arms tan from the sun and his hands bleached by fertilizer but still no black cuts or scars on his arms—the aftermath of his remedy still hidden beneath his undershirt and work pants—Federico de la Fe had drawn a dot on the diagram signifying EMF's position in the battle.

"We are here right now. We are being pushed in this direction. Saturn wants to move us into the peaks and then into denouement. And we must stop before our lives are destroyed," Federico de la Fe said calmly, but with a seriousness that made Froggy and everybody else from EMF spit blood and rose petals.

Every third week Federico de la Fe would update the diagram, but only the position of the dot would change. The map in Froggy's kitchen was one of the early drafts of the war, so it looked very much like this:

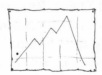

MARGARITA

Using only her fingers and nails, Margarita dug an irrigation canal that reached from the sands of the shore to the furrows of her plum trees. Though she never told her mother, it was in that canal of seawater that Margarita had her first period and her first experience with love. A young fisherman followed the trail of a wounded shark, a diluted stream of purple blood, which led to the thighs of Margarita Cansino.

"I'm a fisherman," the teenage boy said, "but when the sea is dry, I pick lettuce."

And from that encounter the legend was born that Rita Hayworth had sex with lettuce pickers, that the Love Goddess of Hollywood was democratic in her love, giving it not only to Howard Hughes over a neat bed of kleenex but also to migrant workers on the spread leafage of icebergs. But Margarita never saw the boy after that; he left with his fishing net swung over his shoulder and never turned back. And although Margarita lived in a world that predated Technicolor, she always dreamed of the boy in rich pastels.

When her parents moved to Baja California, Margarita wrapped three plum saplings in newspaper, the roots and clumps of dirt slipped into a plastic supermarket bag, and shipped them inside her hope chest. In Tijuana, as she danced in anchored gambling ships and casinos, she often slipped on the shined floors when she thought of the boy who had found her in the irrigation ditch, confirming the theory that equilibrium is always upset by wax and first love. But despite this occasional clumsiness, the Hollywood executives—who lounged in Tijuana, avoiding the injunctions of Prohibition—asked Margarita to dance in front of their celluloid motion machine.

"Rita, you're fabulous," they said, and from that point onward her first name was condensed.

While the celluloid was driven to Studio City, washed in a soup of developing chemicals, and then cut and wound into reels that Hollywood producers would later see and admire, Rita continued to dance, headlining the velvet gambling rooms of Tijuana. And after her shows, lettuce pickers followed her backstage, laid down their own beds of lettuce, and solicited her love. But Margarita turned them away, kicking their lettuce beds and giving them only two things: a bag of her salted fruit and a note to be delivered to the fisherman who had told them about her.

The fisherman received the note two months later:

"There is a certain etiquette to love, discretions that must be observed: You do not tell others about it, nor do you write about it."

But the fisherman thought that story was far more important than the dictates of etiquette and so he replied on the back of the casino stationery, recounting what had happened under the salt water in lucid detail complete with diagrammed pictures and arrows illustrating the strokes of motion. By the time the note had reached Tijuana, Margarita was in Hollywood making a string of B Westerns under her adopted name.

When *Trouble in Texas* premiered, dust from the adobe bricks filled the theaters as the bass from the bullets shook the walls. And when the name or face of Rita Hayworth appeared, jeers overtook the score and the screens were pegged with rotting heads of lettuce.

"She's too good to fuck lettuce pickers," they said, and blew the dust from their noses into their handkerchiefs.

JULIETA

The destruction of El Derramadero continued. The chairs and tables collapsed into lumps of sawdust, but no termite eggs were discovered. Julieta and her mother ate on the stone floor, slurping soup from their cupped hands; the remains of the clay bowls had been swept into the dustpan, then the dustpan disintegrated, flaking and oxidizing, the fragments thrown into the refuse fire.

After two weeks of abiding by its name, none of El Derramadero's adobes were standing, and despite strategically placed mothballs, the linen cupboards had been reduced to sawdust and lint. Julieta's world was falling apart, but as she walked through the heaps of decaying wool and cotton she noticed that a pink button was still intact. Julieta discovered that plastic could survive the fate of El Derramadero.

Shrouded in trash bags, the men of El Derramadero walked down from their native mountain and returned three days later pulling a wagon filled with slabs of plastic. Once in El Derramadero, the wagon collapsed and was thrown into the fire pit where they melted the plastic, shaping it into cutting shanks for butchering and forming forks and spoons, letting them cool before sliding them into their utensil trays. They cleared the clumps of mud from the foundations where their old adobes used to stand and molded igloos complete with plastic hinges. But although the people of El Derramadero were happy for having triumphed over their town's name, Julieta did not want to live in a town made from melted plastic.

FROGGY EL VETERANO

There were no roosters to prep for tournament, no goats to milk or cheese to make. The county had taken away everything. And Froggy, ever honorable, tried to refund the pre-event bets he had collected and all the money fronted for orders of goat cheese. El Monte was no longer a town of flowerbeds and strawberry fields. Stucco houses, paved alleys, and cement riverbanks now covered its soil. And instead of flowers, gasoline pumps and lampposts rose from El Monte, all marked by the EMF tags. Froggy was the last living veterano of EMF, the sole survivor from the years of Federico de la Fe, and out of respect for Froggy's history they refused to take the money back, instead insisting on placing more orders and bets even though they knew that there would be no return. It was a retirement pledge for an old man who had fought and lost a hard war.

And because there were no more flowerbeds in El Monte, Froggy had to tell all the new members of EMF how their gang name came to be. He instilled a pride in them, citing their hometown as the battlefield where one of the greatest wars against tyranny had been fought years before, a war against the future of this story—Federico de la Fe's war. A war waged against Saturn, against the invasion that infiltrated their thoughts and overheard even their softest whispers, murmurs meant to touch only one ear, and to be retrieved only by memory or swabs of cotton.

But now, the EMF members had moved away from wars of volition, dealing instead with the claiming of streets and customer bases. Pride now came in the form of shank marks, scars left by screwdrivers and switch-blades; the indentation of flesh, where the bullet entered, was the highest of decorations. A simple "EMF" on the side of the neck was no longer sufficient; instead a full Old English script stretched from shoulder blade to shoulder blade.

"What we fought against didn't use guns or shanks," Froggy said. The younger generations of EMF listened, while the fragments of bullets and broken blades shifted inside their bodies, finding muscles to nestle among. What Froggy, EMF, and Federico de la Fe had fought against didn't use stones or weapons of steel, nor could it be defeated by such. They had discovered this after firing their guns into the sky and launching a barrage of slingshot rocks, watching their projectiles ascend and then crest before they ducked for cover, sheltering themselves from their own fire. EMF never pierced the sky, always far from reaching Saturn's orbit.

It was never Saturn's intention to destroy any of them, if only they had not rebelled and just lived their lives without looking up. If they had not listened to Federico de la Fe and his crazed speeches, his claims of dignity through privacy and their right to be unseen—it was he who prompted the unneeded war. Saturn wanted only to watch, to see their story develop and unfold.

EMF's battles were now with the human; there was no more Saturn to fight, no celestial adversaries floating in the universe. Before, there was no gore, but now blood dripped from park benches and pooled at the feet of phone booths where corpses lay—their EMF tattoos crossed out with the edge of a hunting knife, the bloody blades later found in the bushes.

Whatever the reason, a member's final exit from EMF was always followed with ceremony. A funeral procession began with a car wash that paid for the casket and a wreath of flowers, and ended in the Church of Guadalupe, where money was collected in soup bowls and then handed to the mourning mother.

RITA

Rita Hayworth bleached her jet-black hair into a light shade of auburn. To emphasize her widow's peak, she used needle-shaped electrodes to push back her hairline. She pinched her cartilage until her mestizo nose was pointy. The in-house linguist at Fox Pictures touched Rita's tongue, teaching her to unroll her *r*'s and pronounce words like *salamander* and *salad* without sounding like a wetback.

Once the linguist and makeup artist had transformed her, the producers sent Rita and a crew to Buenos Aires to make a movie about underground casinos and love triangles. Rita knew about casinos: she had danced in them and sat around their tables all of her life. And she also knew about love triangles: she had been pulled out of and into them many times, once even giving an existing triangle an additional point. The movie was called *Gilda,* and out of the dozens of movies Rita Hayworth made, it was the film she hated most. Decades later, as she sat in her New York City apartment overlooking the East River, her brain dissolving into the dementia of Alzheimer's, Rita Hayworth daydreamed about salted plums and a world where *Gilda* did not exist.

"Every man I have known has fallen in love with Gilda and awakened with me," she said, listing all the men she had married and then left:

1. Edward Judson
2. Orson Welles

3. Prince Aly Khan
4. Dick Haymes
5. James Hill

None of the listed names belonged to lettuce pickers.

In Buenos Aires, between takes, Rita went to the park gazebos and watched little girls as they rhymed songs and played hopscotch. And at night Rita went to the Argentine circus and watched counting cats perform arithmetic while she took sips of maté tea. The tea was bitter and the odor of the gourd and ground leaves made Rita's pointy nose drip.

After the circus, as the elephants tightened the tent ropes, Rita licked the mucus from her upper lip, entered the hotel lobby, and took the elevator to her room. When she lay down on her bed she thought there was something lonely about making movies and counting cats. Her plum trees had wilted and died long ago, so whatever tears she wept seeped only into the worn hotel mattress.

JULIETA

Julieta ran away, leaving the customary farewell note on top of the formica bed before she tumbled out of her bedroom window. The note instantly flaked and crumbled, the paper ashes gathering at two corners of the room, entangling with dust bunnies. She walked down the mountain of El Derramadero, down to the river of Las Tortugas, where doors were shut and wells covered. The people feared that Julieta might spread the destruction of El Derramadero, and though they were generally kind, they drove her from Las Tortugas. The infamy of the town of plastic and decay had spread from the mountains to the foothills and shore, and north all the way to the border. Though never confirmed, there were reports that the path Julieta walked to Tijuana was marked not only by broken blades of grass and twigs but also by soft dirt that collapsed into pits and ditches.

When Julieta reached Tijuana, what was once a border marked only with a line of chalk had been replaced with watchtowers and steel fences; cement barricades had been buried directly underneath the fences and no one could burrow to the other side. Stadium lights shone on the border all through the night until the early hours of the morning. Meanwhile, the people who tried to sleep under the oppressive wattage of the electric lights lowered their heavy curtains and buried their heads into their black pillowcases.

It was not clear whether Julieta had dragged the disease of El Derramadero with her, or if it was just a coincidence that she found a gap in the three-hundred-mile-long fence where the steel had corroded, allowing her to pass into the other side.

FROGGY EL VETERANO

Froggy lamented what EMF had become, one of those pachuco gangs that slung speed and stripped cars, and even the old gang tag had lost some of its formality, now posted haphazardly and sloppily etched. Froggy wanted Federico de la Fe to return to renew the war and take up against Saturn. Froggy did not want EMF to fight for drug turf and street names.

Froggy gathered EMF in his yard. The chain-link fence had been torn down and the dirt and lawn had been raked clear of the droppings and feathers. The barrel grill had been charcoaled and lit and the beer cooled over ice. Julieta flipped the beef, squeezing lime and pouring beer onto the cuts while Froggy passed out tequesquite bread and bottles of beer. Froggy let the EMF cholos eat their limed meat and finish their drinks, realizing that this would probably be the last EMF assembly he would ever lead. Froggy did not raise his voice or stand on the table until well after the coals had cooled from red to gray and the ice had completely melted into water. When he finally stood, Froggy held up one of Federico de la Fe's war schematics. And when the EMF cholos looked up they all sighed, not with awe but with a sense of weariness, because they did not want to fight Saturn.

"Froggy," one of the cholos said, "I say this with respect, but we are not going to fight that war again. The veteranos couldn't win it, we can't either." And everybody but Froggy nodded in agreement. Froggy gave up his campaign; the war would not be renewed. But before dismissing the members of EMF, Froggy told them that one day, when they were old men and were making love to their wives, they would feel a mocking smile staring down at them from the rings of Saturn. And when that happened, they would regret not fighting in Federico de la Fe's war.

RITA

When *Gilda* premiered in the adobe theaters, they did not throw heads of lettuce at the screen. The lettuce pickers, who had spent most of their lives tossing iceberg onto conveyer belts and who lived far from the tinsel and red carpets of Hollywood, were proud that one of its biggest stars had once made love with a lettuce picker.

The next morning, hunched over the iceberg that they tore from the frost and dirt of the new day, their hands double-gloved and throwing the heads into the tractor's wagon, one of the lettuce pickers said, "I fucked Rita Hayworth. I bent her over."

Though it was not true, he believed firmly in his lie.

The foreman, who drove the tractor, asked what Rita Hayworth looked like naked.

"She looks like you would imagine. The way she looks in *Gilda,* except without clothes, and her nipples are dark and her muff is wild and black," the lettuce picker answered.

JULIETA

Like many of the first who fled Jalisco and their small towns of Las Tortugas and El Derramadero, Julieta settled in El Monte, where she picked flowers for a living. And while many had left their hometowns to escape the memory of love lost, Julieta came to El Monte and found it. When she met Froggy she was not thinking of broken whispers at her ears or of chapped lips at the nape of her neck; she was pulling her tarp of flowers, setting it on the scale, and watching the needle register the thirty-six pounds of yellow carnations.

Froggy was barely eighteen. His head was shaven and it took him months just to grow a five o'clock shadow. He was ignorant of the strength of Saturn and had recently joined Federico de la Fe in the war against the ringed planet.

Julieta told him that it was okay for him to grab her belt loop and touch her skin but warned him that she had come from a town named after decay.

"I'm fighting a war against the most dangerous of planets—I'm not afraid of a little rot and rust," he said.

And that night Julieta left the grass-lined furrow where she had slept for a week and entered his stucco. Strewn throughout his house was evidence of someone else: hair ties and bobby pins, bottles of lotion, and intricate knots on the drapes.

"Her name was Sandra, but she is gone now," Froggy said to Julieta, pulling her by the hand and leading her into the bedroom.

The mattress and sheets tore and the bed frame collapsed, but none of it had to do with decay.

CHAPTER
FOUR

█ █ █

The night Federico de la Fe dreamed of his wife
Merced, he awoke to a soaked mattress and the faint
smell of wood rot. A puddle of urine gathered underneath his bed and stained the planks. When awake,
Federico de la Fe could dull the sadness and memory
of his wife with fire, but he could not control the
alignment of the planets or the heavy weight of
Saturn while he slept.

Federico de la Fe pulled his sheets from the bed,
dabbed the floor with bath towels, lifting urine and
drowned termites, and opened the curtains to let in
the sun. Then he walked outside his house and looked
up at the sky.

While Federico de la Fe's stare was dry, with no
sign of tears, the front of his work pants were still
wet, and dead termites stuck to his bare feet. He
stood under the sun with his eyes fixed, neither
blinking nor lowering his head, and Federico de la Fe
was for the first time able to pinpoint the source of
the imposing weight. He looked directly at the second largest planet of the solar system and did not
turn away until Saturn acknowledged Federico de la
Fe's anger and implicit declaration of war.

In the evening, Federico de la Fe spread plastic
over the mattress and slept with a bundle of cloth
wrapped around his waist fastened by safety pins.
Despite the diapers, the urine ran from the side of his
leg onto the plastic sheets and then dripped onto the
floor, stirring the aroma of wood rot and the wet carcasses of termites.

To prevent further drownings and the dreams of
Merced, Federico de la Fe resorted to a self-imposed
insomnia. He bought a sack of Argentine maté, aged
and bittered on the shelves of the curanderos. Federico de la Fe drank the boiling water, letting the
heat scald his tongue. And when the tea was gone he
chewed on the roughage of the leaves while the rest
of El Monte slept.

LITTLE MERCED

I had not smelled my father's urine since we had left Las Tortugas, but now the stench had returned and I feared that his depression would follow. But when he came out of his room, there was no sadness in his voice, just a wet spot around his zipper.

"Tell Froggy I'm not going to work today, but that I want him to come in the evening," he said, and then went out to the backyard to dry his pants and stare at the sky. I went to the weighing station and relayed the message to Froggy.

That night when Froggy knocked on our door, he brought the set of ivory dominoes and three older EMF cholos with him. My father, Froggy, and the three other men sat around the dominoes table chewing rose petals and drinking mescal. Everybody except for Froggy and my father had "EMF" tattooed on the side of their necks.

That night, Froggy won the dominoes pot—a pack of cigarettes, two switch-blades, ten dollars, and a quart of agave mescal. Froggy gave me two folded dollar bills and then my father sent me to bed.

As I lay in bed I remembered the old adobe bricks of Las Tortugas. I used to bore peepholes into the walls with a bit of saliva and my pinky. Through those holes I had watched my father brush my mother's hair and witnessed my mother eating limes and then throwing the shells into the stove's fire.

But now, all the walls were made of wood and plaster and all I could hear was the muffled talk of the men and the sound of ivory hitting the table.

FROGGY

Before Federico de la Fe sent Little Merced to her room, I wrapped the smaller switch-blade I had won in dollar bills and gave it to her.

As we put the dominoes away and got up to leave, Federico de la Fe asked us to sit back down and began showing us schematics of the universe and plans for the war he was asking us to join.

He said it was a war for volition and against the commodification of sadness. "It is a war against the fate that has been decided for us," he said.

I asked who had given us the fate. Federico de la Fe shook his head and said he was not entirely sure. All he could tell us was that it was something or someone in the sky, hidden and looking down on us safely from the orbit of Saturn. And that entity had driven his wife away and cursed him with a perpetual sadness that was alleviated only through fire. And everybody else in El Monte was subject to the temper and whims that emanated from Saturn.

"Right now, as I say this, we are part of Saturn's story. Saturn owns it. We are being listened to and watched, our lives sold as entertainment. But if we fight we might be able to gain control, to shield ourselves and live our lives for ourselves," Federico de la Fe said.

Froggy was the first recruit to join Federico de la Fe's war, but soon others from EMF followed. On the second day of the campaign against Saturn, the fungus that grew on the stems of carnations spread onto Froggy's shoes. From his soles it spread to the brown carpet in Froggy's living room, and then to the walls and ceiling. And as Froggy tried to beat the white mold from his curtains, the fungus spread onto the broom and down to his hands.

And every day, as more EMF cholos joined Federico de la Fe's army, the fungus spread to more houses until all of El Monte was covered in a layer of white mold.

They scrubbed the fungus from their hands with pumice and kerosene, and when mushrooms sprouted from the crevasses in their bathroom tiles they scraped them with spatulas and poured bleach.

During the two-week plague, twenty-three EMF cholos died. When the coroner split open their chests to drain the blood and stuff them with tissue paper, he found toadstools growing between their ribs.

In the midst of sorrow and funeral processions, Froggy survived and at nineteen became the oldest living member of EMF. After the plague, the chain of command was Froggy, Smiley, Pelon, and then Little Oso. But still it was Federico de la Fe who oversaw the war.

Saturn had won the first battle, but instead of surrendering, Froggy increased their ranks by jumping in more cholos and inviting teenage girls to join EMF and the fight for emancipation.

The first girl to join EMF was named Sandra. There were no other women to jump her in and so the official initiation was waived. But there was no need for a brinca anyway, as she had fled from a father who had beat her so much that she could no longer remember what it was like to properly knit.

Sandra had survived the plague, impeding the growth of fungus by sniffing ammonia. And instead of Sandra being initiated at the hands of Froggy, it was Sandra who used her knitting needle to tattoo "EMF" onto Froggy's neck.

I fought the mold with bleach and a wire
brush. I pushed it back from the living
room floor out to the porch and splashed
bleach onto the sidewalk. My father
walked around town sniffing kerosene
from a mason jar and sipping maté. At
night, while I laid in bed, my father sat
bent over the dominoes table sketching
plans and chewing the leaves of his tea.

Once the fungus receded back into the
flower fields, the daily games of dominoes
resumed. Froggy made Sandra subcomandante of EMF and as subcomandante,
Sandra sat next to Froggy.

But unlike the other EMF cholos,
Sandra did not cuff her pants or shave her
head. She cut her pant legs below the
knee and pulled her hair into a ponytail
that she tied with string pulled from fertilizer sacks, loosing her hair only when
alone with Froggy.

Every Sunday morning, as families
walked by holding their soup bowls, new
members were jumped into EMF. When
Froggy and Sandra returned from the
flower fields, my father gave them petroleum and towels to wipe the splatters of
blood from their faces.

They entered the house with their col-
lars stained and smelling of arnica cream
and petroleum. They would sit and study
the charts that my father had drawn.

One of which looked like this:

The three tallies circled:

(III)

"Here is where we attack," my father
said.

And Sandra listened while trying to
knit the tail of her shawl, but her knots
always unraveled, leaving strands of string
strewn wherever she sat.

My father recognized the stitching from
the old tablecloths I had attempted to
make. He followed the hems of my knitting through the town of El Monte and
into my bed. As he picked up the yarn
from the floor and placed it into his
swollen pockets, I lay there wrapped
around Froggy, until I felt the familiar fists
of my father pounding against my back.

And before I could turn, Froggy had
lunged out of bed and dropped my father
to the floor, putting two slits across his
throat with the blade of his carnation knife.

And even though my whole life I
wanted to flee from my father, I did not
like seeing him wrapped in the shreds of
my shawl and buried in the middle of a
flower field.

I remained subcomandante of EMF
but moved out of Froggy's. I could not
sleep in the same room with the man who
had killed my father.

I took only the bureau drawers, two
rugs, and two pillows from Froggy's, and
moved into a stucco at the edge of El
Monte. I slept alone, cushioned by rugs
and pillows. I was a quiet sleeper and did
not thrash about or even snore, but I
began to wake with welts on my arms and
my ribs sore and bruised. It was not until
I looked in the mirror and noticed the
black eye on my face that I knew I had
been dreaming of my father.

SATURN

On the first day of the offensive, Federico de la Fe and the rest of EMF covered their faces with handkerchiefs. This was mostly a symbolic gesture, because Saturn could see through the thin cloth. And despite the smoke caused by the burning of the flower fields, Saturn could still see the maneuverings of EMF and Federico de la Fe. The women fed tires and kerosene into the fire, while the men hopped into trucks and drove south. The plan was to split the army and force Saturn to choose between the two battalions.

Froggy drove the lead truck and everybody else followed, honking their horns so no one could hear what Froggy and Federico de la Fe discussed inside the cab of the Chevy.

Little Merced sat on Federico de la Fe's lap and looked out the back window to see the convoy of pickup trucks and EMF cholos.

They drove past San Diego and into Tijuana—the city of invention and discoveries. Where Margarita Carmen Cansino shed syllables from her name and velvet curtains from her stage, rising, leaving a tail of draperies and scraps of paper cut from her birth certificate, to emerge as a star.

Sandra and the EMF cholas spread kerosene around the fields that ringed El Monte and fanned the fire with rugs and towels until it completely surrounded the town. The handkerchiefs across their noses and mouth covered them from Saturn and from the smoke and glowing ashes that leaped from the flames.

There were two purposes for the fire. The first was for the smoke to cloud the view of Saturn. The second was to mark the town—a circle of ash and melted tires. So when crop dusters and hot air balloons flew over El Monte, the pilots would point down at the town that had engaged in the most impossible of wars.

LITTLE MERCED

Once the war maneuvers began, I dropped out of school. Instead, I rode in Froggy's truck and listened to my father talk about the supplies needed for war.

When we got to the border crossing, the guard made Froggy and my father pull down the handkerchiefs that covered their faces. The guard, holding his empty holster, said that he did not sympathize with gringo or fatalist wars and we could only enter on the condition that we would not spread the conflict.

Once in Tijuana, we parked and gathered around Froggy's truck. My father climbed on the roof of the cab and read from a list he had written. He told Smiley to come back with a milk goat and a billy. Pelon was in charge of fighting cocks and hens. My father read down the list and passed out money wrapped in newspaper until only he and Froggy were left. My father and Froggy were to bring back as many mechanical tortoise shells as possible.

We walked to the mechanic's shop, where my father and I had first stayed, but there were no more turtles, just Japanese combustion engines and a rhyming quatrain written in black grease above the frame of the door. It was a quote from *Centuries* and it was written in French. My father asked for the man who had written the quatrain but they told him that the man he was looking for had quit and run away to the colonia of La Quemadora.

We got into the truck and drove through the center of town, around a turnabout with a copper statue of a shackled Hidalgo that veered traffic to the edge of the city. We continued past warehouses and maquilas, beyond the tin and paper towns. The three-lane road funneled into a single lane that hugged the edge of the rock quarry and then turned into dirt as we entered La Quemadora.

MECHANIC

When the man and his daughter returned from Los Angeles, they were accompanied by an American pachuco who had written the initials of his hometown on the side of his neck. The daughter asked about Nostradamus's warnings, while her father spoke of his need for lead shells. He said that he had once found shelter from an ominous force in the density of the tortoises' dome, and wanted to know my price for the shells and how I had come to them. I explained everything by telling them my story of exile and tortoises:

"I began dismantling the mechanical tortoises when I found one chewing on the meat of a real sea turtle. The carapace of the tortoise had been pierced by the metal jaws, and aside from a little blood and some fleshy pouches of milk, nothing was left of the animal. It was just an empty shell nestling on three eggs.

"I cradled the eggs in my hat and when I got back to the mechanic shop I quit my job and wrote Nostradamus's prediction from quatrain 215, which warns against the strength of machines.

"When the eggs hatched, I suckled the tortoises at the tit of a goat and let them roam in my bedroom until they ate all my sheets and were old enough to return to sea.

"Since then I've exiled myself in La Quemadora, luring the remaining mechanical tortoises into cages and then into scrap heaps.

"Some of the lead shells have been charred and melted by Burn Collectors but there are still a lot of them left. You can take as many as you want. Just leave one—once in a while I like to sit and think without anybody intruding."

The people of La Quemadora had also discovered the cure for sadness. But unlike Federico de la Fe, they felt no shame and did not hide their scars or blisters. Federico de la Fe had entered La Quemadora in search of the carapace remains of mechanical turtles. But as he left La Quemadora, his truck heavy with lead shells, he did not think of the war, but of his wife and the scabs he would peel and replace with the heat of fire.

Before they entered the house of the exiled mechanic, they passed a hotel, a fruit stand, and a charred table where a woman flipped tarot cards while rocking a slobbering baby on her knee.

Her arms were blistered and black, and at times the tarot cards stuck to her hands as the pus trickled to the tips of her fingers.

Federico de la Fe was the first to knock on the mechanic's door, but when no one answered, he let Little Merced press the illuminated button that rang the doorbell.

A woman covered in burn stars opened the door.

Dark strands, bringing the stench of burned rubber, billowed into the air space, reaching heights above the Aviation Administration's jurisdiction. The black smoke braided with the fluff of cumulous clouds, forming patches so dense that Saturn had to shift his weight and push through in order to see the EMF women roll tires and logs into the fire. The crackle and roar of the flames drowned out the words Sandra whispered through the cloth of her handkerchief and into the ears of EMF.

Sometimes not even Saturn could make out the whole sentence, catching only chunks of what Sandra said.

"The heavy feeding will be in the... when the men are to return... Everything into the fire... and smoke into... on my command..."

My father did not want me to touch the stars of Maricela, and as he and Froggy entered the mechanic's study he warned me not to ask her.

In the study, my father, Froggy, and the mechanic talked about turtles and tortoises, and Maricela and I sat in the living room. And because I could not touch the stars, I asked how she made them. Maricela showed me her burners. She poured petroleum into one of them and lit its flame. Then from a drawer that she had lined with packing print she pulled out her screwdrivers, all their Philips heads smoked to black. She held the one that made the biggest stars, and then the most pointed, and then the one that poked miniature stars that could not be seen.

Maricela chose the smallest screwdriver, heated the head until it glowed, then pressed it into her palm, singeing and lifting smoke, leaving only pink rawness.

"Does it hurt?"

"A little."

I asked her when she had started making stars. She said that she had started when she was young, though she was unsure why she had been drawn to fire. There was a man named Tacho who, despite being in love with her, was ashamed of Maricela's stars. Tacho was the type of man who wanted respectability even before love and, instead of accepting the smell of singed flesh and Maricela's marks, he had chosen a career of badge and title over her.

But Maricela did not cover her stars or burn in secret; she was defiant of Tacho and all those who said that Burn Collectors should be anonymous and their scars hidden. Maricela was brash and public and she did not mind if people wanted to touch the constellations that adorned her body.

When the doorbell rang Ignacio was in his study reading *Centuries,* planning new ways to lure the mechanical tortoises into La Quemadora, and I was in the living room dipping the tips of my screwdrivers into alcohol and vinegar.

They immediately asked for the mechanic and I led the two men into the study. The young girl stayed with me in the living room.

Her name was Merced and I showed her my tools and fire, the stars on my arms, and the pattern that ran across my back.

There was no design to where I pressed the screwdriver. At times, I would simply press the head into a healing burn, darkening what was the fading outline of an old star. But Merced saw logic in the placements and pointed at the bust of Santos and at what she assumed were Nostradamus's pet dogs. And there were other constellations still forming that I had yet to complete.

I also told Merced about Tacho, how after many years of always thinking about him and his possible return I had finally settled with someone who was not Tacho, someone who was neither a Burn Collector nor a native of La Quemadora. And while Ignacio's hands were always black, it was not from fire but from the dismantling of machinery and tortoises, a black that would wash away with soap lard and pumice.

Ignacio was never threatened or embarrassed by the permanence of scars, by the pus of blisters or the dryness and cracking that surrounded the burns. He poured water from the retaining buckets onto the agave and aloe garden and then broke the sword-leaves from the plants. And every morning, before I dressed, he pulled off the sheets, and in the bucket were skinned and limp swords of agave and aloe that he rubbed upon my skin, soothing my burns.

The mechanic led Federico de la Fe and Froggy outside, past the woman with tarots and the baby, past the agave and aloe garden, until they came to a lot where the mechanic kept the gutted shells of the tortoises. In a cage a mechanical tortoise bit at the lead bars of her prison.

There were hundreds of shells, some rusting, others gleaming with the luster of metallic blue, and while the mechanic explained to Federico de la Fe how he disassembled the tortoises, Froggy pulled the truck into the lot.

Stacked, roped, and tarped, ten shells fit in the bed of the truck. There were enough shells to fill every EMF truck. Had Federico de la Fe known of the mechanic's collection he never would have sent the rest of EMF in search of goats and roosters.

The flames subsided, the smoke no longer thick ropes of expanding girth but mere strings rising from the hems of the fire. Just inside the circle of abating flames, the EMF women had arranged mounds of tires and lumber—ready to be fed on command to the glowing ring.

On the south side, the flames faded completely, making a gap in the glow of the circle as the heat of the embers burned, deploying the last of their energy before crumbling into gray ash.

While my father and Froggy loaded the
turtle shells into the bed of the truck,
I went to talk to the woman who shuffled
tarot cards. As I got closer to her table,
I realized that it was the Baby Nostradamus and his mother, except that her
arms were now raw and burnt.

I patted the Baby Nostradamus's head
and asked the mother what had happened
to her arms—they were not stars, just
burns without meaning.

She offered to tell my fortune with the
help of her baby. She grabbed my hands,
squeezing my fingers while I stared into
the eyes of the Baby Nostradamus.

As she traced my lifeline, the blister
on the tip of her index finger ruptured,
and the fluid channeled into the ruts of
my hand. The outer lines of my palm
became tributaries feeding into the main
river. I lifted my hand toward my face and
saw that I was holding the river of Las
Tortugas. As I looked closer I saw our old
adobe house and the orchard that lined the
river, the trees heavy with limes. A family
with goats and dinner doves had moved in
and planted maize on the dirt roof.

Downstream, at the cliff of my hand,
there was a couple taking a bath. I could
not recognize the man, but he was pale,
his beard trimmed, his hair unkempt and
curly. At first, I could see only the
woman's back. She stood in the water, her
hair still dry, but as she turned and
grabbed the pumice and soap lard from
the rocks, I saw that it was my mother.

I closed my fingers, collapsing the
trees into twigs and the river and banks
into a clump of mud, and threw it into
the street.

Froggy whistled and told me to get
into the cab. I gave the woman a dollar
and jumped into the truck.

At first croak of the morning rooster, the sun still hours from the horizon, Federico de la Fe and his convoy headed back to the now-marked city of El Monte. The shocks of their trucks were pressed down to a tight coil and the exhaust pipes sparked against the asphalt as they rolled over speed bumps and potholes. The load of tortoise shells and livestock bounced on the trucks' beds. But once across the border and on the highway, the tarred lanes leveled out, and reflectors in the middle of the road led all the way back to El Monte.

They doused the wood and tires with kerosene, letting the fluid run into the knots and woodpecker holes, drowning mites and silverfish. And through nail punctures and knife slashes, kerosene trickled into the inner tubes, soaking wire meshes and air valves. They waited for Sandra's word, and she looked for daybreak and the grille of Froggy's truck to give her command.

Morning light was yet to appear, but once she heard the hum of Froggy's engine and saw the rays of his headlights, Sandra tossed a log into the flame, ordering the fuel into the fire.

The convoy accelerated, funelling into El Monte from its southern opening, trailing in track marks as they drove over soot and ash. Once the last truck passed, the circle was once again connected, the full ring of fire sending heat and thick puffs of clouds to clot the sky, trying to screen Saturn from his view of El Monte as the trucks scrambled and the goods were unloaded and stored.

Federico de la Fe put his hand over his hankerchief and mouth, speaking slowly into Froggy's ear and then going to Sandra.

"Go get some sle... tomorrow... Saturn... is what... cau... ther..."

Sandra cupped her ear but was still unable to hear all of what Federico de la Fe had said.

LITTLE MERCED

When I woke up, it was almost evening.
The fire was now only a ring of ash, flar-
ing at spots, but the smoke stayed low to
the ground, lingering like a fog. My father
stayed awake, not kneading his pillow or
pulling his covers, instead watching the
fire while the rest of EMF went to bed.

By evening everybody was up again,
dousing hot spots and sweeping ash from
windowsills and stoops.

My father brought out two roosters,
training them by waving meat in front of
their beaks, and instead of yoking blades
to their feet he tied rocks to weigh them
down. He kept the cocks from the hens;
instead he caged them and slid in mirrors
so they would peck at their own images.

My father then showed Froggy and
Pelon how to milk the goats. Just as in Las
Tortugas, he tied the hind legs of the goat
together, making sure not to jerk the knot.

EMF was now ready to run its own
dairy farm and host its first cockfight.
After rubbing the milk into the palms
and back of his hands, he told Froggy that
we had almost everything we needed to
sustain and finance a war against Saturn.
All that remained was to retrieve more
lead shells.

CHAPTER FIVE

•

FROGGY

When Sandra moved out, she left the knitting needle that she used to etch "EMF" into the side of my neck. She wiped the stains of India ink and blood from the tip and stuck the needle into the floorboards to mark the spot where her father had died.

She loaded the rugs and bureau drawers onto the bed of my Chevy and drove to a stucco six blocks away. When she returned the truck, mud clung to the walls of the tires. She apologized and handed me the keys.

"Thank you, Comandante," she said. I closed my hand, feeling her residual warmth on the surface of the keys. From that day forward she addressed me with a sterile formality and prefaced everything she said with my military rank. She no longer called me "my Froggy" or "mijo," and when she spoke of me to Federico de la Fe, I was "Comandante Froggy." She discussed only battle strategy and logistics in my presence and refused to acknowledge anything I said unless I called her "Subcomandante Sandra."

Though I had never believed in the medicines of the curanderos, when Sandra did not return after a week and refused to respond to the letters I sent her, I went to the botanica for a cure.

We had just returned from Tijuana three days earlier. The fire had been out for almost two nights, but smoke still lingered and the light breeze that rolled down the San Gabriel range pushed burnt debris and ash against the door of the curandero's shop.

Inside, porcelain saints and candles lined the walls. Officially canonized and recognized saints sat on the top shelf. The lesser saints, whose halos were held up in Vatican red tape, and those whose sainthood had been revoked after it was discovered what they kept underneath their futons, occupied the lower shelf. The Marys and Magdalens all stood on the floor where we could touch their gilded crowns and the stubs of their missing fingers. There was nobody at the counter but I could hear groans and church Latin from behind the curtains. After waiting for some time I shook the tepetate bell.

The Latin ceased, the groans lessened, and the curandero appeared from behind the now-parting curtains. Though he was a shade darker, he looked very much like St. Gabriel, the patron saint of long-distance love who stood in the lower shelf holding international postage stamps and the itemized phone bill that confirmed his vow of poverty. Just below Gabriel's statue was the Mary Magdalen of the second fall, who was of course kneeling with her mouth open and her left cheek protruding and a white glaze across her lips.

"Unrequited love?" the curandero immediately asked.

"It's more complicated than that, but yes," I said.

He nodded and asked for a minute to finish the limpia he was performing. The curandero did not close the curtains. In the back a woman was lying on her stomach, her bare back streaked with blood and flecked with bits of black thorns. The curandero picked up a smoked thorn bush and whipped the woman, and while she groaned he calmly recited Latin verse. When all the thorns had broken off and there was nothing left but a black stem, the limpia was complete. The curandero wiped the blood and spread soaked marijuana on the woman's back. She sat up. I could see her light mestizo breasts and the dark of her Indian nipples. She buttoned her blouse and walked around the counter and kneeled in front of the porcelain Virgin of Arcadia who carried the rotting body of Christ in a wheelbarrow. She said a short prayer in Spanish and then walked out of the shop, the blood from the thorn wounds seeping through her white blouse.

The curandero introduced himself as Apolonio but said that I could call him simply Polo. He then explained that cholos never came to him for problems that had to do with warts or rashes, and that if I was in his shop he knew that I was looking to nurse some ailment of love.

He wiped his hands on a towel and from a drawer took out a parchment that listed the reasons why women deserted comfortable homes. He read and I shook my head at all the offered possibilities.

"Sometimes men don't notice these things. Are you sure there is not another man?" the curandero asked.

I told the curandero the specifics, how I had unwittingly sliced the throat of Sandra's father, and of Sandra's insistence that it was unholy to share a mattress and breakfast table with a man who had killed any of her progenitors.

Curanderos could restore the levels of the drying oceans, they could repair broken teeth and collapsed retinas, and if God was distracted and not looking they could even pull people from the grip of Purgatory—provided the appropriate fee was paid. But they couldn't reach Sandra. For the price of my Chevy and two grand, the curandero offered to retrieve Sandra's father no matter where he was. But his resurrection would not absolve the murder, and then I would be responsible not only for his death but also for reawakening her beatings.

Instead, I left the shop with a paper bag into which the curandero had punched holes with the tip of a pencil. Inside was a songbird from the Oaxacan range, along with a tortoise egg and a banana that I was to fry and scramble and then feed to the bird.

Despite the bird shit and the colony of ticks that clung to its wings, the bird's perpetual song, sung even when it was perched and its eyelids shut, helped to alleviate some of the loneliness Sandra had left.

The memorial Sandra had built with a single knitting needle began to lose its effect. No longer a tribute to her dead father, it had become a scratching post where the songbird shat and against which it flapped its wings. The drawerless bureau where Sandra had once kept her socks and cotton underwear was now a shelter housing a nest made of shredded newspapers and shirt lint. The only time I felt the loneliness was when I scrambled eggs and sliced bananas and the Oaxacan bird stopped its song to eat.

Federico de la Fe understood that when a woman leaves a house there are many things to resolve. Some are simple things, like figuring out how to fold the linens, learning to cook smaller portions, and discovering where the manzanilla tea is kept. And then there are other adjustments— the adjustments that seem to be the simplest but take the longest time to make: the unclogged tub where her hair used to gather, the sterile odor of a lone sleeper, the missing swabs that she always left floating in the toilet. Federico de la Fe said that it was never the cleanliness of women that we missed, but the signs of their fallibility and oversights in hygiene.

And while I listened to the songbird and prepared the scrambled eggs and bananas, Federico de la Fe and the rest of EMF continued to prepare for the war. Sandra coordinated the initiations; though she honored the tradition of EMF, she did so in the kindest way, electing the meekest members for the brincas, sparing as much injury as possible. Pelon and Little Oso ran the cockfights, bringing in ten grand a week in admission and house bets. And Federico de la Fe had managed to set up a goat dairy and a small egg farm to feed EMF. Little money was spent on food, and those who picked flowers after weigh-ins donated a percentage of their pay to Federico de la Fe to help fight against Saturn. Half of the money went south to the mechanic, allowing him to continue his hunt for the tortoises, luring the mechanical beasts into his yard. He dismantled them, keeping the coils and sprockets and sending the lead shells that we transported to El Monte. The rest of the money went to incidentals and to a reserve, anticipating a future time where we would be unable to work or put on cockfights.

During those times that I did not go to the dominoes table, Federico de la Fe would come to my door and update me on his plans. He said it was okay to listen to the songbird and stay in the house for now, but one day I would have to come out and rejoin him at the dominoes table.

"I told everybody that you were fighting tapeworms," Federico de la Fe said, "and that you would return as soon as you spat them out." He explained that there was nothing shameful in taking sick leave because of a woman. It was only for the sake of morale that he had chosen to lie to EMF about the cause of my absence.

Though he rarely talked about it, Federico de la Fe mourned the loss of his wife. Sometimes, after waiting his turn at the table, holding all six ivory pieces cupped in one hand, he unloaded the tile and instead of calling out the double five he had set down, he would instead say the name of his wife. Everybody knew that if she had not left, Federico de la Fe would be a maize and bean farmer—not a war commander. No need to rise against the solar system when you have plenty of crops and a beautiful wife.

I admired his loyalty, the ability to long indefinitely. But I did not have Federico de la Fe's endurance. After one month and the constant serenade of the Oaxacan songbird, I was able to sit at the dominoes table and speak to Sandra with the same confident tone that I used when addressing Pelon or Little Oso.

And it was that infidelity to remorse that drove me to a woman from the old country, a paisana, in the hope that she would be able to inspire in me what Merced had in Federico de la Fe. I thought that because Sandra, like me, was born in the world of asphalt and cement, she could not possibly know what it was to really love.

After an early morning meeting around the dominoes table, during which Federico de la Fe discussed his plans for the tortoise shells and Sandra gave a head count of the members of EMF, I went back to the fields to pick carnations. I had not picked flowers since Sandra had left the house, and there was something comforting in folding up the cuffs of my pants and feeling the sun on my back and the soil trapped in my shoes. I picked until I covered my tarp and pulled it to the scales and stacked my picking basket on top of the others.

At the scales, a woman was weighing the tarp of carnations she had picked. I had never seen her before and she did not have EMF markings on her neck or bruises from recent initiation. Although all those that I approached eventually became EMF, she was the first I had thought of sparing. She wore no shoes and spoke a Spanish like Federico de la Fe's, unbroken by English. She said she had fled a world that was falling apart and had settled in El Monte, lured by the stability of stucco and sidewalks that did not crumble on contact.

"Not even my shoes would hold together," she said, and lifted her legs to show her bare feet.

For one week she had slept in a bed of carnations, nestled between furrows, and had survived on strawberries, an experience that forever ruined her appreciation for flowers and red fruit. Thereafter, no matter the amount of baby's breath or care in arrangement, she saw nothing romantic in bouquets, and she refused strawberries, even when they were dipped in chocolate. And Valentine's Day reminded her only of hardship.

Her name was Julieta and the day I met her I took her home to listen to the song of the Oaxacan songbird. Julieta warned me that she came from a town named after decay, but I did not care. We undressed to the song of the bird and as the box springs coiled and uncoiled the song became louder and louder—so loud that no one could hear the creaking of the bed or the thud of the collapsing bed frame. The concerto of the Oaxacan songbird reached beyond the ashen boundaries of El Monte, past the Chinese village at the edge of Los Angeles, past the skyscrapers and into the hills of Hollywood.

CHAPTER SIX

● ● ●

RAMON BARRETO

Though it was faint, Ramon Barreto could clearly distinguish the melody that entered through his restroom window—a melody he had not heard in more than twenty years. As a young boy, he sat under the weak shade of chaparrals and whistled along with the Oaxacan songbirds. Ramon Barreto's birdcalls were so difficult to discern from the genuine chirps that he was often pelted with rocks intended to scare birds away from the thickets that surrounded the cornfields. But now, as he tried to mimic the tune in his porcelain and linoleum restroom, blood and saliva spilled from his mouth and onto the floor.

Ramon Barreto had slit his tongue and lips while trying to taste the inside of Merced de Papel; he left a puddle of blackening red between her thighs. He ran from the bedroom, through the den, and out to the back deck that overlooked the Hollywood hills. He let his tongue drip on the wood planks until Merced pulled down her dress, walked outside, and helped him wrap his tongue in gauze. The paper cut was so deep that he could not taste the rusty flavor of his own blood.

In time, his lips healed, but the wound on his tongue remained tender and bled so often that he kept a chamber pot in every room where he could spit. Merced de Papel came from a tribe of extinct people and though Ramon Barreto had spent almost a year of his life sleeping happily next to her, he was not surprised when he awoke one day and she was gone. He understood the restlessness of people made of paper.

Often, when a man is deserted, there is a desperate need to fill the emptiness, but for Ramon Barreto there was solace in the loneliness. He felt even a sort of relief: no more tangling with her sharp edges and crumpled legs, waking striped by her dry scratches. Ramon Barreto threw away the dresses and blouses that Merced de Papel had left behind. He scrubbed the newsprint smudges from the refrigerator's handle, from the loveseat's armrests, from the television and radio knobs. The only reminder of Merced de Papel left in the house was a glass jar where Ramon Barreto kept the scraps of construction paper he would sometimes find stuck to his chest or at the foot of the bed.

Ramon Barreto always feared discovering a completely unraveled and torn Merced, and so he was glad that she had gone. But still there were mornings when he woke to a sore tongue and blood on his pillowcases. He would lie there, dabbing his tongue with the sheets, looking at the ceiling and thinking of what he had lost. And on those days, when it was lonely to remember her, he stuffed his mouth with tissue paper and crumpled the Sunday news, and at night he pressed the paper between his knees.

APOLONIO

The meat Apolonio bought was carted by Chinese butchers from the stadium to their market stand. While the groundsmen tilled the sand for the next match, the butchers entered the corridor and pulled banderillas and swords from the fallen toro bravo. They brought out the hooked knives from their apron pockets and slashed and gutted the bull. The horns and hooves were buried on the plaza passageway, and three wheelbarrows, heavy with warm meat, exited the plaza as the trumpets sounded and the next matador was announced.

The sour steaks were sold to the stone-and-shake prisons lining the border and at the Tijuana central market. Apolonio selected the cuts of beef from the table next to dead fighting cocks. He boiled the tenderloin in brown sugar to counter the acidity of anger and fear, but after a day under the flame the stew still smelled of citrus. It was not until Apolonio added bark from a sweet mesquite that the meat gave up its bitterness. He found a solution to the sourness of ring bulls and soon after learned to marinate uncrested and severely pecked roosters in pear sauce, bringing out the sugar from the wing meat and breasts.

Apolonio was not yet a curandero—his broths and fried dishes were intended simply to nourish, not to cure spiritual ailments. Unlike the curanderos from the south, Apolonio had come to medicine not through ancestry but by pure accident. His mother had just suffered the third apparition of the Virgin of Trinidad when he stumbled upon his first remedy. The brightness of the holy mother, as she floated above the headboard with her blazing halo, tanned Apolonio's mother's face and warmed the pillows. It was then, looking to calm his mother's neurosis brought by the sacred visitation, that Apolonio discovered the calming effect of tortoise eggs.

One morning—as his mother lay in bed frazzled, praying with her palms pressed and sunscreen on her face—he cracked open a turtle egg, dropping it into the pan and then scrambling it with his finger. Apolonio instantly recognized the soothing properties of the raw yolk. He cracked two more eggs, sifted the whites through his fingers, and walked into his mother's bedroom, carefully sliding the yolks from his palm and on to her belly. As he punctured the soft sacks and massaged the orange yolk into her skin, she sighed and unclasped her hands, relaxing her fingers and falling into a deep sleep for the first time since the Virgin's initial visit.

Apolonio's knowledge was not one of inherited traditions. He was scientific, setting up control groups and administering placebos, all results carefully graphed and cataloged in the index of his recipe book. The remedies were first recorded in pencil and then traced over in ink, once the trial phase was over. Despite Apolonio's insistence on inking only proven antidotes and ignoring the blind faith of the paisan healers, his parchment was identical to every other curandero's book—the one exception being an entry that dealt with the music of Oaxacan songbirds.

SANTOS

In his home state of Jalisco, in front of the mayor, the reigning flower princess, and fourteen thousand spectators, Santos was unmasked. The challenger, Mil Mascaras, unknotted and unlaced the cloth-and-sequin mask with his teeth as he held Santos' face down on the canvas. He threw the mask out of the ring and two unsuspecting Clandestine Vatican Troops, dressed in their vacationing Swiss guayabera shirts, picked it up from the cobbled floor, placing it in a brown sack bearing the Pope's wax seal. Santos covered his face with his hands and tried to run out of the ring. But Mil Mascaras knew that he had unveiled a saint, instantly noticing the tell-tale cowlick where the halo would one day hover. In a choke-hold, Mil Mascaras paraded the unmasked Santos from one end of the ring to the other, making sure to stand underneath the balcony of the flower princess. As a fugitive, Santos had found the perfect hideaway in the code of the masked luchador, but after nearly four decades of searching, the authorities now knew that Santos was Juan Meza.

After the match, Juan Meza was taken to the dressing room, where a Vatican official touched his Catholic nose and began to administer the qualifying tests of sainthood while the Swiss troops stood by the door. The official, a cardinal on emergency summons, had been educated in Roman seminaries and specially trained in holy and heretic diagnostics.

The Cardinal lifted Juan Meza's arm, sniffing the wrestler's sweat, and then shone a flashlight into his eyes. One of the Swiss troops, prompted by the Cardinal's command, assisted in the final procedure, slicing the side-welts of Juan Meza's unlaced boots and then peeling the split leather and socks from his feet. It was confirmed: Juan Meza was a saint. His sweat smelled of potpourri, his pupils did not contract, and the soles of his feet were pale and marked by fresh stigmata.

On his saintly honor they released Juan Meza and ordered him to present himself at the Saint Juaquin Cathedral the next day, where the canonization process would begin. He shook the smooth powdered hand of the Cardinal, a palm so smooth that it felt like ivory, and promised to arrive promptly and with his hair combed, first thing the next day, and then walked outside to feel the sun on his bare cheeks for the first time in decades.

Juan Meza preferred the life of a Mexican wrestling hero to the quiet, celibate existence of modern saints. He turned down a trip to Saint Peter's Basilica in Rome and a calendar day dedicated in his honor. Instead he fled north to Tijuana, finding refuge in a three-hundred-seat cockfighting ring built on squatted land along the banks of the Tijuana River, where he would fight his final match.

RAMON BARRETO

Ramon Barreto remembered the day Merced de Papel wiped the blood from the deck and looked up at him as he stood leaning against the banister.

"I'm sorry, Ramon," she said.

"Not your fault." The blood began to crust on his lips and chin.

"If I would have known... maybe we shouldn't do that anymore?"

"I'm fine, just a little blood."

"Maybe we should wet it a little. With water I mean. I can do that."

And she did. After Ramon healed, she soaked a face towel and dabbed herself until she was soft and could not cut through the skins of oranges. She put her hand on the back of his head and brought him into her thighs. He opened his lips and put Merced in his mouth. He felt her breaking apart; small wads of wet paper stuck to his teeth, some he swallowed. But instead of facing the fact that Merced was dissolving into his mouth he bit his tongue and drew blood.

"You're still a little sharp," he said and walked over to the sink.

Ramon Barreto wanted to love Merced de Papel from the first day he saw her. He had lived most of his life in Hollywood, splicing film. He made sure no one saw Fred Astaire trip on the stairs, cut Judy Garland's temper tantrums, and marked the celluloid where Rita Hayworth botched her lines and cussed in Spanish. One day, as he hand-rolled a reel and stored it in the fireproof safe, he looked out the studio's window and saw Merced de Papel sitting on a bench waiting for a cable car. Ramon Barreto had fled his childhood adobe town and settled in one made of tinsel. As always, with those estranged from their patrias, it is a woman who reminds them of the maize fields and songbirds. In Merced de Papel, Ramon Barreto could see the handiwork of the old origami surgeon who made flying swans and leaping monkeys. She bent her knees and then closed her fingers as she lifted her canvas bag, revealing the familiar movements of the paper birds' flapping wings and hinged beaks.

For Ramon Baretto, Merced de Papel was a way to return home without leaving the comforts of central air conditioning and reclining living-room chairs. But soon he discovered that Merced was prone to the same fragility as the eroding adobe walls and the endangered songbirds; and though it was Merced who left Ramon's house, it was he who had pushed her away. Ramon's homeland was disintegrating, a disease spread from the mountain town of El Derramadero, and despite his homesickness he preferred the severe melancholia of Hollywood and its people to the pestilence of decay that Merced de Papel might bring.

APOLONIO

Apolonio painted his front door green and lit a red candle that signaled he was open for business. Though he was a self-made curandero, his reputation grew, and even stubborn old southern widows knocked on his door looking for a cure for cataracts. A young Rita Hayworth once came to Apolonio's botanica and asked him for plant food and uña de gato to rub on her callused dancing feet. And though Apolonio knew that Rita Hayworth would one day turn her back on the city and people of Tijuana, he treated her kindly and let her follow her path to unhappiness and Hollywood stardom.

The fourth apparition of the Virgin of Trinidad scorched the south wall, the wooden headboard, the grass futon, and the intent face of Apolonio's mother. She died watching the radiating light of the Virgin's halo—a tragedy that only added to Apolonio's reputation and customer base. Against Catholic injunction, Apolonio crumbled his mother into an urn and walked up the cerro that overlooked the wood and paper towns and the smoking silver assembly plants. On the hilltop, as the wind spread his mother, he first felt the joint aches of lost parentage, orphan pains that would rankle his body every second Sunday of May and the second to last Sunday of June. With alchemy Apolonio tried to conquer his sorrow, but the concoctions of turtle yolks and minced lemon seeds, the special diet of mesquite beans and palm ash, and candle-burning rituals all failed.

During a hot Tijuana winter the smoke from the television factories lingered and mixed with the odor of meat cuts and de la oya beans. Flocks of migrating Oaxacan songbirds flew over the central market and the maquilas but then broke from their formations, dropping like stones onto the Tijuana streets. Some crashed into the chest of a granite Hidalgo raising his shackled hands; the lucky ones collided with the fountains that surrounded the Al Capone casinos. But many broke their beaks against the brick and mortar walls of old slaughter and packing houses.

When Pío-Pío fell she crashed through the thin layer of burnt shingles and landed safely on the charred bed of Apolonio's dead mother. Pío-Pío could flap her wings but was too weak to fly or sing. In the same room where the intense heat of the halo had spelled death to Apolonio's mother, a faint chirping led Apolonio back into her locked and boarded sleeping chamber. By the third week Pío-Pío was flying around the house and singing concertos with frolicking cadenzas. Alchemy and years of santería could not alleviate the grief that the visiting Virgin of Trinidad had brought to his home. But now, the sorrow that the Holy Mother had brought was pushed out by the melody of a Oaxacan songbird.

SANTOS

The Vatican official waited for Juan Meza for two weeks before deciding that perhaps the word of a saint was not always to be trusted.

Juan Meza stitched together a new Santos mask, complete with his trademark silver trim that outlined the mouth and eyes. For days he walked around the city of Tijuana with the mask in his pants pocket. No one asked to shake his hand or kiss his knuckles. He bought sugared meat and chewed on it while sitting on the banks of the drained river. People walked by in plastic jumpsuits, passing the cockfighting arena, and disappearing into the television maquilas.

Juan Meza enjoyed the anonymity of being a Ticuanense, but two days before his final match, he pulled the cloth mask over his face and went to the arena's proprietor, Don Feliz, to discuss the details of his contract. Don Feliz agreed to cut the undercards. There would be no cockfights to upstage, no splattered intestines, shit, or broken blades to slip on. When Santos jumped into the ring, he would smell only the acrid fumes of cleaning ammonia rising from the mat.

Don Feliz offered to split the admission revenue and give the winner fifteen percent of the house bets. And even though Santos refused to acknowledge his own sainthood, he signed over his share to the Virgin of Arcadia, who would be paid in a thousand veladoras made from pure beeswax and braided wicks. Santos agreed to Don Feliz's terms: he would not know the name of his opponent, the thickness of the ropes, or the bounce and pliancy of the mat.

On the day of the match, Santos stretched and oiled his body in the dressing room. He slipped on his wrestling boots and threaded the laces, tightening them to his feet and then shining them with layers of wax, while spectators filed in and took their seats on the bleachers. The Clandestine Vatican Troops were not in the building. They searched for Juan Meza in every farm and church alcove and deployed personnel into the Jaliscon canyons of the Machuca Indians—a tribe notorious for providing sanctuary to AWOL saints. They searched everywhere except for cockfighting arenas and border wrestling circuits.

And while the Pope cursed at the archbishop for losing yet another saint, Chicago gangsters and Hollywood starlets left the horse track, crossed the lounge where the roulette wheel spun, the ball landing on double zeros, and told their chauffeur to drive them to Don Feliz's arena. Don Feliz circled the ring with chairs and made sure to pad the splintering seats and backs with pillows. The gangsters and starlets sat ringside, drinking their own brand of mescal made from tender agave and purple saffron and smoking filtered American cigarettes.

She was wearing a scarf, long gloves, and dark sunglasses, but the distinct wave of her cigarette holder gave her away. From the top bleachers lettuce pickers threw heads of iceberg and chanted, "Rita Vendida!" When she stood up and her bodyguards walked her to the ladies' room, the lettuce pickers whistled and yelled, "Fuck you, Margarita!"

By the time Rita had returned to her seat, Santos had just been introduced, and instead of the pale iceberg lettuce, he was showered with lush romaine leaves and carnations. Santos climbed into the ring. The ropes were unpadded and pulled tight. He undid his cape and hopped on the mat. It was solid. One body slam or a missed flying kick and the match would be over.

Three hours before the match, silk-screened posters were posted on the phone poles, on the bus benches, and in Tijuana's casinos and racetracks. Everybody in Don Feliz's arena knew who Santos was fighting except for Santos himself. Suddenly, from out of the corridor, his head covered with a wet towel, closely followed by his corner man, came the challenger. Instead of flowers and romaine lettuce he was received with animal cookies; loyal fans threw only those shaped like tigers and lions, while the rest of the crowd launched indiscriminate handfuls.

When he pulled off the towel, revealing his orange and black mask, the crowd roared the tiger's growl, welcoming the challenging wrestler to the ring.

Santos knew that his old partner was always received with cookies, but it was not until Saturo Sayama stepped over the second rope that he realized that his last match would be Santos versus Tiger Mask.

RAMON BARRETO

Minutes before Karen Damen knocked on Ramon Barreto's door, he moved the glass jar that held the scraps of newsprint and colored paper from the bedroom to the kitchen cupboard, next to the pasta and the sacks of bleached flour. Though his tongue was always tender, when Ramon Barreto ate Karen Damen the warm wetness was not followed by the taste of his own blood. There were no ink smudges on his back or on the sofa cushions, and for the first time in years he could make love in the shower with the water running. The moisture from Ramon's mouth did not discolor Karen's chest; water slid across her body and down to her untattered toes. The mundane and simple things that the body could endure were miracles to Ramon Barreto.

Karen slept with her hair wrapped in a towel, and when she awoke in the morning Ramon led her into the shower and watched water bead off her body.

"You've never seen a woman shower?" she asked.

"Not in years," he said.

APOLONIO

Pío-Pío descended from one of the flocks that had willingly left the Garden in pursuit of Eve. Pío-Pío's ancestors were faithful to the first couple until they bore Cain. Attending to the duties of a new father, Adam neglected the fields, and when the crops wilted he began to caress the plump meat of the songbirds' wings and bellies. The first bird migration began on the brink of man's discovery of white meat. The flocks were not seen again until the years of Cortez. At that time the mestizos, who had learned from their colonizers, began to cage the Oaxacan songbirds.

And though Apolonio was a perfectly rationed mestizo (fifty percent Machuca and fifty percent Spaniard), he did not cage Pío-Pío. He let her fly through the house and perch on the woven wooden chairs. She ate her fried tortoise eggs and bananas on the kitchen table, and if it hadn't been for the impropriety of lying with feathered vertebrates, she would have slept in his bed. Instead, Pío-Pío rested on top of a redwood table in a nest made from strips of Apolonio's Sunday shirts.

A touring archbishop from Italy had once said, "Where the Virgin touches is forever blessed." And for that reason Apolonio had not informed the local authorities of his mother's cause of death—they would have enshrined her in a glass casket so the whole world could see her burnt face. The house would be surrounded by Vatican officials with pointy noses and Swiss guards, and then they would discover Apolonio's parchment text and santería potions.

Two months after crashing through Apolonio's roof and regaining her strength, Pío-Pío's fevered flights around the house became quick darts that shot from the tabletop to the kitchen counter and then back, and the excited cadenzas shortened into single chirps. At first, Apolonio worried, fearing that Pío-Pío had contracted an avian flu, but when he saw the three spotted eggs in her nest, he knew Pío-Pío's fatigue was only due to her approaching motherhood.

SANTOS

Santos and Tiger Mask shook hands at center ring. Rita replaced the cigarette on her holder and the men dressed in their pinstriped suits refilled their silver flasks. Even before the match began the arena was stuffy and dense with the stench of smoke, sweat, and tub-brewed alcohol.

"Saturo, we can end this quick," Santos told Tiger Mask as they grappled against the ropes that burned and chafed Tiger Mask's back.

Tiger Mask had blown his fortune on Argentine maté and a series of Italian sculptures siphoned from Europe during the war. Now, Tiger Mask wanted to return to the foothills of Mt. Tateyama, raise the collapsed roof of his childhood home, and paint the walls where he would hang his championship belts and photographs from every continent he had stepped on. But to afford the voyage he needed to defeat Santos and claim the fight purse.

Neither Santos nor Tiger Mask would throw the match. Despite nearly a decade of touring, during which time they shared a dressing room and won six intercontinental tag-team championships, they were now at opposite corners. The first three rounds were fought conservatively; both were wary of hitting the hard matting and the air in the arena taxed their lungs.

The Mexican canto written on the ceiling of the Gran Auditorio de Guadalajara said that in the fourth round heroes were either made or broken. And so it was: midway through the fourth round Tiger Mask lifted Santos over his head and slammed him onto the floor, breaking the back of the most celebrated and beloved Mexican wrestler in history. His spine cracked, sending a wince that frayed the fabric of his mask as he blinked for the final time, his holy eyes never to be seen again. The weight of death instantly dropped his eyelids, while a splintered black cross appeared on every poster and souvenir that bore his face.

The impact tore the canvas and exposed the slabs of concrete upon which the ring was raised. The ropes snapped and the spectators at ringside, except for Rita, rushed forward to see the broken Santos. His body remained still and not even the medics dared to unmask him. When it was clear that Santos was dead, Saturo Sayama knelt on one knee and paid his last respects to his former partner. The lone photographer at the event let the moment pass undocumented. The crowd and even the jeering lettuce pickers were silent. If not for the settling dust and floating cigarette smoke, that section of the world, at 117 degrees longitude and 32 latitude, would have been completely motionless.

RAMON BARRETO

Ramon Barreto and Karen Damen ate dolmas and pilaf while busboys danced around them and performed Greek somersaults; for dessert they went to the boardwalk and slurped oysters from the half-shell. In their stomachs they felt the aphrodisiacal potency of shellfish, and on their way home made love on the bench seats of the Lincoln while the chauffeur drove around Los Angeles. They passed Japanese gardens with blowfish rising from their waters, towering Salvi banana trees painted in tropical pastels tilting towards San Salvador, and rings of ashes surrounding furrowed towns. Ramon Barreto and Karen never looked out of their tinted windows; instead they basked in the glory of wet flesh that withstood the rigors of desire and propulsion.

While love thrived at fifty-five miles per hour, moths invaded Ramon Barreto's pantry and cupboards. They chewed through the flour sacks and ate the pastas. They fluttered throughout the house. The powder from their forewings left beige prints on the walls, on the framed Diego Rivera paintings, on the vases. They punched holes through Ramon's suits and ate everything from the laundry basket, leaving only the zippers from Karen's dresses.

When Ramon Barreto returned to the house, with his shirt unbuttoned and his tie wrapped around his fist, he opened the door to a cloud of flour and insect dust. The jar where he kept the pieces of Merced had busted its lid and was filled with moths and larvae feeding on the scraps. Unbeknownst to him, among the newsprint and construction paper, fertilized moth eggs had also been bottled. Despite his fear of decay and the precautions he had taken against destruction, Ramon Barreto had kept a plague incubating in his kitchen cupboard.

APOLONIO

Three days after Pío-Pío's eggs hatched, Apolonio left the house to attend to a woman whose amputated pinky finger had grown back as a brittle mesquite twig. Pío-Pío chewed the fried bananas and eggs and spat the regurgitated food into the beaks of her three hatchlings. After she fed them and picked the ticks from her nest, she began teaching them music scales and harmonies.

Pío-Pío did not feel the heat or see the brightness emanating from Apolonio's mother's old room; Pío-Pío was too busy with motherhood. But the rest of Tijuana—except for those who worked in the maquilas— saw the silhouette of the Virgin of Trinidad over the house of Apolonio. The holy mother had returned to visit Apolonio's mother, unaware that she had already passed away. By the time Apolonio returned, the Virgin was gone; the parish priests had surrounded the house, taking notes on Vatican letterhead, and firemen were dousing the fire that blazed on his roof. Apolonio did not want to be under the scrutiny of God, and instead of answering their questions he went into the house, wrapped Pío-Pío and her hatchlings in their nest, grabbed his parchment text, and ran out. Apolonio did not look back at the smoldering fire until he was over and beyond the chain-link fence and cement barriers that marked the border.

SANTOS

When a saint dies, the smell of potpourri extends out to a five-mile radius. But in closed quarters, like Don Feliz's arena, what was supposed to be a pleasant tinge of flowery aroma was suffocating and nauseating. In three minutes the arena emptied, leaving Santos alone in the center of the ring. The eyelets from his shiny wrestling boots oozed blood. His arms were spread open and the stigmata on his palms widened. Saints were supposed to die in open fields, not on the mat. Their blood was not supposed to drip from the corners of the ring into the gutters and reservoirs where cock blood was strained and wrapped into sausages.

CHAPTER
SEVEN
▌ ▌ ▌

Saturn can see the roofs of El Monte, the surrounding ring of ash, the two-ton trucks that pull in empty and drive away heavy with carnations. The movement of people crossing streets, hoeing weeds, and crouching in the furrows. The tortoise that pokes feet and head from its metal shell and slowly crawls away, escaping by the back door, down the stoop, and into the flower fields. Sights usually reserved for hovering crows and crop dusters.

Saturn's power is of a piercing strength, able to penetrate asbestos and wood shingles, tar paper, plywood, the darkness of the attic where yellowing cardboard boxes are kept, the painted plastered drywall, the spinning lead blades of the ceiling fan that Saturn carefully eludes (after first banging himself against the whirling vanes). He then makes his way through the polyester and acrylic sheets, down to where Little Merced lies sleeping, her feet rubbing against each other and her arms wrapped around the pillows.

Often, windows and doors are left open and what Saturn sees anybody can see. At night, when Little Merced lies in bed, Federico de la Fe sits at the kitchen table singeing flesh and sadness. The smoke and smell of kerosene rises from his chest and floats out into the yard where the lime trees used to be. The elote man pushes his shopping cart. Only two cold cobs of corn remain in his tin pot and the jars of butter-cream are empty, but his pockets are heavy with quarters and folded dollar bills. The elote man passes by Federico de la Fe's house, sees the smoke and the flashes, but does not stop. Nor does he wonder about the possibilities of fire. He knows it boils water and steams the corn and that is enough.

Federico de la Fe then fans the room with a wet rag, and when he no longer hears the plastic wheels of the shopping cart grinding against the asphalt, the rattling noise of the cart, he shuts the door and lifts the cloth placemats from the kitchen table to reveal two slabs of lead cut from the shell of a tortoise.

When I woke up there was sawdust and crumbled plaster on my sheets. I stood on my bed and pulled the cord and watched the fan change from a whirling blur to four slow-turning metal blades. There were cracks on the ceiling surrounding the mount, and when I touched the fan the whole thing wiggled and more debris fell on my face and hair.

My father had launched a war against a force that I could not see but I could now feel, and somehow it had left traces of its presence. I gathered the sawdust and plaster into a dustpan and dumped it in the kitchen's trash tin, covering avocado and orange skins and a burnt handkerchief my father had discarded.

In the old days, when we still lived in the adobe, the days after rainstorms were often followed by dripping ceilings that leaked not only water but also clumps of mud. And though the wet heaps of earth were cold and heavy, I preferred the consequences of rain to the dry weight of an unknown power.

It was not until two days later, when Saturn cut me, that I went to my father. There was no sawdust or plaster, and my blankets still covered me, but there were stains of blood on my shorts and a bit on my sheets. I ran out of my room into the kitchen, yelling for my father. He saw the blood and stood up, but not before covering his notes with a jagged slab of lead.

"It's Saturn," I said.

He laughed and then wrung a wet towel over the kitchen sink and then handed it to me. He said not to worry, that everything would be okay, and then picked up the phone.

"Subcomandante Sandra..."

It was a bit heavy; it should have just been spots. Some blood soaked through onto the sheets, but I told Federico de la Fe that everything was fine. I showed Little Merced how to use the napkins and mix a vinegar wash. Because we lived within the ashen boundaries, Little Merced would start her cycle at the same time I and every other woman in El Monte did.

In El Monte, sisterhood and solidarity were always marked by bloodshed. I pummeled girls on the mouth, their blood spilling out of their chins and onto my knuckles. And then I nursed their broken skin, put arnica compounds on their bruises, and welcomed them into EMF.

I hiked up my dress and pulled my underwear down, exposing the stained quilted pad. "See, I'm just like you," I said. Little Merced nodded. I hugged her and left Federico de la Fe's house.

I passed by Froggy's house, the house where I used to live. His doors and windows were shut. I wanted to at least see his silhouette moving behind the curtains, but I saw nothing, and heard only a faint chirping coming from the house.

Froggy's truck was parked in the driveway, washed and waxed, the white walls of its tires slightly muddy. I felt as if I could walk into the house and lay on the bed, and everything would be as before. And Froggy would be happy and I would be happy too. But there are forces that don't let you turn back and undo things, because to do so would be to deny what is already in motion, to unwrite and erase passages, to shorten the arc of a story you don't own.

If I could walk into the house and say, "Froggy, I'm sorry I left." If I could hug him and unbutton his shirt and pick the petals from his hair. If I could do that, there would be no reason for me to fight this war.

SATURN

At night Federico de la Fe chewed on the leaves of his yerba maté and then spat the spent gabazo into the trash tin, the sawdust and plaster sticking to the boiled and munched wads.

Federico de la Fe was in the kitchen, readying the lead shells to be cut into slabs. He turned the shells on their backs and then walked over to the kitchen table to assemble the torch. As Federico de la Fe screwed the copper cutting tip onto the canister, turning the dial and inspecting the low blue flame, one of the lead shells turned over onto its belly. Its legs poked out and slowly it crawled toward the yard, ramming its head and chipping the paint of the back-door, escaping the scrap heap for the second time.

Federico de la Fe passed the flame over his stomach, singeing his straggling hairs into knobs and blistering his flesh. He then took the torch to the base of the tortoise shell, separating the flat underbelly from the dome and then cutting the scutes, until all that remained was a pile of flat slabs of lead. Federico de la Fe never noticed the escaped tortoise.

Federico de la Fe marked each slab with the wax of construction markers, labeling every piece with Arabic numbers, and then sat back down at the kitchen table. Pressed against the two slabs of lead were Federico de la Fe's schematics for a war of eventual emancipation, safely hidden from Saturn's view.

Some of the parchment paper stuck out from between the heavy sheets of lead. Parts of Federico de la Fe's home-taught cursive, with uncrossed x's, undotted i's, and unlopped Spanish q's, were exposed, along with what appeared to be a triangle with numerical measurements. But Saturn could not extrapolate any of Federico de la Fe's plan from the protruding scribbles.

LITTLE MERCED

My father was preparing for a full assault. But it was an attack without gunfire or mortar explosions. He wanted no sound and little movement. We would expel Saturn from a quiet and clear sky, not one shattered by violence.

Phase One would begin without Froggy. My father told everybody that he was home drinking kerosene, trying to loosen the grip of stomach worms, and that he would return once he had flushed the parasite. But Sandra and I knew the truth: he was home listening to the Oaxacan songbird.

As always we sat around the dominoes table. I sat on Froggy's empty chair next to Sandra. Pelon and Little Oso put down wads of twenties they had collected from the cockfights and selling goat milk and cheese while Sandra counted and wrapped rubber bands around the money.

Smiley drew tallies in increments of five, each line representing an hour that had been lost to war. He kept two running figures: one to account for the actual time engaged against Saturn and another that tracked the hypothetical future days that would also be sacrificed. Because Smiley's only job was to document the disappearance of time he wore a black guayabera shirt with three pockets instead of four, the missing pocket emphasizing loss.

After the hours and bodies were counted and cataloged, Pelon and Little Oso requested funds to buy a new set of cock blades, a rake to till the pit, and two yards of cheese cloth. Smiley wanted nothing, and Sandra asked for arnica cream for the cuts of the freshly initiated.

My father distributed the cash and said, "The rest is for the mechanic. We are going to need more tortoise shells." He hid the money in his shirt pocket.

SMILEY

Two years before the war began I got jumped into EMF. I was only sixteen. But when we learned of Saturn I tore off the left pocket of my shirt.

In the times before de la Fe we had no dairy and no cockfights; we made our money running borders and slinging. When we returned from Tijuana it was not with tortoise shells and farm animals but with the white powder of coca leaves and bales of chronic so sticky and rich that even the curanderos bought from us. We smoked and snorted some but most we sold to the powdered Hollywood people who came down from the hills to watch the horses at the Arcadia racetrack just north of El Monte. There was no ring of ash; we could step out of El Monte without the black soot sticking to our shoes.

My job has always been accounting. I'm a descendant of the Pengula tribe, which invented not only the tally marks but also the marks for nothingness and everythingness. My job was to keep the books for EMF, but when Federico de la Fe came I surrendered the job to Sandra so that I might count things that are unseen.

Froggy says that we are fighting a war that means something and that when we are old veteranos we'll be proud of fighting a war that counted for more than slinging coke and holding turf. We'll be free from the sight of Saturn.

"But what's wrong with Saturn?" I asked Froggy.

"Do you want it looking down on you and following you wherever you go?"

I wanted to say, "I don't mind it, Froggy. Someone has to watch over us. I don't want to look up at the sky and think that nothing is up there. I want to know that something is watching me."

But I didn't.

SATURN

Federico de la Fe took down the ceiling fan from Little Merced's room. He set it down on the bed and swivelled its dented blades, touching the metal and instantly recognizing it as the eighty-second element of the periodic table. He then dragged the bed, reading chair, and desk into the living room.

He brought in planks of two-by-fours made from split lime trees and a bag of lead nails that he purchased from Apolonio the curandero.

Federico de la Fe laid out the planks on the bedroom floor, driving nails through the wood with a single drop of his hammer. He cut studs using only a hand saw and then forced them in between parallel two-by-fours. When he was done he lifted the frame of wood and nails and leaned it against the wall and then laid another set of planks on the floor.

By midday Federico de la Fe had only three nails left. Inside Little Merced's room Federico de la Fe had built a framework that could support lathe, wallboards, and the heavy sheets of lead that had been cut from the shells of mechanical tortoises.

Federico de la Fe placed the lead on the floor first and then used the cutting torch to solder the pieces together. After the floor was complete Federico de la Fe hung lead on the ceiling and walls, fastening and then soldering them in place.

There was no hinged door. Instead, the turn of a handle activated a system of ropes and pulleys that lifted and dropped a slab of lead.

And when the door was dropped no one, not even Saturn, could see into the leaden room of Little Merced.

That night I slept in my room with the lead door down. The next day they brought the dominoes table inside my room and played and talked around it, and whenever the door was raised and Sandra or Smiley went to the kitchen or restroom we stopped talking, dropping dominoes in silence. And if we did talk when the door was open, it was only about picking carnations and roses. Sometimes Pelon would talk about cockfights, but my father said that we shouldn't even discuss that unless the door was down.

At night when the evening breeze from the Hollywood hills came in, heavy with the smell of perfume and steak sauce, Pelon, Little Oso, and Smiley brought in wood planks and bags of nails.

In two nights they framed the inside of the entire house and began to hang and solder the lead onto the walls and ceiling. They took the heavy door from my room and rigged it to the front of the house.

When the construction was complete and the blue, lustrous hue of lead filled the house, we were free to think and say whatever we wanted without fear of Saturn.

We sat around the table and counted bills and coins and Smiley took out the folded paper from the left pocket of his guyabera. And my father talked about lining every house in El Monte with lead.

And although we had gained freedom inside the house, my father instructed us not to talk or think unless we were protected by lead.

"If you must think about something, think about picking roses and carnations, about potatoes, about things that Saturn has no interest in."

There were planks and sheets of metal on every lawn. I followed the sound of the saws and hammers, hoping to find tired and hungry men who would be tempted by the smell of cooked corn, cobs tender and sweet still in their husks and blanched in peppered water. I pulled back their wrapping, plucked the red silk from the ear, and then stabbed the cob on a stick; on request, I smothered the kernels with cream and rolled them over grated cheese.

I seesawed my cart onto the sidewalk and squeezed the pump of my horn, but no one approached. If they came out it was only to retrieve material, to load metal and wood on their shoulders and lug it inside.

"Not today," they said, and I pushed my cart forward.

Despite the pounding and sawdust in the air, no structures rose, no second stories or expanded living rooms appeared. Whatever they were building was contained within their walls.

The foreman, who I had once witnessed burn his own flesh, went from house to house, inspecting the construction material and whispering instructions into the ears of the workmen. He was careful and methodical in his inspections, feeling the smoothness of the metal and squinting to spot termites in the wood. And though he was a foreman, he had tics particular to maize farmers, constantly looking up at the sky, ever-watchful of clouds and thunder showers.

They were all too busy and ignored the call of my horn, so I kept moving, going away from El Monte, crossing the line where pavement and asphalt had been scorched and into the city of Arcadia, a town with greener lawns and streets swept by motorized circular brooms.

SATURN

In two weeks Federico de le Fe and EMF had lined every house in El Monte with the impenetrable element. Even Froggy, busy nursing heartbreak with the help of a Oaxacan songbird, opened his door to a crew pushing wheelbarrows loaded with sanded planks and slabs of lead.

And while Saturn was still able to see people crossing the streets, hoeing weeds, and crouching in the furrows, it could no longer follow EMF into their houses or watch them eat in their kitchen or sleep in their beds or make love on the tile floor.

And even in open air, unshielded, the people of El Monte obscured their thoughts in a loop of irrelevance. Everything they thought of had to do with carnations and farm animals and objects too brown or formless to have any meaning.

Unable to see the notes that Federico de la Fe hid underneath the lead, Saturn had not foreseen this type of attack. De la Fe's plan was to stump Saturn in the midst of the story, to hide their lives behind lead walls.

Fringed petals and green stems. Pink and white carnations bloom from tight buds and the air is scented by fertilizers and flowers. Crop dusters mist the petals with insecticide and plant food is tossed at the foot of the stalks, spread by the hands of flower pickers.

Federico de la Fe looked at me and said, "Pelon, once you're out there don't talk or think about anything you've heard or seen in here. Feed the roosters. Brush their feathers and keep them away from the hens. Whistle, think about tilling the dirt, the color of the rooster's crest, the braided loop and string that you tie to the rooster's leg. And if you must, you can think about the rooster fights but not about where the money goes or what it is for.

"After you're done, come back here. We will all sleep here tonight, and tomorrow we'll put lead on as many houses as we can, so you can go and sleep in your own home."

That's what he said, but I can't think about that anymore. No, Pelon. Think about the brown dirt, the black ashes that float in the sky and land in the pit and then stick to the rake, the red crest of the roosters, the red blood on the razor blade that cuts the fighting cock's crest, the sharp beaks of the hens that pick at the severed tuft, the brown eggs they lay, the ropy mucus that covers the blind hatchlings, the yellow puffy chicks that choke on the shelled corn, the furrows where they are buried, the corn stalks that grow from their mouths, the stalks of carnations that suck the minerals from the soil and into the petals, the chapped hands of the flower pickers that gather the flowers on tarps and drag them to the scales and from the scales to two-ton trucks and then to flower shops, from the flower shop to a wedding, to a vase at the center of a long dining room table, and if not a centerpiece as a bouquet thrown on a porch as a thank-you, or on a grave also as a thank you, flowers, flores, El Monte Flores gang, no, don't think about that, think about the brown dirt, the black ashes that float in the sky and land in the pit and then stick to the rake, the red crest of the roosters, the red blood on the razor blade that cuts the fighting cock's crest, the sharp beaks of the hens that pick at the severed

91

They thought of nothing but flowers and frogs. And the times when they strayed, they quickly returned to dreams of carnations and dirt, or they ran into their lead houses and lowered the door. And when they were stranded deep in the fields, their feet steeped in mud, they bit their tongues until their minds went to bursts of pain and blood, scrambling thoughts into indecipherable throbs.

But there is more to El Monte than Federico de la Fe and EMF. Not all is about gangs and a sad man who wets his bed. There is time and space for everything, to observe the thousands of tragedies of a single growing season. To watch the flower stalks burst through the soil, interweaving their roots with the neighboring plant, tangling their wires under the privacy of soil, tightly gripping, gradually pulling themselves to each other to feel the brush of leaves against their stems.

When the fertilizer is tossed and the sun beams down, the foliage wilts and the stems burn with an itch. The plant on the edge of the furrow cups the morning dew underneath its leaf and extends its arm to drip the moisture onto the scabs of bark on the neighboring plant. The bead of water falls and then a sudden flash of steel collapses the stalk, which is then tossed into a basket. Four weeks later the harvest is done and the dirt is upturned by a tractor plow, exposing tightly braided roots still clutching each other.

LITTLE MERCED

There were two crop dusters in the sky. One held level, surveying all of El Monte. The second plane cruised behind and at a lower altitude, diving into the fields and spraying insecticide on the budding flowers. At the furrows' end it pulled up, leveling and then turning around for a second pass, this time against wind and closer to the ground, grazing long stems as the propeller spat out petals.

SANDRA

In the rainy season, a season that lasts only six days, water gathers and stays in the furrows. You unlace your shoes and pull off your socks and step bare through mud and water; tadpoles squirm between toes, bursting from colonies of eggs, losing their tails and pushing out legs, their jelly turning to leather, underwater blindness giving way to blinking eyes, and as the water evaporates and soaks into the watershed, they leap out as frogs, their croaks filling the night. They called him Little Tadpole at six years old, spending the whole of the day swimming up and down the irrigation ditch. When he leapt into the bed of a speeding truck, he shed his tail and they called him Froggy. In the summer the frogs hide where the moisture gathers underneath tarps and forgotten nylon fertilizer sacks. Pull the plastic and you reveal embarrassed amphibians as they wink and straddle, spreading their long legs to accommodate both the missionary and canine positions.

SATURN

Shake roofs at the center of town, the wood bleached
pale by the sun, bright moons, and the proximity of
the ringed planet. The gaps where tiles had flown off,
patched by scraps of plywood nailed down and
caulked with oakum.

Surrounding the shake stuccos, roofs made from
newspaper and rags dipped in tar; the sticky layers,
spread like blankets, in the morning light, cooled by
the western breeze. Workboots and socks pulled from
feet by the thick gunk, tarred over by broom and
mop. Six pairs of mismatched shoes, footprints size
nine and a half, and a swarm of june bugs preserved
and four centuries later unearthed as fossils.

The oldest clay roofs were built decades before El
Monte's official township. Roofs of cooked mud,
baked in Spanish ovens next to husk-wrapped corncakes. Once baked, the tiles were loaded on a sling
and the backs of heathen workers, who climbed the
ladder and arranged the pieces on the top of the bell
tower and church. Two hundred years later, from
inside the rectory, water stains revealed the leaks
where corncakes and not clay had been placed.

I watched the planes fly out of El Monte,
fading into dots and then disappearing,
and then I went inside and shut the door.

Through a short lead tube he gripped in the fist of his hand, Federico de la Fe delivered his war speech. He pressed one end of the pipe to my ear and brought his lips to the rim, into which he whispered:

"I once had a wife. She had twenty-two birth marks and a sneeze that sounded as if it was blown through a flute and Saturn drove her away, just so that there would be this story. So that I would venture out from Las Tortugas and he could follow and mock me.

"One day, Smiley, you will have your own wife, maybe a daughter and son, and you will not want a looming Saturn watching you. We attack now. Go to your stucco and close your door. We are shutting Saturn out. If we are to be free and sovereign people, free from the tyranny of Saturn, this is what we must do. When under the uncovered sky, say nothing, and think only inconsequential things and in a jumbled logic. We fight now, so that we may be free."

He finished his speech, patted me on the shoulder, and walked away. I obeyed, but I took the long route home, walking under a naked sky while contemplating what he had said. How did Federico de la Fe know that it was Saturn who had taken his wife away? Was Saturn really so ominous and threatening? Could he not be protecting us?

SATURN

The sky was growing gloomy, a cloudy and saddened sky. The meteorologists cleared the weather map, taking down the yellow sunrays and replacing them with gray magnetic clouds.

Federico de la Fe and EMF bunkered down, coming out only for quick chores and then shutting their doors. Only Smiley stayed outdoors, but even he, who often stared at the sky, not in contempt but with a faithful sense of wonder, eventually also went inside and shut his lead door, leaving only the mechanical tortoise.

The escaped tortoise was making its way south, propelled not by a forward crawl but by pushing dirt behind its legs, bringing Tijuana closer one scoop of earth at a time.

In the morning mist the dirt became muddy and heavy and the tortoise tucked its head and feet into the shell to rest, leaving its tail hanging, waiting for the heat of sunrise. Everybody was encased by lead, every thought protected, nothing left to hear or see. It was a lonely day, much like the meteorologist had predicted, the whole world shunning Saturn.

Federico de la Fe and EMF would not notice because they also could not see through lead, but something was happening. Saturn was unhinging from its orbit and slowly moving deeper into the solar system, away from the roofs of El Monte, eventually becoming the farthest planet from the sun, its glowing rings dulling to rust and cumulus clouds cloaking its atmosphere.

```
00000111000110001100100010111100
10010101010101011110000100100101 0
10001001001010101001100100000
1000101000100000111110001010101 01
010010010100000001000011111000001
000010101001010111000010000100101
001010100100100011101000100100001
010001000010010010100000010101101
111001010101001000101001101000011
001001001010101001001010001000010
010101000001010000101000010100100
000100000000000111100101010001110
101000001010001000010101001 01110
110100010010001000101000010100000
001110001100011100100010111100100
101010101011110000100100101 0100
010010010101010101001100100000100
010100010000011110001010101 01010
010010100000001000011111000001000
010101001010111000010000100100101
010010010001110100010010000101000
100001001001010000001010110111110
001001001010101001001010001000010
010101000001010000101000010100100
000100000000000111100101010001110
101000001010001000010101001 01110
110100010010001000101000010100000
001110001100011100100010111100100
101010101011110000100100101 0100
010010010101010101001100100000100
010100010000011110001010101 01010
010010100000001000011111000001000
010101001010111000010000100100101
010010010001110100010010000101000
1000010010010100000 0101011
```

PART TWO

Cloudy skies and lonely mornings

CHAPTER EIGHT

•

SMILEY

I ignored everything Federico de la Fe said. I spoke and thought without protection. While I respected Federico de la Fe and EMF, I did not want to live under the heavy luster of lead. I was part of the Flores gang long before de la Fe had come, before EMF had taken up against Saturn.

I entered the war for volition, the revolution against tyranny, unwillingly—obliged by my EMF membership. Had I a choice, it is Saturn who I would join.

I knew that the defeat of Saturn would bring our own end, that everything would conclude with its crash. But I was not worried about the galaxy and the fall of its satellites. I thought of my own existence, of my own place in this novel, and so I went to Apolonio the curandero to inquire about Saturn.

As always there was a fee, so I left the shop and did not return until I had a basket heavy with roses, three dozen eggs, and the two slabs of lead Apolonio had requested with which to bind his Santeria book. It was only after Apolonio had inspected each egg, the stems and thorns of the roses, and the density and potential pliability of the lead that I was allowed to address him.

I asked no preliminary questions and gave him no opportunity to stall or confuse me with his rambling curandero answers.

"What is Saturn?" I asked.

"A pseudonym. A name to hide behind," Apolonio said, still inspecting the scutes of lead.

"So what is Saturn's real name?"

Without hesitating or double-checking his parchment or the formations of candle smoke, he answered, "Saturn's real name is Salvador Plascencia. Salvador Plascencia de Gonzales, to be exact, though he dropped his maternal name long ago."

"How can I find him?"

Apolonio did not say anything. Instead he turned and searched his cabinets and alcove shelves until he located a folded map that had been stitched at its creases, holding its sections together even after decades of unfolding.

"It should be extra for this," Apolonio said, and carefully began to unfold the map. He never collected the extra fee; instead, he laid a sheet of tracing paper over the map and, using the sharp point of his fountain pen, began tracing the route and copying numbered directions, meanwhile telling me the story of the monk who had brought it to him.

Apolonio had learned of Salvador Plascencia from an apostate monk who had abandoned not only the piety but also the marching formation of his ministerial sect: a wandering tribe of Franciscan monks. The monk deserted his assigned position, the fifty-third slot in the line formation, but he was regretful and shamed by his decision. In penance he gave up his birth name and called himself simply Fifty-three, to forever remind himself of what he had left. In his quest for forgiveness he had written *The Book of Incandescent Light*, a manuscript that took three decades of research and twenty-six months of fevered writing to complete. It was published posthumously but lauded as the greatest apology since the blood letters of the expelled seraphim angel Juan Vincente, who wrote with his index finger and the ink of his own veins, standing on his head and shaking his wrist when the ink began to fade.

But *The Book of Incandescent Light* did not emerge from the Vatican until many years later, after the monk had already written his own blood letter on a cinderblock wall. For years and years the altar boys, who received the mail, passed over the book in favor of more traditional catechism pamphlets, before forwarding it to the Vatican press.

While searching for his marching Franciscan order the monk had accidentally stumbled upon the living quarters of Saturn—a discovery uncited in the manuscript, but that the monk traded to Apolonio for a hundred veladoras of hand-braided wicks and pure beeswax and a single chambered pistol that he exploded behind his left ear, splattering ink, the whole of the wall illegible except for the complimentary closing at the foot of the structure: *Amen*.

Apolonio handed me the instructions and the map on tracing paper. "With God," he said, sprinkling a bit of saint's spit on me as I exited his shop. I followed the directions faithfully, walking beyond the ashen boundaries of El Monte, stepping over the soot, taking the meandering path that started in Arcadia, circling around the horse track, climbing the foothills, and ending at the peak of the San Gabriel range.

As instructed by the numbered text of the map, I raised my hand, feeling for a rough spot. Once I found it, I began peeling at the deteriorating glaze of blue, collapsing part of the sky and exposing a layer of papier-mâché. Flakes slipped into the pockets of my guayabera, while the rest of the scraps floated down until they caught on chaparral or landed on the soil.

I stood directly underneath the spot where the monk had once patched the sky. I began sawing through the layers of newspaper and glue, hiding my carnation knife once the manhole in the California sky was complete.

I grabbed at the edges of the hole and pulled myself into the house of Saturn.

It should have been the moment when the creator acknowledges both the necessity of my existence and the reader's role as witness. But it was not the dignified meeting one might expect: the author sitting in his chair, wearing a starched dress shirt with a double-stitched collar, smoking hand-rolled tobacco, awaiting the visit because, after all, he is omniscient, foreseeing all surprises.

But when I came to Saturn he was no longer in control. He did not have the foresight to see that I was coming, nor did he care. He had surrendered the story and his power as narrator. I found him asleep, sprawled and naked, laying on his stomach, pillowcases beneath him but the pillows tossed against the wall. And despite the order he had provided in the form of columns and chapters, he applied none of that logic to his sleeping quarters: his shirts and pants crumpled and pushed against the corners, the linens and towels unfolded and dirty, books stacked in badly planned towers that disregarded alphabet and size, falling and collapsing into rubble. And paper, unbound and scattered everywhere.

On his wall: a map of Los Angeles, the city of El Monte scrawled in with pencil; the framed picture of a woman, her hair black and spilling out of the frame; and a poster of Rita Hayworth with a cigarette holder in hand, wearing her strapless *Gilda* dress.

When Saturn finally woke up he did not notice me. I stood in the corner of his room, his papers and clothes beneath my shoes. Without turning over, Saturn reached for the receiver and began to dial.

—

"Hello," he said.

—

"Can we talk?"

—

"Then when?"

—

"Is he there?"

Saturn hung up the phone, clicking on the base, and quickly dialing again.

—

"Just a minute. You owe me that much."

—

"'Not now?' What does that mean?"

Slowly, and unbeknownst to him, I walked out of his bedroom and into the living room, where the embers of the fireplace still glowed. I was very far from El Monte. The California weather and palm trees had been replaced by coats of snow, the crackling sounds of frozen branches, and the smell of grained salt spread over roads. And so after seventeen years I had finally come to discover winter.

When in the house of Saturn there are things an EMF member must do, instructions that were given to us, drawn up under roofs of lead. Things to be done if one is ever lucky enough to be in proximity to the enemy. The carnation knife must be pulled out of the waistband and then put to the throat of Saturn, dragging the blade across the skin and stubble of his neck, letting his ink drip. Because if that is what he wants, to write, let him write his own blood letter on the cloth and foam of his mattress. A dense, warm prose that stains the floors and always reappears six coats of paint later. Something that will remain longer than any novel will.

At the very least, if rushed, steal the plot lines and the hundred and five pages that have been written. Leave nothing behind but the title page and table of contents, on which you write, "You are not so powerful."

But I left my carnation knife in my pocket and was careful not to touch anything. Sabotaged nothing, simply waited for Saturn to rise and walk into the living room.

Even if I believed in Federico de la Fe's cause and in the fall of Saturn, there is an etiquette that must be followed, even in war. You cannot kill or steal from a man while he is asleep and heartbroken. While it is said that everything is fair in love and war, the dictum is nullified when both love and war occur simultaneously; then, the rules of battle become more stringent. The politics that lead to war can always be argued, but there is an undeniable sympathy that must be extended when a woman leaves a man. Saturn waited ten years from the time Merced left Federico de la Fe before he decided to invade the privacy of Federico de la Fe. I would only be extending the same courtesy.

Although Saturn was now blind to the progression of the story and what was to come, he was not startled by my presence. He came into the living room wearing only his undershorts.

"Are you another lost monk?" he asked solemnly as he tried to wipe the sleep from his eyes.

"No, I'm Smiley."

"Smiley?"

It was similar to the devastating sadness one feels when a father fails to recognize his own son; the nails on my fingers and toes ached and the bitterness of crushed lemon seeds filled my mouth.

Sensing my disappointment, Saturn sat down and explained that there are many characters, plots, and devices, and in the jumble of things sometimes minor characters are forgotten, even by the author. He said it would be silly to try to hold him accountable for everything, especially now that he had surrendered the story. But still I asserted myself.

"I am Smiley from EMF. I wear the three-pocket funeral guayabera,"

I said, putting my fingers in my shirt pockets, pulling out bits of sky. I cited every identifiable trait I could think of, but Saturn gave no sign of recognition and simply shrugged.

"Smiley, you can tell Federico de la Fe and the rest of EMF that they won. They can leave their lead houses up or they can knock them down, but they don't have to worry about me staring down on them anymore."

And that was all Saturn said. He then walked to the kitchen, drank a glass of water, pulled down his underwear, and retreated back into bed.

CHAPTER NINE
● ● ●

SATURN

Saturn's great-grandfather, Don Victoriano, who outlived a century by two years, always warned of the dangers of falling in love with Ticuanenses and Gypsies.

"They are people without a homeland and of a bohemian fidelity," Don Victoriano said, not as a condemnation of the races but as an explanation of their nature. But despite the warnings of his great-grandfather, Saturn fell for a woman who descended not only from a tawny family of Gypsies but from Ticuananse blood as well. Her name, which is cited on the dedication page of this book, was Elizabeth of Helen, but was abridged to simply Liz.

Saturn reviewed the blood maps and charts: all Gypsy and Tijuana blood. But still he hoped that the bloods united would quell, bringing forth instead a recessive desire: the want for a single stable home, a home not set on axles and wheels.

Fidelity came from the most unlikely of places, sometimes occurring despite genetic predispositions.

"All the blood charts say that you are leaving," he said to her.

"I know what they say," she said, "but I'm still here."

"And tomorrow?"

And tomorrow happened.

"Still here," she said.

"And tomorrow?" he asked.

And tomorrow again:

"You need to stop worrying," she said.

And Saturn went off to war. And the news that was predestined, written into the Gypsy's strains of DNA and on the XY sperm cell of every Ticuanense throughout history, finally came. On that same day that she said she was leaving, Federico de la Fe and EMF advanced on Saturn, raising lead to the sky. That day Saturn pulled the sheets from his bed and held them up to his nose, sniffing for the stench of urine, trying to remember the last time he had wet his bed.

"What pee? You have never peed the bed," Liz said, but Saturn was unconvinced. He promised he would never do it again, he would go to bed thirsty and sleep with his hand tucked in his shorts. He would do his own laundry and not forget the fabric softener, and he would never put his shoes on top of the bed. He promised all those things men promise when they are far away and can feel the phone lines stretched too tight, the wires and cables rapidly unraveling from their braids, snapping, recoiling, collapsing the poles along the way.

And the poles gave way, crashing down on the Queen Anne porches, on the factories of Pittsburgh, on Chicago slaughterhouses, then south upon the churches of the Bible Belt, harmlessly in the fields of corn, then on the quartz sand and cacti of Arizona, and finally in El Monte on the potted plants that Liz's grandmother had carefully planted in rusty coffee cans while eating sugared bread and ignoring her diabetes.

The phone lines were down and Saturn's pleas too heavy for messenger pigeons, leaving only the inept brevity of the telegraph. So he left the front lines, allowing Federico de la Fe and EMF to enjoy the privacy and volition they had long desired. Saturn boarded a plane that followed the trail of collapsed telephone poles from New York all the way to El Monte.

RALPH AND ELISA LANDIN

The news of Saturn's war on Federico de la Fe and EMF arrived belatedly at the penthouse of New York millionaires Ralph and Elisa Landin. They sat in their library late at night, sipping maté and eating chocolate slices of Rigo Jancsi—a pastry that had been named after a Gypsy violinist and infidelity.

Ralph Landin had once spooned swastika soup in his native Hungary, feeling the sharp bends of the noodles on his tongue before they tore the walls of his cheeks. He saw fractures and holes in the brick and mortar of buildings and trails of ink spilling from bodies, writing desperate love letters on sidewalks in the shape of bloodied snow angels.

Ralph Landin spent two years of his youth covering his ears from the deafening thunder of cannons and crumbling walls, and eating stale zwieback sprinkled with brown sugar. And now when he thought of war he pushed foam plugs into his ears and sipped cups of milk of magnesia. But despite the indigestion and dizziness that memories of war brought, he knew that Saturn's war was different, that it was somehow about love. It was with a muffled symphony in the background and a milk mustache that Ralph Landin decided to sponsor a war.

"I think we should help Saturn against EMF," Ralph said to his wife, as he wiped his lip and clipped on his hearing aid. After a pensive stare Elisa nodded and called for her accountant.

DON VICTORIANO

At a hundred and two, Saturn's great-grandfather Don Victoriano had never left the Americas but always dreamed of a Spanish musket with a silver-worked handle and trigger, of wine from French vineyards, and of kissing the Vatican cobblestones that led from the souvenir shop up to Saint Peter's. Though Don Victoriano's eyes were scathed by cataracts, his hands callused by the years of ropes and sickles, his tongue cooked by decades of lime juice, he was never fooled by cheap cabernets, by carved wooden handles, or by rocks brought from the wash oiled with musk to simulate centuries under Roman air.

He turned away the con men who tried to swindle him and then picked up his cane from the coffee table and walked to the park. Once there, Don Victoriano would take his seat while the seventy-year-olds shuffled the deck and dealt him a hand.

As was customary, between hands, when the stern and serious poker faces relaxed, the men talked about the new archbishop of Guadalajara, the street sweepers that had not come in weeks and the accumulating piles of litter, and the grandchildren recently born.

And one day, after the request of the self-appointed dealer, Don Victoriano brought the scroll of his family tree. The scroll, with its amendments taped and pasted, extended across the whole of the poker table and onto the ground. The family line began with Don Victoriano and ended with three pregnant great-great-great-granddaughters.

Among the two thousand and six descendants of Don Victoriano were: the first settlers of Las Tortugas; eight lawyers; a professional soccer player; the first origami surgeon; two altar boys and a priest; a banker; a novelist; four bakers and a gourmet cook; and six carpenters, all of whom refused to assemble coffins to avoid the grim specter of Don Victoriano's imminent death.

After Don Victoriano ran his hands across the cured pigskin that had been stretched into rough parchment, cracking and with hair follicles still in sprout, he rolled his family tree back into a scroll, fastening it with a cord and using a knot he had first learned on his wedding night. It was without the thought of generations or legacy that he had pulled at the lace of his wife's dress and carried her onto the straw mattress.

On Don Victoriano's one hundredth birthday, when the radio microphones filled his house and the reporters asked about the generations he had come to father, he responded only with the name of his wife, who had died thirty-three years before.

"She is the one you should be talking to."

SATURN

On the airplane he tried to write the perfect sentence:

Without you there is nothing, not even drizzle.
~~Without you there is nothing, not even drizzle.~~
I will build you bookshelves like you always wanted.
~~I will build you bookshelves like you always wanted.~~
Missing you is worse than Pittsburgh.
~~Missing you is worse than Pittsburgh.~~
I will wash my foreskin every day.

Saturn arrived in El Monte, the El Monte where he had first touched her waist and tasted her split ends and dandruff, this El Monte, not the

El Monte of warfare and lead houses. There were only remnants of her: the hair in the blankets and the light underlines she had made in books—signs of her that would remain undiscovered for years. Saturn could feel her absence even in the asphalt; as he drove, the roads became uneven and pitted.

El Monte had no hospitals, no wet nurses or delivery beds, no native daughters or sons—the whole township adopted. And because El Monte could not bear its own, it was with greater sorrow that it felt the desertion of those it had come to love and claim. And when she left—walking to a city with neat shrubs and painted mailboxes—the lemon blossoms wilted, the crows that gathered in her grandma's backyard refused to meet, and the elote man who pushed his cart every day ratcheted the tires from his cart and went on strike, refusing to honk his horn.

While El Monte felt the absence, it was Saturn who suffered most. He would not eat, turning away even his mother's cooking. He extended his daily walk around the block into a jog that lasted hours. When he finally returned, his midday nap outlasted the night. Not even the droning sounds of crop dusters could wake him.

His mother, naturally, was concerned, but she was comforted by the curanderos who displayed a chart of the food pyramid, informing her that one could survive on the taste of sadness for years:

El Monte was ravaged, the telephone poles splintered in half, the roads eroded, the crows dispersed, cart pushers on strike, and the tags of EMF etched everywhere—on trees, on windows, and on the bakery walls. Only the church of Guadalupe was spared. And every time Saturn came across one of the tags he crossed it out:

Saturn knew that it was on account of the war against EMF that she had left. It was impossible to be loyal to a war commander who was always away, busy examining maps and charts, lost in the strategies he tried to untangle from his brain. So while Saturn was tracking Federico de la Fe and EMF, Liz was in downtown Los Angeles, twelve miles west of El Monte, receiving a tour of a Russian-style apartment.

"This is where I cook," the tall man said, "and this is where I sleep."

And as Federico de la Fe advanced, his ever-swelling army accumulating a surfeit of lead shells and planks, Liz was shown the contents of the cupboards—the jars of tomato sauce and sacks of potatoes—and the different strata of the made bed, the comforter peeled back, exposing blankets and sheets.

And like Liz, Merced had surrendered to the voice and bristled face of another, gradually lured from Federico de la Fe by a voice that came through a tiny carved window. Merced resented the smell of piss and the wet bed, but she was driven away by the drip of Federico de la Fe's penis. As Federico de le Fe slept next to Little Merced, warming her with his wetness, Merced would go to the kitchen to eat limes and to pull the cob of corn from the adobe wall, exposing a tiny window. It was through that opening that Merced was courted. And on the day that Merced left Federico de la Fe, the window widened, the packed dirt moistened into mud, and what was once an opening three fingers in width could now accommodate two fists. For three years words had been whispered into the wall, mutters that smelled of peppermint and rhymed in rehearsed couplets, trying to woo Merced away from her husband. It was with the wall between them that the affair was consummated. They copulated with their faces pressed against the adobe bricks, tasting not lips but baked dirt and blades of hay. Their perspiration ran down from their foreheads and armpits, gathering where their bodies touched, softening the wall into mud, the wet soil and straw clinging to the hair between their legs.

When Federico de la Fe discovered the hole a week later, it was without suspicion that he patched the opening, never inspecting the outer wall where half a beard was pressed into the clay and a pattern of curls and matted ringlets framed the window. Federico de la Fe was convinced that Merced had left because of his pee.

When Saturn finally located Liz, in her new Pasadena apartment, nestled between trees and the houses of lawyers, she did not blame anything on urine.

"He's tall and has a beard, and he's very funny. And has no foreskin," she said.

"And he is white." But she did not say this.

And while Saturn had always sympathized with Napoleon, it was not until Liz left him for a taller lover that he fully understood the little corporal's compulsion to unsettle worlds and then weep.

"Sal, it is time for you to leave," she said, and opened the door for him. And though Saturn wanted the annals of the affair to show that he simply nodded and quietly left, he did not. He tried to touch her, to kiss her, and when she turned him away he refused to leave the room. And it was not until Saturn cried, soaking fibers on her hand-knotted rug, and she insisted six times, that he finally complied.

She turned the bolt, locking the door, and then gashed her hand as she pulled on the cord that shut the blinds.

RALPH AND ELISA LANDIN

Ralph and Elisa agreed to fund Saturn's efforts against Federico de la Fe and EMF, but while the millionaires were trusting, their lawyers were not. There were many provisions that had to be met: everything had to be inventoried and cataloged before the first installment was given to Saturn. When the lawyers returned, their legal pads full of figures and lists, they lined up with their sports coats unbuttoned and methodically began to read their findings to Ralph and Elisa Landin:

> Number of times the word "sad" appears (inclusive of "sadness" but excluding "Pasadena" and "asada"): 53
>
> Number of times the word "happiness" appears: 4

Inventory of heartbreaks:
1) Maricela and Tacho
2) Federico de la Fe and Merced
3) Ramon Barreto and Merced de Papel
4) Froggy and Sandra
5) *The Book of Incandescent Light*

They went through everything, page by page, with a mechanical counter in hand, clicking for every instance of sadness and using tally marks for happiness. Even those things that were only slightly evocative of melancholy, like origami hearts and the empty shells of tortoises, were recorded. And only after quantifying the breadth of sorrow and calculating the probability of Saturn's martial success was the contract drafted and the money allotted. While Ralph and Elisa Landin believed in the war and shook Saturn's hand with approval, the following disclosure had to be included every time the millionaires appeared:

> The completion of this book was supported in part by a grant from the Ralph and Elisa Landin Foundation. They are not responsible for the views expressed herein.

DON VICTORIANO

In his many years living under Catholic occupancy, Saturn's great-grandfather had never witnessed a miracle. It was not until the old mayor in his Easter robe and stiff collar was replaced by a secular baker who worried more about gutters and street sweepers than about pledges to the Vatican that Don Victoriano began to commune with God.

It was a string of miraculous transformations, the first miracle occurring while Don Victoriano walked home from the market with a bottle of mescal in one hand and six fish wrapped in newspaper tucked underneath his arm. The miracle took place somewhere between the market and the kitchen table. When Don Victoriano poured the mescal into his tea cup, the liquid had already become tap water. And the next day, when he pulled the newspaper from the refrigerator and tore open the package, instead of six onyx-tailed carp it was only one fish and two handfuls of river gravel.

The second wonder of the Lord's occurred when Don Victoriano placed a twenty-pound turkey in his gas oven, letting it roast as he took his evening walk around the park. When he returned, the drip pan was full of herbed broth, but instead of basted bird on the hot rack, there was a baked clay doll of our Lady of Guadalupe.

Don Victoriano felt privileged in his newfound proximity to God but still he went to church and knelt at the altar: "Lord, these miracles of yours are going to starve me," he said solemnly, careful not to adopt a heretical tone.

So the miracles stopped, and it was not until twenty years later as he lay in his Indian hammock that Don Victoriano's son Antonio came to him holding a resuscitated cat patched with newspaper, completing the trilogy of miracles. While it was not the raising of Lazarus, it was, for once, a miracle that did not cost him anything at the dinner table.

But there were also the miracles that never happened: the day that his son Antonio sat in the back of a speeding taxi cab looking down at his hands as he fumbled and folded, trying to give shape to paper lungs. Meanwhile, Don Victoriano's wife was tied to the bars of the hospital bed, her legs restrained by rope, while Don Victoriano looked on and the doctors and nurses tried to keep her lungs from collapsing using a drinking straw and an inflating latex glove. When Antonio finally arrived and entered the hospital room holding two paper lungs in his hands, it was only Don Victoriano who stood over the bed.

"She's gone," Don Victoriano said, and then pulled the sheets from the hospital bed and stuffed them into his grocery bag, never to let anybody else touch the linens on which his wife had died. That night, after Don Victoriano had returned from the market, he peeled the sugar canes and ground the flowers he would put inside his wife's coffin—to neutralize the smell of death.

SATURN

When Saturn left El Monte, boarding the plane to the cold of upstate New York, El Monte did not mourn, no one went on strike, and the lemons ripened at their usual pace. And once he was in New York, the snow did not cease, not even for a day in mourning for Saturn's heartbreak. Instead, the white accumulated, and the porch swing, where Saturn often sat on spring days but which was now heavy with ice, broke from its hanging chains and crashed down on the porch.

RALPH AND ELISA LANDIN

The completion of this book was supported in part by a grant from the Ralph and Elisa Landin Foundation. They are not responsible for the views expressed herein.

DON VICTORIANO

Don Victoriano mourned the death of his wife for so long that by the time he decided to stop wearing his funeral shirt and pants, all of his wardrobe, even his soccer socks, was dyed the deep black of nestamal kettles. But resolve had finally come and he would no longer be a mourner, so he blew out the scented candles that had burned for years and, rather than go out one more day in black, he stitched a shirt from his pillowcases and the valances on the windows. And while he was no longer a mourner, he still walked to the graveyard to pay tribute and consult with his departed wife.

"I'm thinking about going to Europe to see the Pope, and maybe shoot a Spanish musket, and with your permission drink a little wine," he said to his wife. And while he knew that she had always wanted for him to see the world, he postponed the trip every year. Although Don Victoriano never admitted this to anyone, except once in the confessional, he never boarded the plane because he was afraid of dying away from his wife.

CHAPTER TEN

||

SATURN

The roof caved in yesterday. Today the legs
of the dining-room table gave way. And
the bathtub has been leaking for days.

> I'm sorry.

I opened the kitchen drawer and there was
nothing but rust and the plastic rings from
the napkin holders.
    I stayed up all night writing you a
letter. It had perfect sentences—sentences
that took years off my life. All the things
I wanted to tell you. But when I woke up
the letter was flaking and tender as ash.
I touched it and it disintegrated.

> I never meant to do any of this.

You weren't supposed to spill out of the
dedication page. But then you fucked
everything. Made holes in my ceiling,
cracks in my ribs, my whole wardrobe
to dust. All for a white boy.

> I didn't do all of that.

That is what happens, the natural physics
of the world. You fuck a white boy and my
shingles loosen, the calcium in my bones
depletes, my clothes begin to unstitch.
    Everything weakens. I lose control.
The story goes astray. The trajectory of the
novel altered because of him. They colonize
everything: the Americas, our stories, our
novels, our memories...

> You went away to fight de la Fe and
> ▓▓▓▓ was here.

Don't say his name. I don't want him
in here. I will scratch him out.

I have to call him something.

You should come back.

I can't.

I'm sad without you.

It's not my fault.

Without you there is nothing, not
even drizzle.

...

I will build you bookshelves like you
always wanted.

It's too late.

Because missing you is worse than
Pittsburgh.

Nothing is worse than Pittsburgh.

I will wash my foreskin everyday.

Stop this.

I will pull it back.

I have to go.

I don't know what they are called, the
spaces between seconds—but I think of
you always in those intervals.

I'm sorry.

You are awful. Worse than Rita Hayworth.
Too good to fuck us lettuce pickers.

That is not what it's about.

You sell-out. Vendida. You are worse
than the Malinche, worse than Pocahontas.
Fucking white boys and making asbestos
fall from the attic.

What about your girl? Your
white girl?

She was after you, when you would not
answer the phone or my letters.

You are leaving things out. I love ▨▨▨.
I have to go.

Sometimes, I call her names that are not
her name. And she says, "That is not my
name."

And again I say the name that is not
her name. Don't touch me, she says. So
I don't touch her, or I say no names and
touch her. But still I think of the name
that is not her name. But your roof does
not fall. Maybe I need to say her name.

Tomorrow, I will break your roof.

Your kitchen chairs are still strong
and mine are piles of sawdust. I want you
to have dust for spoons and dirt in your
closets, clothes that become string on you.
Everything that is you to break and disin-
tegrate. Everything that you touch. Your
windowsills, the steps that lead to your
door, all to fall apart. And when you touch
him, his bones to break, the splinters into
his pancreas, into his lungs, pelvic bone to
snap, the spilling blood to rust. For him
to rot and decay and fade.

CHAPTER ELEVEN
● ● ●

CAMEROON

S he sat alone in her upstate New York apartment holding a jar of honey-bees, pressing stingers into her forearms. At night, when the poison brought the fever, she peeled off her shirt and pulled down her panties, stretching, her feet pushing Saturn from the bed and onto the floor.

Underneath the bed: shoes, tangled bras, the smell of loneliness, and small mounds of spent and desiccated bees.

"Cami, what are these?" Saturn asked, holding two curled insects in the cup of his hand.

"I don't know," she said.

Cameroon kept the bees a secret, hiding them deep in her closet and covering the jars with towels. In the bathtub, while pretending to shave, she plucked the stingers from her arms. And the fever that kept her hot and sweating she blamed on the pneumonia she could never shake.

But at night a faint buzzing emanated from the closet doors. She slept, her fever warming the sheets and walls, melting the ice on the windows. As cliffs of snow crashed down, Saturn stepped out of bed, took the jars from the closet and filled them with water, drowning all of the insects. In the morning, when she awoke, Cameroon tried to salvage the bees, but the stingers were limp and soft, unable to stab, and the poison she tried to suck from the ends was diluted by water and traces of honey.

"No more bees, I promise," she would say, the heat of her fever increasing, forming a halo at the crown of her head. And so Saturn lay in bed with her for weeks, holding her, feeling her body shake and cleaning mouthfuls of chewed bread and fruit she had tried to eat. He brewed manzanilla tea and rubbed arnica cream on her belly and breasts; he squeezed out the thorns, using his teeth to pluck those that had gone deep into her meat.

The halo finally faded. Saturn left the room, only for a couple of hours, walking outside and over gray and salted snow, trailing dirt and melting ice into the supermarket, through the dairy aisles.

"I could have built you bookshelves," he thought, pulling the dedication page from his pocket, looking at the grocery list he had scribbled below the typed text.

He crossed "potato bread" from the list and placed the loaf in his basket. He crossed out other things too.

~~eggs~~

~~milk~~

"And for Liz ~~who taught me that we are all of paper~~," and then wrote: "For Liz who fucked everything."

While Saturn unloaded his basket and the cashier tallied the items, Cameroon was in the apartment dialing. Twenty minutes, they said. And then they came, dressed in their wire veils, still holding their just-extinguished bee smokers. They traded two Mason jars of honeybees for three twenty-dollar bills.

This time she was careless—she made no attempt to hide any of it. He discovered dead bees on the carpet and in the trash bin, and others crawling up the curtains. He said nothing. He lay in bed, his back turned to her, the buzzing spilling from the Mason jar. Cameroon slowly silencing the whole jar, pocking her arms with bees pressed to her skin, singeing her hair, warming the room with the glow of her halo.

NATALIA

Natalia had only one request: She asked that on their honeymoon Quinones would take her to a place where she could touch and eat real snow. She had tasted shaved ice, covered in eggnog and sprinkled with crushed almonds and cinnamon, but machine-made ice was never as soft or delicious as the flakes of a fresh flurry that landed on her tongue as she watched the roaring falls of Niagara.

After thirty-five years of the perpetual summer of Ensenada, Natalia wanted to feel the joy of wearing a sweater and drinking a pot of hot coffee. She wanted, for once, to lie with Quinones and not have the sheets turn into sweat rags; and she wanted goose bumps that were raised not by embarrassment or nails scratching on blackboards.

"We have lots of winters to make up for," she told Quinones.

Quinones had always known that he loved Natalia, but it was not until he gave up sunbathing, the taste of tropical langostas, and the sands of a warm coast that he understood the price of love. What was supposed to be a weeklong honeymoon in the cold country was extended into a fifty-year residency on the frozen banks of the Georgian Bay.

JONATHAN MEAD

After three years of searching, Jonathan Mead finally located his daughter. The investigator provided him with the phone number and descriptions of her hair color and its length (black and to mid-back) and estimates of her height: around 5'6", 5'8", always wears sneakers, except during heavy snow.

He had not seen his daughter since she was seven, and now, sixteen years later, he wanted what every remorseful and estranged father wants: to reconcile with the child he had abandoned. Jonathan Mead held the piece of paper, imagining what it would feel like to dial the number and hear his daughter's voice. He practiced what he would say and the tone of voice in which he would speak, and then began dialing.

CAMEROON

When the first installment came, sealed with the saliva of millionaires, Saturn did not use the money to fight Federico de la Fe and EMF. Instead he forged war reports and sent them at regular intervals to New York City, and he used the endowment to tend to Cameroon's bee stings and to alleviate his own sadness.

He filled a thermos with manzanilla tea and gave Cameroon two jars of arnica cream that she packed between her sweaters and pants next to an empty Mason jar. The doctors and curanderos recommended repose and wet towels—that is how you fight the swelling and muscle cramps, they said—but Saturn opted for the road. A route with no honey crates or bee-keepers. But there was another agenda: he knew that the true mission of Napoleon Bonaparte was not always to conquer, but to travel. To see foreign lands and forget the women who had hurt him. On the trip Saturn would concentrate. He would touch Cameroon and look at her, calling her by the name that was hers. He would write his grocery list on different paper, on sheets of paper that did not allude to anything but toiletries and edibles. He would not think of her or of the white boy who colonized his memories. He who had spread his imperialism everywhere. All over her, spilling it on her chest and stomach, coating her lips, and throat, lining the esophagus and intestines.

"There will be no more of you," he said as if she were there. "Only Cami, only Cami."

The first stop on Cameroon's and Saturn's journey was what was initially known as the seventh wonder of the world but had been demoted by auditors to the ninth position, displaced by the Flamingo Casino and the city of Needles, which claimed the largest thermometer on earth.

It was from the window of their hotel that Cameroon and Saturn watched the crashing waters of the ninth wonder of the world, the sound barely muffled by the soundproof windows of their honeymoon suite.

"People actually spend their honeymoons here?" she asked.

"Honeymooners and tourists," Saturn said.

"So what are we?"

"Just passing through."

When he went down on Cameroon he transfered everything that he knew about love onto her, no grocery lists or white boys in his mind. Just her softness and warmth, the taste of dissolving paper absent, but she was as white as *The Book of Incandescent Light*. He dragged his tongue across her and felt nothing but smooth flesh. When he reached her ear he whispered:

"Cami, you should let it grow."

"Why?"

"It's nice to feel something."

Then it was she who went down. The taste of foreskin filled her mouth, slowly she pulled away, handling it, and then folding back skin, hurting Saturn and exposing meat. No salted milk spilled. Not until the church-sanctioned missionary position was employed and the halo, which scorched the pillows and warped the headboard, was extinguished by the sweat of their bodies, only then did his starch come forth.

Saturn had not registered with the papal embassy for years, yet he retained a very Catholic idea of love. He followed the procedures faithfully, adhering to all church recommendations and the advice his devout great-grandfather had given him: caressing and never pulling hair, pinning 'em down and mounting, rocking gently, but never pounding—unless, of course, they specifically said to do so.

"Always from the front and never call her by the name that is not her name," his great-grandfather had said. After proper love there were symptoms: a sweaty forehead; the limbs sore and bruised; a philistine rawness on the foreskin; and a nearly insatiable and debilitating appetite, a hunger that had been specially invented for postcoital love, a hunger that never came to Saturn.

Niagara Falls was only the trailhead of the honeymooners' voyage, followed by the Caledon Hills, the incline of Kolapore, the limestone caves of Kimberly, terminating at the tip of the Bruce Peninsula. At the Niagara escarpments Saturn vomited a meal he could not recall eating and Cameroon purchased a sandwich to silence the growls of her stomach and then they drank water from the glacial melts.

At the end of the honeymoon trail, on the most northern part of the Bruce Peninsula, sat El Hotel de los Novios, founded by Natalia and Quinones Hernandez—a hotel that upheld the strictest honeymooner policies, accepting only those who could provide a marriage certificate no more than two weeks old, with rare exceptions granted for paper and platinum anniversaries. But no anniversary, regardless of its years, would take precedence over those newly wed.

Using the same ream of paper on which he had forged war reports, and with the help of Cameroon's penmanship, Saturn drafted a marriage certificate that he handed over at the reception desk.

The suite had no television, only a radio with an emergency weather station and two FM channels, each playing a constant rotation of love ballads. The bed was sturdily reinforced at its legs and dip, the linens starched, and the wedding lasso that hung above the bed was braided from four strands of rope. The bathroom was equipped with a French bidet and a wood-burning boiler, in which Cameroon put too much coal, scalding her shoulders and Saturn's chest when the boiling water spat out from the showerhead.

In El Hotel de los Novios, Saturn renounced the papal guidelines, folding and stretching Cameroon. She held onto towel racks and the backs of chairs, while he pretended to be impervious to her whimpers and cries. And she, as if to reciprocate, sat on Saturn, bending him and chafing him until his skin reddened and flaked, the friction sparking a halo that would burn through the front of his pants. And as an emphatic dismissal of the Vatican dicta, Cameroon and Saturn avoided any position that even hinted at the civility of love.

And though Cameroon had said she loved Saturn, whispering it over and over while underneath him—never when on top—she went into the washroom and sat on the bidet. She tossed a small log into the boiler and when the warm water spouted from the faucet in a low voice she recited the bidet prayer:

"I'm gonna wash this man right out of my hair, I'm gonna wash this man right out of me. My apologies to the Georgian Bay where he will go."

NATALIA

Natalia and Quinones dedicated their married lives to each other and hotel management. And as Francophobes, never forgiving the French invasion of Puebla, they also dedicated much of their free time to dispelling many of the aphorisms Napoleon Bonaparte had popularized. Quinones helped Natalia with the hotel duties, replenishing bundles of wood and inspecting the authenticity of the marriage certificates, and when his duties were done, he sat at his mahogany desk writing to the French Museum in Montreal and to the Parisian Hall of Archives.

While he had yet to address Bonaparte's largest claim—"I believe love to be hurtful to the world, and to the individual happiness of men. I believe, in short, that love does more harm than good"—Quinones had argued against every other Napoleonic declaration.

So when Napoleon wrote, in his diplomatic letter to Alexander I, "All women in the world would not make me lose an hour," Quinones refuted, not by citing the names of all women in the world, a list that would take three months, six days, and two hours to read, but by simply writing one name: "Marie Louise."

And in response to Napoleon's assertion that he had "autre chose à penser que l'amor," Quinones submitted photographs of the uniform Napoleon's troops had worn and a diagram of their battle formations. Every uniform bore the same decorative pin that Marie Louise had given Napoleon when they first met, and when sent to battle, the troops were always deployed in the form of her initials.

The French, as always, were unimpressed, and aside from the occasional porcelain bidet that Quinones received, packed in Parisian headlines, there was never any official acknowledgment that they had read his letters. Quinones was never discouraged. In the morning he installed the bidets in the hotel's washrooms and then returned to his desk and wrote late into the night.

Natalia's critique of Bonaparte took a more subtle form, a critique manifested in the décor and menu of the hotel. There were no vanity stools to stand on and not a single topographical map hung on the wall, and in the kitchen the cooks were forbidden from ever preparing crepes or Napoleon's favorite pastry: the mille-feuille.

JONATHAN MEAD

He let the phone ring once and immediately hung up the receiver. He had rehearsed what he would say, how he would say it. He would speak with regret but not guilt.

There were run-throughs and simulations. Calling his own number to hear the tone of busy signals, calling restaurants after-hours for the string of endless rings, dialing ex-wives for the click and crackle of answering machines. Old friends for the sound of voice. Wrong numbers for terse goodbyes.

CAMEROON

Saturn picked up the phone. At the other end the hotel proprietor requested that Saturn come down to the front desk.

"The marriage certificate..."

"Yes?" Saturn said.

"I'm afraid it's false. This is a hotel for honeymooners."

Saturn did not argue. He told Cameroon to pack her bags and with bags in hand walked down to the reception desk and returned the room keys and the knotted and tangled wedding lasso.

"Nothing against you. We are not to say who is in love and who is not. We just need something official that proves it."

"I understand," Saturn said.

On the drive out of the Bruce Peninsula, the clouds collapsed, covering everything, stranding Saturn and Cameroon underneath the white. They pulled the car to the side of the road, turned the engine off, and unpacked their bags, huddling into each other and wrinkled clothes. They shivered and did not sleep.

Saturn kissed Cameroon and called her by the name that was her name and for once felt the hunger pangs that he was supposed to feel, but did not know if it was love or signs of starvation.

"Your stomach is growling. When we thaw out we'll get some food," she said and then touched his hair.

When the snowplows and thaw came they drove past a land that had disintegrated into a thousand islands. Once over the bridge, the earth consolidated and the spring weather began to encroach, melting snow from the roof of the car. They drove for the rest of the day until they reached the city of Philadelphia.

In Philadelphia, the redness from the stings subsided and the halo on Cameroon's head completely disappeared and Saturn finished plucking the last of the remaining thorns from her body.

"Why the bees?" he asked.

She said that when one is sad there is only insects or sex.

"Honeybees or fucking," she said.

Cameroon's sadness was not a biblical one like Federico de la Fe's, but it was a sadness that could not be suppressed by fire or by honeybees or by fucking. De la Fe's sorrow ran deeper, infecting even the tiny alcoves of his lungs, but there was always the possibility of a cure—the return of

Merced. But for Cameroon no returns or reconciliations were possible. No way to forget a lonely childhood and the parade of fathers who tried to have a hand not only in her rearing but also underneath the elastic and hems of her clothes.

There were no indigenous bees in Philadelphia. They were imported from the South, from the islands of the Caribbean, some from the Florida panhandle, transported in punctured shoeboxes, in jars and screened crates. And she, with her empty Mason jars, her scarf blowing, and her feet on the banks of the Delaware river, waited for the beekeepers to come. They arrived wearing their wire veils and gloves, replenished Cameroon's empty jar and walked away.

NATALIA

In the fifty-year history of El Hotel de los Novios, a history that included three expansions and four different decorating schemes, Natalia and Quinones had uncovered only three fraudulent marriage certificates.

The first, though written in careful calligraphy and stamped with the justice of the peace's seal, was brought in by a fifty-year-old man who carried his suitcases and his thirteen-year-old bride in his arms. Though the certificate was authentic, the groom could not provide identification for his bride and Natalia and Quinones were forced to turn the couple away.

The second was an Argentine couple whose marriage certificate was written with the cheap, faint ink of squids, in a cursive so illegible that Quinones could barely make out the newlyweds' names; on the required supplementary page, the names of witnesses had been purposely obscured with bird droppings. When Quinones tried to scrape the bird shit from the parchment, the bride protested, explaining that the witnesses could not be revealed without endangering not only the lives of those listed but also those who read the names. Natalia and Quinones left the names unexposed and the certificate invalidated, referring the couple to a motel that required no documentation.

The third came in the final years of their ownership, before Natalia had begun sniffing tanning oil and importing sand and coconut milk. The certificate was printed in sterile ink, the names of Cameroon and Saturn underlined and bolded, and all the required signatures neatly written on the dotted lines. The document was so convincing that Quinones could smell the scent of holy water emanating from the paper and see the oily stains of musk left by the priest's hands. And when he saw the couple, the bride tall, her face burned by cold and wind and a halo above her, the groom short like Napoleon, holding the luggage and snow umbrella, they seemed convincingly wed. And though Natalia was suspicious of Saturn's short stature and of the red of Cameroon's arms, she gave them a room on the third floor that faced the waters of the Georgian Bay.

At first, it seemed only a typographical error, but when Quinones reread the certificate and tried to find the location of the ceremony, consulting both maps and church directories, he came to realize that the place existed only in the imagination.

Natalia would have disapproved, but Quinones did not immediately evict the couple, waiting instead until morning.

JONATHAN MEAD

He let the phone ring. Four times and then hung up. He dialed again, fully aware that no one would pick up, letting it ring until his ear was warm. He had placed the call three days too late. His daughter was gone, in the passenger seat of a rented Buick heading toward the ninth wonder of the world.

CAMEROON

Saturn watched Cameroon as she slept. The Mason jars were empty again and her arms were freckled with the thorns of insects. Two bees buzzed around the room, another tried to untangle itself from Cameroon's now full and unshaped muff, and a pile lay on the carpet torn in half, their stingers missing.

He watched as the bee threaded its way through Cameroon's hair, emerging on her stomach. He lifted the bee by its wings and pressed it into his arm. When the poison entered his body, suddenly swelling his veins and slowing the blood, all these things disappeared from Saturn's mind:

1) The war on Federico de la Fe
2) Cameroon
3) Liz

For once in a very long time Saturn felt the singularity that children sometimes feel when they are left alone on the lawn—as if there is nothing else in the world but the softness of grass.

CHAPTER TWELVE

•

SATURN

A diatribe against womanhood: In his final battle, the one he lost, Napoleon used the most predictable of military strategies. He replaced his troops' rifles with flowers and filled their canteens with Marie Louise's favorite perfume. They were sent into battle with roses and scented breath, marching over vineyards on the tips of their feet, the initials ML clear to those who looked down at the soldiers from hot-air balloons. Three thousand troops sent to slaughter, their bodies piled high, rotting and spilling ink on her garden. The reinforcements came, their pockets stuffed with chocolate and earrings, and they too perished. The ink of their bodies gathering at the foot of her door, forming letters and introducing a new word to the French lexicon: *cunt*.

Marie Louise researched the etymology of the word and precedents where it had been used. The citations were mostly biblical but she found others:

in the fall from Eden
cunt.

in the story of Sampson
cunt.

in the undoing of Val Kilmer in *Heat*
cunt.

in the story of Saturn
cunt.

in love
cunts.

in the fall of civilization
cunts, cunts, cunts, cunts, cunts, cunts...

CHAPTER THIRTEEN

•

BEEKEEPER

She did not smoke but there were always cigarette burns in the sheets and dead bees in the folds. Her muff was untrimmed and wild.

"Because of Saturn," she said.

I doused her with water and she did unholy things, but still the halo glowed. Two pairs of sheets later and after the near-arson of the closet the halo seemed to disappear. But still she took precautions: she slept sitting up and staring at the ceiling, her head cocked back, soaking in the sink to prevent further flare-ups. But by morning the water had evaporated and the porcelain of the sink had bubbled and blackened.

This is what it is to live with saints.

But there were also unexpected details. Details that are never taught or even mentioned in catechism. She spoke in words that were not becoming of sainthood and she wanted to make love in ways that were not love. She was not reserved and quiet and, though she spoke softly, it was mostly slander.

"Fuck Saturn," she said. "He is not telling the whole story." And this was why she had left him, because he was a liar.

There were nights when we did not talk. She would pull off my gloves and mesh hood and we would press honeybees into each other and then make love in the dark, illuminated only by her halo. And there were days when she would have me take notes as she listed all the lies Saturn had told:

63. Rita Hayworth was never Mexican.
64. There is no cure for sadness.
65. The bidet is not French.
66. There was no television during Prohibition.
67. I never said I loved him.

The list went on for sixty four-pages.

"Have you read *The Book of Incandescent Light?*" she asked. I had not read beyond the second sentence, but I nodded thoughtfully, as if to say, "It is the most beautiful thing I have ever read."

"That book is such drivel. No one thinks that way," she said, and her halo intensified.

CHAPTER FOURTEEN

●

I was going to stay quiet, let you write your story, let your history as you see it stand. Because I was the unkind one, the reckless one, deserving of whatever you may say. But this is a novel—it is no longer between just you and me. You have involved too many people, brought in too much of the world, and I will not be the villain. I deserve your hate, your resentment, even your cruelty, I will not argue that. But that is your right, your entitlement for what I did wrong, not something that can be shared. You cannot pass that right on to others.

But that is what you are doing, turning the readers into lettuce pickers and me into your Rita Hayworth. The sellout, the faithless one, the Malinche, the whore. And you of course are the loyal and kind one, the only one true to Monte. The romantic hero.

Raising your army of lettuce pickers who will toss their insults and rotting heads of lettuce. So every day I awake and must smell the pile of rot that has been thrown against my door, and somehow you think that will make me lament what I did to you? But I don't need the smell of wilting lettuce to remind me. I did wrong, I know that, and I carry my own rot.

But, Sal, I will not be your Rita Hayworth.

I loved you, I loved you very much, but things changed. You went away to fight de la Fe and then there was someone else who was not from

Monte, who could not speak a word of Spanish, and who had never heard of EMF or tasted the tripe of menudo. And I fell in love with him. And because of this you want to cast me not only as the woman who hurt you but also as the woman who turned her back on Monte, as the sellout.

So I have moved house and replaced you with a white boy, but that is nothing compared to what you have done, to what you have sold. In a neat pile of paper you have offered up not only your hometown, EMF, and Federico de la Fe, but also me, your grandparents and generations beyond them, your patria, your friends, even Cami. You have sold everything, save yourself. So you remain but you have sold everything else. You have delivered all this into their hands, and for what? For fourteen dollars and the vanity of your name on the book cover.

But I'm not here to punish you, or to make you feel guilty. Do what you will. I have only a request: You need to remember that I exist beyond the pages of this book. One day, I don't know when, I will have children, and I don't want them finding a book in which their mother is faithless and cruel and insults the hero. Sal, if you still love me, please leave me out of this story. Start this book over, without me.

cunt

THE PEOPLE OF PAPER

by
SALVADOR PLASCENCIA

Para mi papa, mama, y hermana.

PART THREE

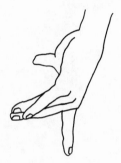

The sky is falling.

CHAPTER
FIFTEEN
❚❚❚

In the sky there were only clouds. Apolonio tested the rainwater, dripping dye into the glass beakers and then straining the solution. After three samplings the test was conclusive: there were zero particulates of Saturn in the atmosphere.

Froggy phoned the planetarium to confirm. "Only eight planets in the solar system," the astronomer said.

And my father, who always felt the weight of Saturn on his shoulders, now walked with perfect posture and a step so light that it did not ripple even the shallowest puddles.

Slowly the news reached every house in El Monte. People came out of their shelters and began trimming their hedges and tipping the stale, putrid water that had gathered in the birdbaths. They looked underneath the hoods of their trucks, pouring gasoline into the carburetors and scraping corrosion from the battery posts.

But we were not convinced: while the rest of EMF tidied their lawns and tuned their engines, Pelon climbed the water tower and rigged a siren to the roof of the retaining bin. Froggy, Sandra, and my father each carried a flare gun in their waistbands, tucked next to their carnation knives. This was our warning system.

My father did not venture far. He sat on the steps of the porch talking to Froggy and Julieta, constantly looking up at the sky.

Sandra passed by the house, the flare-gun hanging from her belt like a gunslinger's; she waved hello and everybody waved back except for Julieta, who lowered her head and squeezed Froggy's hand.

I excused myself and followed Sandra down the sidewalk, along Ferris Road and into Medina Court. There, Apolonio was airing his shop of the incense, waving a cloth towel, pushing the strands of smoke out of his door and into the liberated sky.

Before me there was Sandra.

In the cushions I still find yarn, traces of her inept needlework: loose knots and snagged string.

But on Froggy's neck the pattern is intricate and skilled, the "EMF" written in the same ornate Old English script used by the monks who transcribed copies of *The Book of Incandescent Light*.

Froggy rarely speaks of her and that is how most would want it. You don't want your lover speaking of the one before you, but you still look for some acknowledgment—evidence that the past has been dealt with, that the wounds suffered have been treated, that there is nothing festering, no remnants of love incubating.

I find strands of string, old stockings, and half-empty bottles of lotion. I hold them up to Froggy and he simply says, "They belong to Subcomandante Sandra," matter-of-factly, ignoring how the items came into the house.

"Do you still think of her, Froggy?" I asked.

"Yes, of course. In any tactical decision I consult Subcomandante Sandra."

"No, Froggy. Do you think of her in other ways?"

"No, Julieta. All of that has passed."

"So when you see her at the dominoes table you don't think of the times you were with her?"

"We are in the middle of a war. I don't think about that. I think of ways to defeat Saturn so that you and I can have our own lives. So that there will be no onlookers when we are in bed or at the kitchen table. Julieta, a lot has passed since me and Subcomandante Sandra, and you are the only one that I think about in the way that you are asking about."

But at night, I would kiss his neck, moistening him with saliva, trying to wipe the ink from his skin.

SATURN

148

Some tribes are benign: Glue Sniffers and Monks who want only alms and prayer. And then there are the other tribes, the ones that my father prohibited me from even greeting. Gypsies who came with sugar cane slices in hand and rope netting hidden in the back of their pants, and Ticuanenses who sold real estate and building contracts—tribes with reputations as kidnappers and architects of shoddy construction.

And then there were the curanderos, like Apolonio, who my father trusted. Curanderos did not travel in packs or in formations; they were solitary and of a happy loneliness. They held no grudges but also no allegiance, not to the principles of Newton or Hippocrates, disregarding both cardinal and papal authority. They operated under their own tenets of the market economy, faithful only to the individual needs of each customer. And if anything it was this neutrality that was suspect—the fact that Apolonio would not side with either Saturn or EMF.

The business of the curandero was one of pure mercantile exchange, of tending to the needs of the clientele: selling arsenic to an angry flower picker and days later the antidote to the yellowing scale attendant who had been cheating workers for years.

But the curandero, in his strict professionalism, was also a confidant. A confessor with no duty to the Vatican. What was said to the curandero, unless otherwise requested, stayed with the curandero.

So when you enter the curandero's shop and ask for a bag of limes, he asks no questions, he quotes a price, you nod, and he hands you a brown sack brimming with limes. And that is all that is ever said of the exchange.

El Monte for once in a very long time was living the carefree life of a complacent California farming town.

I sat with Federico de la Fe, shuffling dominoes and then holding my seven ivory pieces, careful to unload the double sixes before gameplay choked the tile. War was not in our minds; our thoughts were relaxed, able to wander into those places we had avoided while under Saturn.

It was not just military strategy that we had stopped ourselves from thinking about. We also denied ourselves those quiet and reflective moments when we pondered the alternatives, the could-have-beens, those paths that might have led elsewhere.

The moments where we look back and think about other loves and towns. Places we have visited and think that maybe we belong, among the orchards and shade of oaks, that place with real rivers and seasons. Or with that other person, perhaps, with her in that other town where there are no flowers or ash. Rarely does anything come of this, but at the very least you exercise the memory and the muscles of nostalgia.

And while we were free to think and reminisce inside our leaden houses, Julieta was always there, perceptive to any signs of pensiveness.

"Froggy, tell me what are you thinking," she would say, not understanding what the war was about.

But today, I walked the Monte streets, at times imagining I was elsewhere. The breeze carrying the smell of flowers and manure, returning me to Monte, to thoughts of Sandra and then Julieta. To the day that Sandra inked my neck and I stuffed her dress with petals, celebrating our love and our gang that had sprung from carnations.

SATURN

There was no Saturn or school, nobody to beware of but my father. I spent the afternoon shaded under an outgrowth of carnation plants, using the switchblade Froggy had given me to cut the whole limes into rinds. I did not have to be locked in my room chewing the bitter meat of seeds and the waxed skin; instead I spit the seeds into the air and let the peels fall on the ground.

This is what emancipation allowed, what it was to live outside the casing of lead.

I ate my limes and returned to Apolonio's with my sack empty, my tongue burnt by the citric juices, and my lap and hands stained and sticky.

"My father will know," I said, showing him my fingers and then sticking out my tongue.

He was calm, squeezing soap lard into my hands, and then sprinkling pumice sand.

"Lather. That will take care of your hands. And there's a sponge for your dress. You can chew flower petals for your breath."

I stuck out my tongue again so he would see the peeling skin, but he just shook his head. There was nothing he could do for my tongue.

I never told de la Fe. I unbuttoned my shirt, shaking it until all the bits of sky were emptied from its pockets. At night, from my porch I could see the gap in the sky. The unpatched hole, twinkling as the light from Saturn's bedroom was turned on and off.

"Smiley, do you think Saturn is gone?" Froggy asked.

"It is just sad," I said.

"Planets cannot be sad," he said.

"What about Pluto?" I asked.

"Yes, but that is a very small planet."

Froggy was of the belief, grounded in ancient philosophy, that after a certain amount of accumulated mass, sadness ends. And so he cited:

Saint Nicholas
Don Ho
Winston Churchill
Sir John Falstaff

All fat and jolly people. Though jolliness was the saddest form of happiness, it was a happiness nonetheless.

But Froggy did not mention the nights when Don Ho wept on Hawaiian sands, not rising until long after the tiki lamps had been extinguished. Or the hours Saint Nicholas spent pulling splinters from his fingers and sniffing turpentine. He never even mentioned the sadness of the Elder Elvis. Or the saddest of them all: Don Francisco, always tangled in velvet with hired women while commercial jingles played in the background, ditties for soap and mops. The women were not the prettiest, but they all resembled his first love, and he asked them if they would not mind very much if he could call them "Porfedia."

SATURN

When Saturn finally returned it was with a
Napoleonic fervor. Federico de la Fe instantly felt the
presence, the weight dropping him to the ground.
The siren sounded and two flares shot into the sky,
coloring everything with flashes of red.

EMF rushed out of the fields, from underneath
the hoods of their cars, from the pleasant shade of
trees, and then ran into their houses.

When Froggy saw Federico de la Fe face down
on the lawn, he instantly knew what had happened.
He fired the flare into the sky and then went looking
for Julieta. And when the pulsating light began to
fade, Sandra shot the second flare.

Federico de la Fe crawled into his house, heading
straight for his bathroom. He shot the gun into the
sink, propelling the flare into a ricochet around the
porcelain. He trapped it with his bare hands, cupping
it until it exploded. The warmth from the sparks
soothed him and singed his eyebrows and lashes.

"It misfired," he said to Little Merced, and she
said nothing, concealing her tongue.

Outside, the dominoes were scattered, tarps and
flower baskets abandoned and still unweighed, lawn
trimmings spreading onto the sidewalks, carburetors and alternators dismantled and soaking in gasoline, screwdrivers stabbed between sprockets and
timing belts.

All of EMF ran back inside and there was no one
left to enjoy the sunny skies. No one, that is, except
for Smiley, who was determined to make himself
known. Taking off his guayabera and then his undershirt, he lay down outside his house, tanning his
shoulders and then turning, exposing his belly to
the sky.

LITTLE MERCED

The shrill of the sirens came through Apolonio's windows. He handed me a small sack of limes. I paid and hid the fruit underneath my dress.

"You better go," he said. "Saturn is back."

I ran home, the ring of the sirens and the palpitating light of the flares slowing everything, as all of El Monte scattered.

"Little Merced, go home!" Froggy yelled, dragging Julieta by the arm. And Pelon wiped the grease from his hands, smearing it on his pants, and then jumped into his truck, driving beside me and pulling me into the cab.

When we got to the house the inside glowed red and then suddenly filled with smoke. My father came out of the rest-room holding the ashing flare in his hands. He doused the flare and tossed it into the dustbin and I went to lower the front door.

SUBCOMANDANTE SANDRA

I shot the flare. I watched it crest and then fall, bursting into star clusters before crashing into the flower fields.

The gray clouds floated away, replaced by the heat of the California summer and a looming presence that thickened the air and shifted weather patterns.

The cool breeze from the west had been diverted around the ring of ash that surrounded El Monte. In the weather maps the cooling fronts were represented as arrows carefully avoiding one particular circle:

It was then that the flower company, long absent, sent their irrigation team to patch the leaks and drag all the sprinklers into the fields, diverting all the water from the tower to the flowers, ensuring that the petals were kept moist and cool. Inside the walls of lead, the faucets and showerheads spilled only warm air and dust. Not until sunset did the valves siphon water back to the houses.

And so the nights were spent plug-ging bathtubs and sinks, and then filling boiling pots, pitchers, and every single glass, stockpiling water before the daytime drought returned.

SATURN

When they finally cut the siren, El Monte was vacant. The only sounds were the hourly bell tolls and the spitting and ticking of sprinklers. The town quieted, the bustling town of flower pickers and sidewalk mechanics who pounded out oil filters and dropped pieces of ivory while whistling tunes from Rita Hayworth movies, all its clatter and noise halted.

Whenever a member of EMF opened his door he kept silent and thought of nothing, or what he imagined nothing to be: dirt, water, cracked pavement, the webbing between feet, the buttons on mattresses, and the wide expanse of the blue sky. They dragged in blocks of ice and standing fans, and then quickly shut their doors.

Sandra shut her door last, watching the star clusters fall, looking at the townscape of stuccos and fields, for a moment imagining what El Monte would be without flowers or furrows, without EMF and war.

And then there was Smiley, who stayed outside all day, entering his house only in the late evening and then spending half the night tearing the lead from his walls. Exhausted and his clothes stiff, crusted by the drying sweat, he slipped into bed.

In a persistent but never-remembered dream, Smiley drew his knife and slid it across Saturn's throat. Blood covered the blade and a stream of red ink ran across the floorboards, draining into the hole Smiley had cut, the blood dripping into the blue sky, staining the horizon and turning the afternoon purple.

In other dreams, the ones that he remembered as they came to him at dawn, it was only he and Saturn sitting at a table. Sometimes sipping maté and chewing rose petals, other days playing dominoes.

"Comandante Smiley," Saturn would say and a smile came over Smiley's slumbering face.

LITTLE MERCED

"Water is not a complete thought. It has no shape. You may think of that if you wish," my father said. And so I thought of cups of water and bathtubs, of water towers and reservoir tahoes, lakes and rivers. Rivers that we may hold in our hands, rivers that we palm and toss. The rivers where my mother may be.

The river that ran from my father, warm and meandering across the plastic sheets, the flow dammed along the side of my mother. And then there were no rivers, instead irrigation ditches and piping and obedient streams at attention, channeled by furrows.

And rivers in suspension, the ones that we carried in cubes and blocks of ice.

PELON

When the siren sounded, I was hitching the plow to the tractor so I thought about how before tractors and John Deeres, it was a wooden yoke strapped to the shoulders of oxen who pulled a hand-guided plow. Their mouths muzzled, so they would not eat the seeds or stalks. Their shit splattering on the metal plow and fertilizing the soil. The oxen slowly walked forward, pulling the plow, digging one furrow at a time.

When the tractor came they unyoked the oxen and sent them to a pasture where all the animals that had been retired by machines went. There they grazed on alfalfa and Saint Augustine grass, next to broken-back donkeys and pigeons that had been laid off by telegraph operators.

They set diesel drums at the edge of the field and the driver who drove the tractor from the foothills, where there were orchards and not flowers, would siphon gas from the drums into the tractor's tank. He would oil the hinges of the attachment plow, a mechanical wonder that dug four furrows at a time, simultaneously upturning dirt and planting seed. Perhaps the greatest invention since Galileo's telescope.

SATURN

In the field, eight furrows over from where Pelon
hooked the plow, the escaped mechanical tortoise
brought Tijuana closer, moving scoops of soil from
south to north, compacting land with its legs and
then lurching through the rises of furrows. Official
measures said San Diego was now half a mile closer to
Los Angeles than the week before. This is what
machines did—they bridged the distance between
cities. Nevertheless, there were mechanics who wanted
to destroy the tortoises, to dismantle and scrap what
they themselves had created. And so the tortoise
flipped soil onto its shell, disguising itself as a mound
of dirt, and every hour bringing El Monte and the
border ten inches closer to each other.

LITTLE MERCED

Water from the spouts of the sprinklers,
piped from the Mulholland aqueduct,
delivered through cemented channels,
tapped from roaring rivers that become
trickles, replenished by the rain of the
storm that pours from the violence and
thunder of cumulus clouds, clouds formed
over oceans. From the brine of the Pacific,
the height of its waves pulled by the
moon, the tallest crest breaking when
both Saturn and the moon are aligned.

CHAPTER SIXTEEN

● ● ●

BABY NOSTRADAMUS

After the death of the Baby Nostradamus's mother, a death that the all-knowing infant began to mourn the day of his birth, it was Apolonio the curandero who assumed parental responsibilities. The network of old ladies with cataracts and deep maternal empathy relayed a family tree that linked Apolonio, albeit by grafted and tarred branches, to the Baby Nostradamus. Along with the document was the baby, wrapped in a quilt. They passed the bundled Nostradamus from house to house until he reached Apolonio, outside his shop, trying to repair the broken hands of a porcelain Mary Magdalen.

Apolonio received the baby with an anonymous note pinned to the burlap of his diaper bag, warning that the Baby Nostradamus's powers must never be used for profit. He took the warning seriously, making sure that the Baby Nostradamus was at least ten feet away from any transaction and when possible protected by a wall or a curtain division. It was during those times, when Apolonio tended to his customers and Little Merced entertained the Baby Nostradamus in the adjacent room, that the Baby Nostradamus took her under his wing, instructing her through telepathic lessons.

He started with a simple lesson.

He said, "This is a thought:"

There are three Merceds:
  1) your mother
  2) you
  3) Merced de Papel

The Baby Nostradamus used a thought that was composed of common knowledge and derived from simple indisputable facts, devoid of emotion and judgment.

"So this is a thought," the Baby Nostradamus said, speaking not with his lips but by touching Little Merced's palm. "Right now Saturn can see it. He can see anything that you or I think, but we have the power to hide ourselves without using lead."

And so the Baby Nostradamus demonstrated, concealing what was a perfectly legible and discernible thought:

Though at times forgetful, Saturn knew most of what was contained within the covers of this book: the esoteric allusions to *The Book of Incandescent Light*, the hidden jar of bees at the bottom of Cameroon's hamper, the organic composition of El Monte's soil, and the weight and grain of the paper on which these words are printed.

But Saturn had never been able to penetrate the black of the Baby Nostradamus. Every time he attempted to pierce the protective layer, only further and deeper darkness was revealed. Saturn, like many others, simply assumed that the mental capacity of the Baby Nostradamus had shriveled to black.

But behind the shield more than prophecies incubated. The Baby Nostradamus could do more than predict the future, an artless talent performed by the most simple of savants; his knowledge extended beyond the plot and details of this book, reaching not only into the future but beyond it, circling fully around, intersecting with the past and resting wherever he wished.

The catastrophic events, the collapse of towers, the inadvertent uprooting of the tree of knowledge (shaven and sawed into French vanity stools), the failed revolutions of red flags—all of this was neatly ordered and cataloged in the Baby Nostradamus's mind. But he also knew things that were inconsequential to historians and their records, details never written or photographed. The measurement on the Richter scale when Tiger Mask bodyslammed Santos onto the mat. Santos's soul, still wearing the sequined mask, lifted from his body, as he closed his hands into fists and clenched his teeth, trying to weigh himself down.

The Baby Nostradamus knew the intimate trivia of couples. The night Saturn and she whose name is no longer cited on the dedication page rolled off the bed and she landed on the tip of the unplugged iron, bruising the whole of her left buttock. In the hours that followed Saturn pressed his index finger into the purple, trying to locate the epicenter of the bruise.

There were also those quiet resolves impossible to chronicle or verify, those occurring in the early morning and in the private minds of somber war commanders. Things that were sometimes mouthed but never spoken. But the Baby Nostradamus was able to read their lips and pensive frowns. Through this ability he learned of Napoleon Bonaparte's secret spinach diet and regimen of stretches intended to add inches to his height and girth to his penis. And centuries later, the Baby Nostradamus listened to Saturn's morning affirmations; Saturn looked at Cameroon as she slept, and at the pile of upturned and torn bees on the lamp table and he told himself that there was only her. Only Cami, only Cami.

But after months and months the sheepskin still came loose, slipping during love, and when Napoleon climbed down from bed it was always with the help of a vanity stool. And Saturn, who slept on a futon and used a latex that wrapped firmly around him, struggled to call Cameroon by the name that was her name.

The range of the Baby Nostradamus's knowledge was of epic proportions, but now his energies were concentrated on tutoring Little Merced.

MERCED DE PAPEL

Merced de Papel discovered fire. The flames spread quickly, running up her elbow before she was able to reach the toilet bowl. The smell of burnt newsprint permeated the curtains, and the flakes of ash, buoyant even in whirlpools, floated in the toilet for nearly a week.

She rested her burnt and waterlogged arm on the kitchen table and tore the tattered blackened scraps, gathering a neat pile before dumping it in the wastebasket. She called the gas company to request a stoppage of service. They asked if she was moving, but instead of explaining that she had no need for stoves and hot water she said she was going on a long trip.

Merced de Papel was the only known survivor of her people, and as is always the case with those nearing extinction, she chronicled everything. Her manuscript began with an explanation of cunnilingus, noting the pleasures of human lips but also the aftermath of those who touched her, describing blood and the bits of paper pulp they would have to floss from their teeth.

In the last entry, the dangers of fire were cited, followed by a brief tutorial on the use of paper sacks and newsprint to repair what had been burned.

But it was not just burns that demanded repair. The friction from shoes tattered her toes, and simple things like holding a dinner fork wore away at her fingers. And so every weekend she walked down from the second floor of her Hollywood apartment, turned two corners to the newsstand, and returned with the Sunday edition. She sat at the kitchen table peeling away layers of paper, repairing what she had stripped with fresh, tight wraps of newsprint.

Compared to her creator Antonio, her origami was crude, often resorting to glue and tape. The messy folds and crusts of paste were hidden beneath her blouse and skirt. The sloppy tucks and cuts revealed themselves when she undressed and the lips of men tasted paste and jagged creases.

SMILEY

Smiley lived with the knowledge of Saturn. He knew his true name, the color of his sheets, and the position of his sleeping sprawls: always face down, his hands gripping the cliffs of the mattress.

But Smiley said nothing. He walked to de la Fe's dominoes game wearing only his pants, his chest and back bare to the sun and to the fluorescent light inside Federico de la Fe's house. It was there, standing above the dominoes—an absurd game where the greatest value ended in loss, a game that Smiley saw as a direct parody of the mathematical principles his ancestors had pioneered—there over the table, as the ivory pieces were shuffled, Smiley resigned.

"I can't do this anymore," he said. "I don't care if Saturn sees me."

Federico de la Fe simply nodded, but his wrists and hands tightened and arthritis of melancholy inflamed his joints, and he shut his eyes trying to suppress the pain.

Eventually Federico de la Fe and EMF forgave Smiley, understanding that they were involved in a war for volition. They banned Smiley from the dominoes games and military meetings but still extended a kind civility to him, allowing him to retain his dairy privileges and complimentary admission to the monthly cockfights. But Smiley's EMF membership was revoked and the letters that ran across the side of his neck were blotted into black blocks.

BABY NOSTRADAMUS

At first Little Merced's attempts were unsuccessful. Simple exercises involving only fragments of thought and singular words ended in disaster.

The Baby Nostradamus would demonstrate:

And then Little Merced would make an attempt:

Instead of hiding the letters, they became more pronounced. But after three days, as Little Merced practiced under the protection of her lead ceiling she was able to obscure not only basic acronyms but also simple sentences:

After the simple phrase, she hid compound sentences that utilized semicolons and commas, and soon could manage even full paragraphs. Her skill level increased, allowing her to take on complete, sophisticated thoughts. Thoughts that branched and strayed into tangents and then returned, only to split and sprawl again. She became so proficient that she was able to elude even the Baby Nostradamus:

When she succeeded and her thoughts were impenetrable, as a courtesy to her teacher Little Merced whispered the contents into the Baby Nostradamus's ear.

MERCED DE PAPEL

The men who came to love Merced de Papel did so with caution. But when they left her apartment their lips and penises glistened, and the tube of Neosporin was left empty and flattened, its twist cap carelessly dropped and disregarded on the restroom floor.

They left cut by her edges, knowing that they would never sit with her again and watch her as she tore off the scraps where their blood and salt had stained. The crumpled paper collecting at the center of the table, men sometimes hoping that she would let some of the stains remain, if only for the afternoon.

But Merced de Papel never allowed history to accumulate, her skin changing with the news of the world. She peeled away the story that reported the unearthing of a dead Samson; his healthy hair had sprouted from the ground and tangled itself around the shovels and pickaxes. And the following day, she wrapped a headline around her fingers that announced, in a follow-up report, the death of two Philistine archeologists choked by the locks of hair.

She peeled away every mark and scribble her lovers left, rarely saving any of the notes, grocery lists, and small reminders that men had written on her: pick up shirts from cleaners; dentist appointment 9:00 a.m.; milk, bread, cereal. And once she had to strip the whole of her back where someone had written the name Liz a thousand times over in blue ink.

Merced de Papel remained unmarked by her lovers, but men left with split lips and tongues, cuts that scarred, remaining deep into old age. The men walked into the Los Angeles streets, encountering others with the same distinctive paper-thin scars. They introduced themselves, casually licking their lips to reveal the depth and age of their cuts, at times flicking cleft tongues as quick as lizards.

But this was an unspoken fraternity; never were Merced de Papel or the cause of the scars mentioned. Their conversations were about the cities they had lived in and jobs they had worked. With the exception of a gourmet chef whose tastebuds had been shredded and now had to rely on memory and precise measurements when stirring his sauces, there were no regrets.

Merced de Papel had many lovers. On any given night, when the wait for a table at Musso & Frank's exceeded half an hour, the chef who poured salt into a teaspoon and minced two cloves of garlic, two waiters (each carrying a plate of Caesar salad and a bowl of unsalted lentil soup), a patron on table eight wearing pleated slacks and a wool sweater and two at table twelve who asked for their steaks medium-rare with a side of chef's marinade, the supplier who personally delivered the French and Napa wines, and the electrician who on an emergency call, forgetting to wear his rubber-insulated steel-toe shoes, had to replace two fuses that blacked out the west side of the restaurant—all of them licked their lips. A gesture that was both a greeting and a sign of solidarity with those who had been cut by paper.

SMILEY

Smiley tore down the lead scutes from his walls and opened the roof, transforming his living room into a courtyard. And in his bedroom, above the desk where he toiled over geometry problems, he installed a skylight.

This is what becomes of reformed gangsters: they leave the life to become mathematicians. But Smiley was not one of those studious types who disappeared into hermitage or exile. He was an exhibitionist who slept naked and solved theorems while the glass from the overhead skylight magnified his derivations and graphs.

BABY NOSTRADAMUS

The Baby Nostradamus knew how *The People of Paper* ended. It concluded with a plain, nine-word sentence that read, "And there would be no sequel to the sadness." He knew the fates of all the characters, his visions extending beyond the constraints of this book. He knew the different grips of the readers, how some cradled the open covers while others set the book on a table, licking their fingers before turning each page, saliva soaking into the margins.

And there were those readers who, when alone, opened the book and licked the edge of the pages, imagining that they too were going down on Merced de Papel, their blood gathering and channeling in the furrows of the spine. And they, these readers who were intimate with paper, went out into the world licking their lips, showcasing their scars and sore tongues, adding to the loves of Merced de Papel.

The weight of knowledge weakened his muscles and divinations battered his limbs, leaving him unable to lift his bruised and welted arms. Omniscience ravaged the Baby Nostradamus's nerve tissue, and when he looked more than fifty years into the future, migraines rankled his brain. But it was not just the wear on the body; the strict and demanding moral codes tortured his conscience. Rules that every moral prophet abided by— seers from Apollo's Cassandra, whose predictions were always disbelieved, to Johann von Trittenheim, whose circle of pupils surrounded him everywhere he went, following him even down the waterfall and into the rocks, as he had foretold.

The three umbrella laws of soothsaying were written first in hieroglyphics on sandstone walls and later transferred to papyrus—a copy to be sent to each continent. The papyrus, jagged at its edges and inscribed in colored ink, read:

LAWS OF COMPORTMENT FOR THOSE BLESSED BY THE STARS,
GIFTED WITH THE SKILL OF SOOTHSAYING

1. Seers shall not be under commission of state by either threat or hire.
2. Services may not be exchanged for coins or touch of flesh.
3. Impending deaths are not to be announced, whether kin or water.

These were the laws for seers of the future, but the Baby Nostradamus could look forward and backward. He was able to look into locked safes and unscramble coded documents written by men who adorned their lapels with military pins, all battle plans within the reach of his telepathy. He could see into shoe boxes stuffed with carefully folded letters that had never been sent, all addressed to the same woman in which the words, though differently written and arranged, all said the same thing: One day I will forgive you; until then there are scabs everywhere that you have touched me.

Because of the Baby Nostradamus's great powers, supplemental laws governed his abilities, further limiting his actions. The Baby Nostradamus had the power to undercut Saturn by prematurely disclosing information and sabotaging the whole of the novel. Ending everything here by simply listing the character fates: announcing who would win the war, revealing whether Merced would return to Federico de la Fe or whether Liz's diaspora would eventually bring her back to Saturn.

A terrorism of summation, prematurely bringing everything forward. But the Baby Nostradamus was honorable, never violating the codes of his profession, endowing Little Merced only with what the rules allowed.

Even when he knew the date and time of his own mother's death, the Baby Nostradamus revealed nothing. On the day his mother passed away, a Tuesday of relatively pleasant weather and low humidity, the Baby Nostradamus simply touched the palm of her hand, telling her, "I love you, mum," before she stepped out of the house. She returned three days later in a cherrywood coffin with a ring of carnations and a procession of rosary nuns behind her.

MERCED DE PAPEL

Merced de Papel never came to believe in the permanence of love. To her the idea of a romance enduring even a season was a baffling absurdity.

"It's something that burns and disappears into ash." This is what she said as she swept the floor, pushing the flakes of newsprint into the dustpan.

Any combustion, regardless of its intensity, must ultimately extinguish. Some fires last only for the strike of the flint, while others burn for millions of years before the day of their supernova arrives, leaving only embers and cold debris. And so love need not burn forever, just long enough for paper to smolder.

Merced de Papel never let any man spend more than a month in her bed. She never understood the contrived melancholy of those she had dismissed, or their insistence on sending her letters years after they had parted. Some even sent packages. In one, plainly wrapped in brown paper, came a recording written and performed by a man who had spent two years in seclusion trying to write the perfect love song. Despite his achievement, Merced de Papel never responded, listening to the tape without sentiment or memory, as if it had been sung by one of the unknown voices that filtered in through the airwaves on the AM dial. And then there were the other gifts, always wrapped in printed Japanese paper: flowers, chocolate-covered fruit, and reams of archival paper scented with perfume.

And the bitter and indignant gifts: two pillowcases made of plastic that would resist the stains of bleeding lips; a set of photographs of fifty different men with scars across their lips entitled "Pictorial of a Paper Whore." And once a motorized paper shredder.

These gifts she understood; her own bitterness had once unleashed a swarm of moths that destroyed the apartment of Ramon Barreto. But she was annoyed by the thought of men standing in the post office waiting to send their parcels, not in anger or with hopes of revenge but with a sincere nostalgia, their pride lost somewhere amongst the lint and car keys in their pants pockets.

SMILEY

Through the skylight Smiley could see the starscape: the Big Dipper, the bust of the original Nostradamus, and the mocking twinkle of Saturn. During the day, light filled the room and Smiley moved his potted plants onto the desk and tables where the rays hit the foliage. Smiley was dedicating his life to domestic agronomy and to the art of theoretical mathematics.

He learned how to graft roses into carnation stalks, cultivating a flower of tight petals but no thorns. On graph paper he uncovered the saddest of all polygons—not the scalene triangle, as previously thought, but the love triangle.

Smiley added fertilizer as readily as integers. He speculated about photosynthesis in the margins of his geometric proofs. While Federico de la Fe took refuge in inane thoughts and under the weight of lead, Smiley walked outside and gathered goat droppings to scoop into his pots. And after watering his plants and removing his clothes, he lay down on his bed, enjoying the rest and carefree comforts that came with peace. But still he stared up at the sky, hopeful that perhaps Saturn would look down and notice the nude wunderkind of botany and mathematics.

CHAPTER SEVENTEEN

•

SATURN

Saturn wrote Cameroon only one letter. He said he missed the smell of her. The honey, the wax underneath her fingernails, the way she kicked off her soggy shoes and left them in bed. If only it were a different time, he said. If there were no wars or Gypsies or Ticuanenses.

He closed the letter by writing: Cami, you are the bee's knees. I miss you. Love, Saturn.

He folded the letter, stuffed it into an envelope, and affixed postage. Saturn did not know her zip code or apartment number or the city where she had gone. He put her name on the envelope. Below her name he described the types of places where she might be: cities with rivers, streets with breezes, apartments with steps, rooms with canopies.

Still, three weeks later, there was no reply—just an itemized bill from the Postmaster General requesting reimbursements for maps of cities and waterways, for wind-velocity meters, and for all the man-hours spent climbing steps and peering into strangers' bedrooms.

CHAPTER EIGHTEEN

•

APOLONIO

In the Church of Thieves everything was nailed down: the pews, the porcelain saints, the confessional cushions. The candles were locked behind rails, along with the alms crate, six feet beyond arm's reach but an easy toss for quarters and wadded bills. During the service the Cardinal stored his wallet in the Eucharist vault, and the collection plate was passed around by heavily armed Swiss guards.

The Cardinal, who held a seat in the Vatican congress, was stern but of glowing and warm hands. His brow was wrinkled and the corners of his eyes grooved with crow's-feet, but no age showed on his hands. His palms were smooth, clear of liver spots, and so white that parishioners said they were made from carved elephant tusks. But as you approached the altar you knew that they were not prosthetics. Though at times his grip slipped as he tried to knot the ties of his robe, he easily held the fragile Eucharist between his fingers while swaying the incense lamp with his other hand, performing the ritual with a dexterity not possible with stiff ivory fingers and wire ligaments.

I entered the church with empty pockets, holding the Baby Nostradamus in my arms. The patron saint of pickpockets, cast in porcelain, hung above the arc of the door. His palms, almost as smooth as the Cardinal's, held three crucifixion nails he had stolen from the Romans—a theft that absolved every Gypsy from the seventh commandment.

During mass the congregation listened to scriptural lessons while learning tricks of the trade. Pockets were slit, gold watches were switched for cheap digital imitations, and purses were emptied and filled with gravel. Despite the saying that there is no honor among thieves, once the sermon ended and we were dismissed, the thieves gathered outside in the church's atrium. There they returned watches, mended pockets, and dumped the gravel into the rose garden. Even my shined Sunday shoes, which had been carefully unlaced and slipped off using a technique involving a shoehorn and tissue paper, were returned.

"You curanderos are worse than thieves. Shame on you, stealing in church," said a man with a smirk that wrinkled all of his face, "taking my shoes."

I looked down at my feet and the whole congregation laughed as I stared at a pair of worn tire sandals stuffed with kleenex while he walked around in my shined shoes. The thief's smirk retreated into a friendly smile and he offered to hold the Baby Nostradamus while we traded shoes and I tied my laces.

"You have to double-knot around here," he said, again smirking.

The Baby Nostradamus's mother had many regrets. In all her years in Tijuana she had never managed to cross the border; she was always caught while resting under the faint shade of chaparrals and rocking the Baby Nostradamus to sleep. Despite her persistence she never trespassed further than seven yards into San Diego County and her dream of walking among flamingos and panda bears in the San Diego Zoo was never fulfilled. Her other regrets were mostly religious: her estrangement from the church she was raised in, and a profound guilt for using the Lord's and Holy Mother's names in vain. And so, in her will, her estate consisting of a paper swan folded by the legendary hands of St. Antonio, a deck of tarot cards, and custody of the Baby Nostradamus, she left only two instructions: that the Baby Nostradamus be taken to the San Diego Zoo once every year, and that he be baptized.

I came to the Church of Thieves, a remote structure located on sovereign land, because I was a fugitive from the Church, wanted for failing to report the apparition of the Virgin of Trinidad and for being a curandero. Charges I could not deny.

In the Church of Thieves, the most lenient of all Catholic parishes, old men with bolt cutters and skeleton keys tangled in their beards and women whose pockets bulged with forged checks and counterfeit postage stamps came to be baptized. But despite the church's tolerance for fraud and larceny and its loose interpretation of Vatican law, I was never at ease. I felt the Cardinal's eyes always on me. His hands were tucked in his robe, but as he turned he pulled out one of his shiny palms, motioning to the altar boys. They looked at each other, then fixed their stare on the Baby Nostradamus and on me.

When the Cardinal turned to face us he stood at the foot of the stained glass window that extended from the tile to the ceiling beams. In metal and colored glass the six circles of hell were reconstructed. At the first circle the smoke, made from solder, warmed the feet of shoplifters and alchemists who gilded lead and watches. Though their pants were sooted by smoke, their countenance was pleasant, smiling as they diluted gold and pinched wallets and slit the straps of purses.

Moving downward into the second circle, the strips of solder forked, opening up to yellow flames where gluttons roasted cuts of ham at room temperature. The fat from the meat, depicted in clear glass, dripped on the hardwood, while those of sloth slipped on the lard, never again to rise; their bodies sprawled out on the greased floor, staring upward, seeing only hanging bellies and hair as scraps of meat fell on their faces.

The heat intensified. Red flames dovetailed into the yellow shards of glass burning the hair and eyebrows of the French count who was spread across the third circle, contorted in a position that allowed seven women, wearing only bobby pins and perfume, to sit across his body. The most beautiful, her hair crimped and her almond skin oiled, sat on the count's face, suffocating him, her muff carefully chiseled into the window, the strands of hair made of shattered glass.

Below the count, a general decorated with military pins on his lapel and broken bayonets along the back seam of his tan coat rounded the fourth ring in his military jeep. The road was rutted and the tires worn down to the rim. He approached a woman who extended her thumb into the scorching wind as she ran away from her cozy cottage and a bathtub filled with warm water and the three floating bodies of her daughters.

In the final circle, completely engulfed in red, the floor tiered by coal, a German priest nailed parchment to a wooden door and a pensive Nostradamus wrote his heretic predictions into rhyming quatrains, his fingers melting and glops of skin dripping on the paper. On a table, hoodoo doctors, santeros, and curanderos played a neverending game of dominoes, setting down tiles on a cookie sheet, every piece etched with double sixes.

The Cardinal extended his arms, pulling his hands from the robe's pocket. The gleam from his shiny hands illuminated the stained-glass coals, lighting the flames below the curandero's feet and spreading fire onto the dominoes table and into the general's jeep engine, exploding battery acid and sparks into the Count's chamber, sending billows of smoke and ashes through a kitchen packed with hams and sleeping bodies and into the workshops of alchemists and pickpockets who practiced their techniques on bell-rigged dummies. Some of the smoke floated into the blue sky, passing through clouds and atmosphere and reaching the first choir of angels, their wings newly sprouted by the rings of bells. Their shoulder blades were sore and they winced every time a pickpocket botched his attempt, remembering the chime that had burst wings from their backs.

The baptism ceremony was a small one. A motley trinity: the Baby Nostradamus, a retired atheist whose laboratory work had failed—he was unable to synthesize a cure for loneliness—and a Chinese woman who had given up her state of Zen for a round-eyed god.

We grabbed the rails that surrounded the altar. The altar bar joined us, transferring the heat of our palms throughout the rail and assuring the Cardinal a view of everybody's hands.

"How will you christen this child?" the Cardinal asked.

"Nostradamus," I responded, and the Cardinal scooped a cup into the baptism tub and then poured water on the Baby Nostradamus's head.

"May you be blessed and predict not only prosperity but also righteousness," he said, and then poured water on the scientist.

"May you discover that there is no god in test tubes."

And then he poured water on the Chinese woman but said nothing, honoring her silent tradition.

After the ceremony, as he signed the baptism certificate and readied the ink pad, the Cardinal casually asked where we were from. I helped him press the hands and feet of the Baby Nostradamus into the black sponge and told him we had come from the east, from a town of citrus and date orchards.

"Your clothes have the scent of a flower town," he said, as he rocked his hand on two fingers, daubing off ink on a scratch pad but leaving no fingerprints, only the dark profiles of his thumb and pinkie.

He made the Baby Nostradamus step onto the certificate. The left footprint proved what I had always suspected, a low arch—a near-flat foot—while the right foot of ink revealed things I had never even dreamed of. Intricate maps and timelines of the world, fortunes we were never intended to see. I lifted the parchment before the Cardinal would notice the topography of the footprint and with my fingers smudged the future into an ink blur.

I rolled up the certificate and handed an envelope with my donation to the Cardinal. Light reflected from his smooth hands, illuminating the contents, exposing the green of a hundred dollar bill.

"Thank you," the Cardinal said, and I walked out of the Church of Thieves. Hearing a faint shuffle behind me, I looked back and saw the two altar boys trailing me, so I walked east toward the orange groves, turning west to El Monte only as the sun set.

CHAPTER NINETEEN

•

EXCERPTED AND TRANSLATED FROM
THE BOOK OF INCANDESCENT LIGHT

THE BALLAD OF PERFIDY
The silent hymn sung on the days of snow and bees.

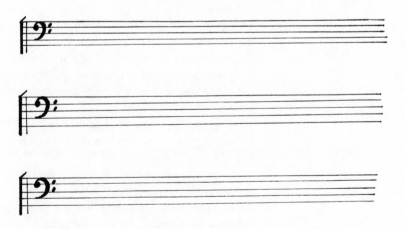

CHAPTER TWENTY III

It was the heat that got to Froggy. The cool breeze was now an arid wind, and all the clouds skirted around the town. Wet towels lay on the floor, the paint blistered and peeled from the lead walls, and the green fruits Julieta kept wrapped in newspaper ripened down to their pits. She tried to stop Froggy, pulling at his arm and shoving the last remaining ice cube into his mouth.

Froggy slipped his arm from her grip and walked out of his house wearing only his shorts, sweat beading and streaking down his body. He flopped down on the field, face down in the furrows, the mud cooling his face and the mist from the sprinklers collecting on the flower plants and then dripping on his back.

Federico de la Fe stepped outside to fetch Froggy. But before leaving his yard Federico de la Fe propped a clean and sterilized nail on his front steps, stomping his left foot into it. A whiteness shot up from the gash in his sole and into his mind, clearing all thoughts except for the rankles of pain, flushing all strategies and battle plans from his mind. Federico de la Fe made his way toward Froggy, carrying nothing, except for a matchbook and some forgotten change in his pant pockets. He bent down and tried to pull Froggy up. Mud oozed into his shoe and mixed with the blood.

"Froggy, let's go inside. Saturn is back. You can't be out here, not like this."

But Froggy refused. "No, I'm staying here," Froggy murmured, squeezing mud into clumps and promising that he would think of nothing but dirt and sprinklers.

Froggy kept his promise while awake, but then closed his eyes, set his head on the furrow's rise and fell asleep.

Soon it would not be just Froggy who ran outside and fell to the ground. The lead that protected EMF from Saturn was leaking into the air and was absorbed by the standing water in bathtubs and sinks, the drought reserves poisoned by lead. They drank the water and lead entered their bodies and circulated through their veins, thickening their blood and clotting in their vessels.

My father poured rubbing alcohol into a pot and then let it boil. He reached in and pulled out a long nail. He said that he was going out but that I must stay inside, and told me to shut the door behind him. But as soon as I closed the door, everything became heavy and the air inside was thick and dried my throat. I went outside and sat on the stoop of the house. There was fresh blood on the steps and a stained nail jammed into the cement's crevices. I looked at the blood and turned my head and vomited on the lawn.

Julieta called and told de la Fe that I had run outside.

"Froggy, get up," he said.

I said nothing at first, then told him that I was not going back inside, that I was staying in the mud and under the spray of the sprinklers.

It is a bright morning and there is water in the tap, a glass of water on my nightstand. The window is open and a breeze enters. Julieta is there on the bed and sometimes it is Sandra. Sandra's father enters, and I reach for my carnation knife, but I can't find it. So I do not slit his throat. Instead, I push him off the bed. Punching and kicking, I throw him out of the stucco and onto the lawn. A trimmed and perfect lawn woven from Sandra's strands of yarn. The sky is light and clear and there is no more Saturn.

Sandra's father returns every month, and every month I bloody his nose, but Sandra is there. There are no Oaxacan songbirds in my house but still you hear their melody coming from the trees, songs that Sandra loves, and I open the windows wide so the sound may enter. They perch and then fly away, sweeping down into the furrows, rising with worms and beetles in their beaks. Sometimes their grips loosen and they drop their prey back onto the dirt.

Insects crawled out of the mud, leaving tracks across his back, walking around his face and ears, careful not to wake him. When he finally awoke it was to the sound of puking.

All of EMF, even Pelon (who could eat and digest bark), had opened their doors and run out to their lawns, hunching over and vomiting on the grass.

Little Merced regurgitated only water and lime seeds, no bile or stench of digesting food. Federico de la Fe failed to notice the smell of citrus on his daughter's breath as he too was bent over, emptying his stomach onto the lawn.

Everybody in Monte, except for Smiley, who had torn down his lead walls, and Apolonio, who had never erected them, was under the malady of lead. Froggy's stomach held the longest, but by midnight bits of bread and pork and chewed flower petals floated on the surface of the water in the adjacent furrow.

EMF was vulnerable, sprawled out on their lawns, their throats and ribs sore, no longer protected by lead. The vomiting and sickness was so consuming that they thought of nothing but their own stomach cramps.

When he heard the sounds of phlegm and raspy throats, Smiley left his theorems and plants and brought water to Federico de la Fe and then to Sandra, carrying a pitcher and a plastic cup. After pouring the last drop of water from the pitcher, he pulled the sprinklers from the flower fields and set them on the roofs, a mist of water reaching every lawn.

For those three days of June, from the thirteenth to the sixteenth of the month, the clicking and dripping of sprinklers and the sounds of puking filled the hot El Monte air.

I was the first to recover.

I helped Apolonio pour his aged milk
into small paper cups, while Smiley
plugged leaks and rotated the sprinklers,
the intervals of rain helping to cool the hot
summer day and dull the stink of puke.

The milk had been aged by a group of
dairymaids under the instructions of
Apolonio and was sealed in wax-lined bar-
rels. The remedy was goopy and bitter,
coagulating even as we swallowed.

My father sat on the lawn, unable to
hold down the milk, vomiting as soon as
it touched his lips.

"Let him rest a bit more. He'll try
later," Apolonio said, the Baby Nostradamus strapped tightly to his back as he
distributed the cups of milk.

Sandra had not changed her shirt, and
despite the spray of water washing down
on her, bits of fruit and rice and chewed
seeds and mucus stained her blouse.
Slowly, she sat up from her slouch and
gulped the milk. It went down easy and
her veil of drowsiness began to lift. Soon
she was able to stand and eat the slices of
banana Apolonio offered.

Sandra chewed the bananas and
walked toward my father.

"We have to tear down the lead," she
said.

My father did not argue. He simply
nodded, again trying to drink the remedy,
but instead puking on the grass.

Blarghhh

Smiley and Froggy tore down the lead walls from de la Fe's, piling the scutes and slabs next to the puddle of puke on his lawn.

Little Merced walked Federico de la Fe into his room and helped him onto the bed. She lifted the cup of milk, tilting it to his lips. For the first time he was able to drink, but as Little Merced set the empty paper cup on the bedroom bureau, the milk spilled from de la Fe's mouth and onto his shirt and lap.

If there was ever an instance that Federico de la Fe wanted his privacy, his right to be shielded from the sight of Saturn, it was that moment, when Little Merced began to unbutton his long-sleeve shirt, opening the collar and exposing burns and scars that he had hidden from her for many years.

He was too weak to pull away and stop Little Merced. He surrendered, allowing his daughter to peel away his shirt. He had always insisted on wearing long sleeves, telling Little Merced that he was very sensitive to the sun, never removing his work shirt until she was safely asleep.

When Little Merced saw the black cuts and blisters, she thought they were further symptoms of lead poisoning, festering from the inside and surfacing to the skin, but Federico de la Fe did not try to deceive her.

"Sometimes I really miss your mother," he said.

LITTLE MERCED

"These are the days I miss her most," my father said, touching two of his deepest gashes.

"How did you...?" I asked. He said nothing, simply pointing to a box underneath his bed.

I pulled out the wooden box, unhitched the leather strap, and lifted the lid.

Inside were knives, their blades warped and smoked into black, hundreds of loose and booked matchsticks, small mayonnaise jars filled with petroleum, and underneath a layer of ash and burnt matches, a framed picture of my mother wearing a green dress trimmed in white.

"She's in my mind every day. Some days I just want to stay in bed and think of her. I think that is enough, just to think about her. But there are days when I want to go and look for her. Find her and say, 'It is me, Federico de la Fe,' and promise her that I will never wet my bed again."

And it was those days that were heavy with memory and longing for the touch of my mother that were the hardest, because he would not go and look for her. Instead he opened his box and heated his blade, preferring infection and the stench of burnt flesh to the possibility of finding my mother walking down the street holding the hand of another man.

And it was perhaps this fear that kept my father from going to Apolonio and inquiring about my mother. I never told my father what I knew about her, what I had learned that day from looking into my palm: that she was still living by the river of Las Tortugas, but with a man who was pale and tall and kept a trimmed beard.

SUBCOMANDANTE SANDRA

While Federico de la Fe rested, we tore the lead from every house in El Monte, piling the slabs in the beds of pickup trucks.

We drove the trucks out of El Monte, south into the Whittier Hills. There we dumped the lead, giving the canyon its hue of blue.

Two days later, as Federico de la Fe began to recover and think of a contingency plan, Monte was once again under the full view of Saturn, unprotected. And while we could occupy our minds with irrelevant and pointless ideas, momentarily hiding, we would eventually surrender to our own thoughts.

We dumped the last load into the canyon. Smiley was at the wheel as we drove back to El Monte, shirtless, his EMF tattoo blotted into blocks, but still he was one of us.

"Smiley, do you want to come back to Flores? Be part of EMF again?" I asked him.

He kept a steady eye on the road and did not turn to look at me when he finally spoke.

"Sandra, I want to be part of EMF, but not if it means being at war with Saturn."

And that was all that was ever spoken about Smiley returning to EMF. When we arrived in El Monte, Smiley returned to his mathematics and flowerpots and stared through his skylight into space, hoping to be recognized by Saturn. Smiley was one of us, raised on flower fields, his breath always scented by petals, but unlike us he did not want a quiet and private existence. Smiley wanted some form of celebrity, even if it came from simply lying naked in his bed.

SATURN

Though Little Merced often worried about the threat of Saturn, it had always been her father's war. At times she even wondered if the war was necessary. But she had never felt Saturn so keenly as on the day she opened her father's wooden box and discovered the tools of fire, and Saturn looked down on her.

She had always seen Federico de la Fe as the heroic leader of EMF, as her kind and caring father, and while he was all those things, he was also a very sad man who had never recovered from the pain of losing his wife.

Saturn lacked the decency to look away, the ability to empathize with Federico de la Fe and his daughter and their need to be alone and unseen. Instead, Saturn focused on the vomit on Federico de la Fe's lap, slowly panning upwards to his bare stomach and chest, revealing the dry and ashing skin, the scars, and the still-blistering burns. And then onto Little Merced as she tended to her sick father, Saturn listening to everything that they said.

"I'm sorry," Federico de la Fe said to his daughter. "There are some things that are better kept hidden."

And Little Merced quietly nodded, sensing Saturn's presence. She began to feel her own resentment, not only toward Saturn, but also against those who stared down at the page, against those who followed sentences into her father's room and into his bed, watching as he pressed matches to his skin, perhaps even laughing and saying to themselves, "Get over it, old man—it is only a woman."

Little Merced wanted to protect her father, hide him from mockery, from the pity of strangers, and to conceal her own rage. She was still under the tutelage of the Baby Nostradamus, but she tried, closing her eyes, attempting to raise her own shield.

Apolonio, who had always refused to make house calls, brought over a quart of the aged milk for my father.

"Just keep giving it to him until he takes it," Apolonio said.

After two changes of sheets and a roll of wadded paper towels, my father finally drank the milk. It was during that time, as the sheets soaked in rose petals and soap, that my father began to recover from the effects of lead.

He spoke to me about my mother and fire, how one had brought the other, but always speaking kindly of her, how it was a wonder she had stayed so long with a bed wetter. And while I had been taught to love my mother, I did not see the kindness in a ▮▮▮▮▮▮▮ daughter and husba▮▮▮▮▮▮▮▮▮ man. And as my fath▮▮▮▮▮▮▮▮rst time, I felt pity ▮▮▮▮▮▮▮ devotion he held fo▮▮▮▮▮▮▮▮t that there shou▮▮▮▮▮▮▮itions to love. That love should not cause burns and blisters. I wanted to hide my father, to protect him from others, so that they would not see him and feel the same pity I felt for him. My father was Federico de la Fe, the leader and war commander of EMF. And I could not bear Saturn or anybody else looking at him as he sat in his bed, burned, his lap damp with water and puke, rummaging through books of matches and blackened flower knives in his wooden box, looking for a picture of my mother. And although there was no more lead in Monte, I tried my best to protect him.

I brought the aged milk to Federico de la Fe's house; I gave Little Merced the Baby Nostradamus to hold while I poured the milk from my carafe into a plastic jar.

I walked from the kitchen into his room, where Little Merced and the Baby Nostradamus looked over Federico de la Fe. Though I had seen him many times, walking through El Monte, at the weigh station with his tarp of flowers, and at the Papal Pawn & Loan with Little Merced, I never suspected that de la Fe was a Burn Collector.

There was always a faint odor of petroleum lingering around him, but I assumed it was from the solvent they used to cut engine grease and the scent of flowers from their skin. But as I saw him sitting on his bed, his shirt wide open and his body ravaged by burns and black cuts, I understood Federico de la Fe's need for combustibles.

I had not seen a Burn Collector in many years, not since I had left my mother's house. Back then the Collectors were flamboyant and unabashed, using fire to decorate the whole of their bodies and quoting the scripture that decreed that we were all of ashes and to such we would return. The Collectors always righteous, shedding ashes, ever closer to our eventual fate.

But Federico de la Fe was bashful, hiding everything underneath his shirt and bed.

As Federico de la Fe began to recover, Little Merced's power grew progressively stronger, and by the time de la Fe was able to eat bread and pork, she had spread her protective shield beyond her own boundaries, cloaking even the thoughts of others.

The shield spread, unbeknownst to Federico de la Fe and EMF. So while Little Merced sat in her room in deep concentration, occasionally reaching into her burlap sack and pulling out a handful of limes, Federico de la Fe and Froggy sat at the dominoes table planning the next assault.

"We cannot hide from Saturn," Froggy said to Federico de la Fe. "Perhaps it is time that we took control and pushed him out."

Federico de la Fe did not say anything; he emptied the dominoes box and then turned the tiles face down so that the unmarked ivory faced upwards. As Froggy spoke of new battle strategies, Federico de la Fe took three dominoes, arranging them like this:

Froggy grabbed the blocks from Federico de la Fe, turning tiles and then adding to the formation:

And while nothing was said, Froggy and Federico de la Fe had devised a new plan to combat Saturn.

I sat on my bed peeling the skins from limes and then eating the meat. Father and Froggy sat around the dominoes table. I closed my eyes and followed the procedures that the Baby Nostradamus had taught me, focusing but making sure not to deny my own thoughts.

I thought back to the bus that has

br
pa
as
I
sli
co
bl
ge

pr
pr
pa

I
wh
an

wh
M
r a
go
dr
le
M
to
th
those with the past written upon them.

Froggy called us to the dominoes table. We all gathered around and looked down at the blocks of ivory.

"This is how we stop Saturn," Froggy said, pointing at the dominoes, "but we will need more than just EMF."

"It is their war too," Federico de la Fe said.

Federico de la Fe and Froggy were tending the war, recruiting beyond the then boundaries that surrounded El Monte.

And so the preparations began. We combed our hair and tucked in our shirts and practiced the pleasant smiles of salesmen. We then drove out of El Monte to the cities of Alhambra, San Gabriel, and South Pasadena. We knocked on doors, asking people to join us in the war against Saturn.

Some answered their doors and politely declined.

"You want to destroy the only thing that is holding us together," they said. We apologized and moved on.

We also came upon veteranos who had fought their own wars.

"I fought in Chromos, in Locos, and Chimera," they said.

And because they had lost every war, they too declined.

After three days and four cities, only two new recruits had agreed to join in the battle against Saturn.

EMF kept recruiting, knocking on doors until the skin on their knuckles was tender and bruised.

Even Little Merced, now proficient in her powers and able to quickly spread the protective shield, went door to door asking for help, at every doorstep dropping lime seeds and peels.

Federico de la Fe's initial strategy had called for patience, a war of waiting and hiding, hoping that Saturn would eventually tire and withdraw. It was not direct combat but a slow defense eventually undermined by the toxicity of lead. De la Fe realized that it was time for full engagement. Time for an all-out war.

Saturn was prepared for whatever assault Federico de la Fe launched. In trying to displace her from his mind, she whose name he now refused to say, he pulled several tomes from the library's military wing. He read about every naval, land, air, and epistolary battle in the history of the Americas. He supplemented his knowledge by familiarizing himself with the autobiography of Napoleon Bonaparte, which the Little Corporal had written while in exile. The main body of the work was a rumination on offensive philosophies, with a short chapter on defensive considerations. The epilogue consisted of recipes for rotisserie chicken and a health regimen.

The regimen consisted of six basic rules that Napoleon followed religiously, except in his last two campaigns, when he was defeated by the Fifth Coalition in the War of Liberation and by Marie Louise in a battle that was never named.

From the two hundred twenty-third page of the biography, Saturn carefully tore out the six basic rules a commander must follow:

1) Breakfast: 2 eggs, 1 oz. of lard, and a glass of milk.

2) Before lunch: one hundred pushups, two hundred sit-ups, and one Hail Mary.

3) Abstain from writing love letters.

4) Do not think of her (even on her Saint's Day).

5) If you think of her, do not do it again.

6) At night use sleeping goggles.

CHAPTER TWENTY-ONE

●

From the notebooks of Smiley, mathematician and botanist:

METRIC CONVERSIONS

(from the Good Book, New Testament)

2.482 liters of water	=	1 gallon of wine
68 oz. of baked dough	=	30 baskets of bread
1 can of salted anchovies	=	3 full nets of fish
the death of Lazarus	=	a short nap
1 lost unhinged halo	=	300 acres of scorched forest

(from The Book of Incandescent Light)

a smile (gap between teeth)	=	how he remembers her
mornings waking in her bed	=	happiness
grandmother's knitted blanket, crackling turntable, two prophylactics	=	first love
1/2 bruised butt	=	Sana, sana, colita de rana
two bags of Susan B. Anthony dollars and a wad of two-dollar bills	=	her savings account

16 inches of snow	=	sadness
round-trip ticket (NY to LA)	=	failed mission
a girl with stings on her arms	=	redemption
a novel	=	the apology
a phone call in which she says: I don't want this book to ruin my life.	=	It won't, he says.

CHAPTER TWENTY-TWO

● ● ●

LITTLE MERCED

Froggy found Little Merced on Sunday morning, lying on her back, surrounded by lime skins. Dew was still trapped underneath her and the seat of her dress was stained by the grass. Froggy lifted Little Merced but there was no breath in her, only the smell of citrus. Her lips were chafed, cut by the limes' acid, the cold dabs of blood absorbed by Froggy's shirt as he carried her from the patch of grass to Federico de la Fe's house. When Froggy arrived his cheeks and chin were streaked by the drying salt tears and his left sleeve and shoulder stained by rusted kisses.

When Apolonio arrived at Federico de la Fe's house, carrying the Baby Nostradamus in a back sling, he propped open Little Merced's mouth and pulled out her tongue, confirming what everybody else had already suspected.

"Citric poisoning," he said, and tucked Little Merced's marinated tongue back inside her mouth.

At the wake, only the commissioned nun who led the rosary prayer and the Baby Nostradamus did not cry. Even Apolonio, who prided himself in his professionalism, took out his handkerchief and after weeping went home and covered all his porcelain saints with velvet mourning sheets.

Froggy and the rest of EMF chewed rose petals and covered their tattoos with tar and kneeled for the three days of the rosary, leaving the room only to spit out the wads of petals. Their exhalations filled the room with the aroma of flowers, and everybody that passed by Federico de la Fe's house and smelled the air believed they were witnessing the wake of a saint.

Those were the saddest days of Federico de la Fe's life, days so sad that he violated even his own rules of decorum, bringing fire to his neck and to the back of his hands where everyone could see the burns.

Federico de la Fe kneeled only for the first day and night of the rosary. On the second day he went into his room and brought out a stationery kit and fountain pen that had been given to him as a wedding present. The paper was made from hand-pressed papyrus and the flaps of the envelopes were lined with real wax. Federico de la Fe had not written a letter to his wife in nearly twenty years.

He sat at his desk, scribbling and drafting, trying to think of a way to announce the death of their only daughter, while in the adjoining room the rosary prayer, uttered by scented lips and tired tongues, entered its sixth cycle.

"My dear Merced," he began, and as he finished writing the salutation he felt a trickle of urine running down his leg and into his left shoe, soaking his dress sock. Though the content of the letter was sad, he felt a strange excitement in writing to the woman he had loved for all those years. After informing Merced of Little Merced's death, Federico de la Fe double-checked his spelling and then used the last line of the letter to tell her that he still loved her and that he no longer wet his bed. "Dry as the desert," he wrote, and then folded and tucked the letter into the envelope. With the same warm blade that he used on his hands and neck, he melted the wax and pressed the flap closed.

In his years in El Monte, Federico de la Fe had never gone to Apolonio, but he knew that if his letter was ever to reach Merced it would have to be through the curandero's network of widows and postmen.

"I don't know where she lives," Federico de la Fe said as he handed over the envelope.

Apolonio simply nodded and took the letter.

MERCED

Jonathan Smith had come from England to Spanish America to colonize and help plant the seeds of Protestantism, but in his many years in Las Tortugas he never spoke one word against the Pope. Aside from a canvas tent that he used to shade himself from the sun, he never came close to establishing even a small building, let alone a colony. In his tenure in the Americas he succeeded in doing only two things: 1) falling in love with a married woman; and 2) luring her away from her husband.

The day the letter from Federico de la Fe arrived in Jonathan Smith's and Merced's mailbox, Merced was in Guadalajara buying sacks of sugar and salt. Jonathan Smith, who possessed very European manners, did not open the letter, leaving it instead on the kitchen table with Merced's name facing upward.

When Merced arrived she set the bags of sugar and salt on the table and picked up the envelope, carefully tearing the side and sliding the letter from its sheath. It was scented with flowers. At first Merced mistook the aroma of roses for a love letter, but the handwriting was unsteady and struggled to keep the horizontal, every sentence derailing from the blue guidelines.

When Jonathan Smith entered the kitchen, stroking his trimmed beard, the salt and sugar were spilled across the table, cascading down to the floor. Merced sat with her head down, her hair covering her face and the granules of sugar glittering.

Jonathan Smith lifted her head gently, watching her tears drip onto the table, her grief staining deep into the grain of the wood.

MERCED DE PAPEL

On a rare stormy Los Angeles morning, Merced de Papel pressed the brakes of her automobile. Her car slid across Wilshire Boulevard, stopping only after crashing into the grille of an oncoming Chevy. The ambulance took away the driver of the Impala, untangling him from his steering wheel and wiping the blood that covered his face and mouth. The second driver was never found. The cleaning crew came, sprayed fire retardant over the two vehicles, and then scraped away shreds of wet paper that clung to the shattered windshield and hood, some of the pulp falling to the asphalt and washed into the gutters by rainwater. As with all people made of paper, there was no official record of Merced de Papel's death, no death certificate or funeral announcement; even the accident report refused to acknowledge her. Her history was on the lips of her lovers, the scars that parted their mouths. But that was the history of Merced de Papel the lover, the loved one, the history of the pain of touching her. Merced de Papel was cautious of a legacy left in scar tissue, and for this reason she kept her own account, written on the scraps that she shed. She compiled her own book, which she titled in her native Spanish: *Los Dolores y Amores de la Gente de Papel.*

LITTLE MERCED

After his resignation from EMF, Smiley had sworn that he would never again wear the black funeral guayabera. But the morning that he received the news of Little Merced's death he got up from bed, his body tanned by the stars and sun, and dressed himself in mourning, slipping on the black guayabera once again. He filled the pockets with the petals of roses and the ruffles of carnations and headed to Federico de la Fe's house.

On the fourth day of kneeling their knees went numb and their mouths dry from chewing rose petals and reciting the names of each of the holy mothers. The commissioned nun had come prepared, wearing heavily cushioned kneepads under her black drape and a hidden canteen inside her slip. The nun, who had studied with the last living Swiss saint, followed Catholic law to the letter, upholding the most esoteric of doctrines: refusing to attend the white wedding of a pregnant bride, washing her utensils only with holy water, and observing the Old Testament custom of eating pork only after the animal had been quarantined and cleaned for three years.

And so when the nun witnessed the resurrection of Little Merced, her first inclination was to alert the church pastor and inform the Vatican office of thaumatology.

Little Merced's death was a short one. It lasted five days, three hours, and twenty-six minutes. When she awoke, she wiped the sleep from her eyes and licked her chapped, dry lips. Federico de la Fe ran to his daughter, while Froggy walked toward the nun and casually flashed his carnation knife.

"You didn't see anything here," Froggy said to the nun. As she tried to explain the importance of documenting the miracle and filing official records of what had occurred, the rest of the members of EMF pulled out their knifes from their waistbands.

"You don't want to die a martyr over this," Froggy said. "Thank you very much for your services." Froggy handed the nun an envelope with the church donation and walked her out of the house.

MERCED

While Federico de la Fe's grief lasted just over five days, Merced's was even shorter. Exactly three hours after she read the letter, a telegram arrived. Jonathan Smith received the message, signed the release, and read the machine type to Merced. "She is alive again," the telegram read.

She wiped her tears and brushed the salt and sugar from her hair, and then swept the floor, gathering everything into a neat pile. She watched as Jonathan Smith used a sanding block to work away at the stains her tears had left on the wood. Sawdust accumulated on the tabletop and fell on the freshly swept floor around his feet, but the dark stain remained deep in the grain of the planks.

Merced poured a splash of diluted paint thinner and then rubbed it with a bit of sheep's wool, lifting the stain. Despite Jonathan Smith's own embarrassment, Merced was never frustrated by his ineptitude and found his inability to perform the most basic of ranch chores endearing. His knots were never tight enough and he spent countless mornings climbing down the well's walls, retrieving lost buckets. And from the bottom of the well, his voice echoing, Jonathan would sing to Merced and teach her how to curse in Gaelic, a talent he had learned while trying to spread Protestant teachings in the Irish isles.

In the wet season Jonathan spent most of the morning yoking the oxen, and then worked late into the evening. He forgot to muzzle his plow team and so they followed their noses and tastebuds across the field, ignoring his prods and orders. As a result, his furrows were always shallow, often crossing into each other. But even this Merced found romantic. Sometimes amongst the crossed *X*'s she would spot an *0*, and Jonathan, using his European wit, would say, "It's a field of hugs and kisses."

Other days the oxen rebelled against his weak commands and pulled him through barbed wire, dragging him through the neighbor's green stalks of maize and tangles of stink squash and green beans. But despite his ineptitude as a farmer, he displayed a restraint and skill that Federico de la Fe could never approximate. Jonathan Smith never wet his bed.

Merced loved Jonathan Smith. She was happier with him than she had ever been with Federico de la Fe, but there were still those who asked her about her first husband.

Once, a touring priest, who carried his rectory on the backs of two mules and had administered Federico de la Fe's first communion, asked Merced why she was with a Protestant.

"They don't wet their beds," Merced responded, and proceeded to name the many other endearing qualities of white Protestant men. Merced cited their height, the ease with which they made allusions to real literature, and the exceptionally funny, yet dry, humor they possessed. And because they were better educated, having actually read scripture, they knew an extensive catalog of sexual positions that they had discovered in the footnotes of the Good Book.

"This is the King David," Merced said to the priest, using her hands to describe the motion and mounting position.

She reconfigured her fingers to arrive at a different position. "And this is the saddest way to make love; it is from the Book of Job." And indeed it was the most melancholy of ways, a position Saturn had used many times in hotel rooms after going down on Cameroon, turning her over and spreading her limbs, distributing the whole of her weight on her palms and knees.

MERCED DE PAPEL

On the sixtieth page of Merced de Papel's book, a page that was once the skin of her stomach, there was an entry that spoke to Merced de Papel's own affinity for white lovers. While she was not opposed to the idea of other men, she preferred those who were pale and whose tongues had not been stretched by the long vowels and double *r*'s of the Spanish language.

But when Merced de Papel dissolved from paper to strings of fiber and pulp it was not the mild-mannered and short-tongued men who mourned her most, but those with the scarred and long tongues. People who very early in life had been trained for mariachi bands, men who turned the tragedies of love into guitar ballads and into résumé lines on their Vatican applications for martyrdom.

The other men simply commented on the death of Merced de Papel—reminiscing while drinking iced tea. But the men with musical instruments and those hospitalized by sadness lay in their beds reciting the rosary, thereby ensuring that the soul of Merced de Papel, a soul that took the shape not of a dove but of an origami swan, was safely received by the soft hands of the Holy Mother.

LITTLE MERCED

Federico de la Fe was not interested in the science of miracles. He accepted the resurrection of Little Merced on simple faith and never looked for an explanation.

"God works in ways we should not try to explain," he said, and while he said nothing else about the matter, every Sunday as the collection plate was passed he added an extra ten dollars to his usual donation. And on Tuesdays, when the porcelain saints and confessionals were dusted, he brought two candles to the altar.

But God was only one explanation. Federico de la Fe never stopped to think that perhaps Little Merced was awakened not by the hand of God, but by one of Apolonio's concoctions. While EMF kneeled and recited the rosary, Apolonio hid in his shop, the Baby Nostradamus strapped tightly to his back, measuring and mixing the most complicated of formulas. On the fourth day of Little Merced's wake, as he returned to Federico de la Fe's house to pay his last respects, he dipped his pinkie in a vial, and as he caressed her hair, Apolonio stuck his finger in Little Merced's mouth. And so when Little Merced awoke, the horrible stench of her breath was not the remnant of death but simply an oversight on Apolonio's part: forgetting to add peppermint to his potion.

Little Merced never noticed her own death; when she awoke to a roomful of mourners, she asked Federico de la Fe who had died.

MERCED

On a Sunday morning, as Jonathan Smith left the milk boiling on the stove, he spooned himself behind Merced, rocking her until she lay on top of him. Jonathan Smith made love to Merced holding onto the two bed posts, the force collapsing one of them, the milk boiling over, evaporating and condensing on the ceiling.

"That is the Samson, from the Book of Judges," Jonathan Smith said, and tossed the broken bedpost to the floor.

By the time Merced entered the kitchen, the silver plating had melted from the pot, and the milk that had condensed on the ceiling dripped onto the floor. Merced's best pots and two days of milking had been wasted by Jonathan's carelessness, and for the first time Merced was not endeared or amused by his futility.

"There must be a leak in the roof," Jonathan said. "It's raining milk." But Merced did not smile or give her usual approving nod, and it was not until a drop of milk hit her lips and trickled into her mouth that her frown subsided. Jonathan Smith, however clumsy, was endowed with refined European manners and an extraordinary knack for serendipity. The milk, as it hung from the ceiling and dropped onto the floor, pulled the sugar from the whitewash. And so what had been a potential kitchen fire instead became the discovery of caramelized milk.

Jonathan Smith's harvest for the season yielded only eight ears of corn and two vines of stink squash, but the revenue from the caramelized milk was enough to provide the basic food staples, two flocks of dinner doves, and a Portuguese spice rack that he used every Sunday in his cooking.

Every morning, when Jonathan Smith and Merced made love, the milk boiled over and gathered on the ceiling, dripping into the pots they had laid out the night before. For two seasons, steamed milk clung to the ceiling. But in the summer the walls lost their sweetness and the bitter taste of birdlime overtook the milk.

MERCED DE PAPEL

Antonio, the old origami surgeon, was the first man hurt by the edges of Merced de Papel. In all his years of folding and tearing paper, none of his projects gashed as deep as the paper cuts that Merced de Papel had left on his hands.

THE PEOPLE OF PAPER

On the day of her creation, Merced de Papel, still unnamed, walked out of the factory and into the rain. Antonio was unconscious, his bleeding hands wrapped in newspaper, opening his eyes only for an instant before the faintness overtook him and the crisp newsprint softened into red tissues. He saw only her back as she walked away from him, but he felt no sadness or abandonment. He knew that he had finally created something that would live long after his death, something that could not be discredited by medical journals and operating-room gossip.

Antonio's creation, which had endured a thunderous rainstorm, the saliva from hundreds of lips, and the ensuing spite of old lovers, was undone by an unfastened seat belt and a shattered windshield.

And as the sirens approached the collision, a light but steady rain soaked the shreds, flushing her into the anonymity of gutters. And those shreds that were not washed away clung to the hood of Merced de Papel's car, hardening days later as the clouds cleared and the heat of the sun beat down on the wrecking yard.

CHAPTER TWENTY-THREE

●

FEDERICO DE LA FE

Two weeks after her resurrection Little Merced was still weak and dehydrated. Her breath, despite the constant chewing of mint leaves, still smelled like the stagnant water of tadpoles.

I consulted Apolonio the curandero, welcoming him into Little Merced's room, but even he had no remedies.

"You can't shake off death so easily. Something must remain of it, at least for a while. Give it some time. Lazarus's halitosis lasted two months, though that was in an age before mouthwash and toothpaste," Apolonio said, walking over to Little Merced's bedside.

"How are you feeling?" he asked Little Merced. She covered her mouth with her hand and in a muffled tone responded.

"I feel okay, but the stink..."

"Just keep chewing the mint leaves and tell Froggy to bring you some rose petals. You'll be smelling like a saint in no time."

Apolonio and Little Merced exchanged goodbyes and then I walked Apolonio to the front of the house.

"Any word from Merced?"

He shook his head.

"She received the letter?"

He nodded.

"And the telegram?"

"Yes."

"Are you sure?"

And he nodded again.

Apolonio, despite practicing a profession of trickery and witchcraft, was candid and did not speculate beyond his faculties. When he spoke of Merced he said everything with a kind reserve, cautious of both wording and tone.

"I don't know about Merced—every woman is different—but sometimes women leave and they never return. But sometimes it is good to wait, because sometimes they do return. Some come back on their knees, leaving a trail of blood and bandages behind them, scraping flesh on cobblestones, then asphalt, finally reaching the cool and smooth surface of their old lovers' Spanish tile.

"Others take a much easier route, kneeling only as they approach the house, using sandpaper on their knees to feign miles of hiking. Either way, you must tend to their scrapes and wounds. And then there are those women who never return, who are never heard from again. Women with soft skin and lotions who don't have a scratch of remorse or penance."

And that was all Apolonio said, never hinting at what kind of woman Merced might be. I thought that perhaps she was on her way, slowly headed in this direction. Pausing to wrap her bandages and eventually reaching the porch of the house.

I wanted to make the homestretch as soft and cushioned as possible.

The next day, as Little Merced slept, I turned over the yard's dirt, weeding it and then seeding saint augustine grass. Letting it grow but not too tall, just enough to keep the knees of Merced from touching dirt. And on the steps I laid out a pad of foam, covering it with a soft rug.

CHAPTER
TWENTY-FOUR
▌▌▌

SATURN

The first postcard, which came on the day
that EMF and its recruits launched their
assault, was covered in Belgian postage,
addressed not to Saturn but to "Sal
Plascencia."

The back of the postcard read:

> Today, I sat on the sand dunes eating
> chocolate. I thought of you.
> Love,
> *Cami*

Saturn turned the postcard over, looking at the glossy picture of a lone row-
boat, its oars missing, docked on the
banks of a canal, tied to a post with only a
strand of yarn. A Flemish greeting floated
above the boat and across the Belgian sky.
He could not understand what it said but
it was written in a bright yellow, glowing
like the heat that once hovered above
Cameroon's head.

For a moment—a very brief moment
—he thought of Cami: her body supine,
her breast tender and pink as he used the
pinch of his fingers to pull stingers. And
when the thorns were too deep, using his
teeth, at times swallowing what the bees
had deposited. The residue of poison
whetting his tongue, but he did not spit;
instead he laid next to Cameroon, fading
into sleep with the aftertaste of insects in
his mouth.

But there was no time to think of
her. Saturn heard them approaching,
crowding into the page, pushing and trying to press Saturn further and further to
the margin.

I couldn't concentrate. I topped the trash
with wads of chewed rose petals and mint
leaves, but still the smell crawled into my
thoughts. Even as I slept, I dreamed of trash
dumps and the smell of a waning sea, the
water draining, leaving only fish and clams
to spoil under the sun. Clamped oysters
slowly hinging open and flopping fish shedding their scales, crabs crawling out from
underneath and then everything was still,
except for the rising waves of stink.

I closed my eyes and tried to spread the
sheet of black, but every time the smell dis-
rupted my concentration, forcing me to start
again. I was never able to stretch the black
much larger than this:

I asked Apolonio for something else but
he had no more cures. But it didn't matter.
We were no longer hiding from Saturn.
Froggy had rallied everybody to say and
think whatever they wished, hopeful that
the streams of talk and thought would
drown the voice of Saturn. Still, I wanted to
protect my father, to cover him with the
sheet and leave him with his wooden box
and picture of my mother, let him do what
he had to, to remember her in his way without anybody looking at him with pity or
mocking stares.

And so I tried again before the nausea
overtook me:
It spread wider than my first attempt
but I lost some of the sharpness; the corners
were blunted and I could not anchor it
down. The shield swayed from side to side.

I swallowed minted mouthwash and
quickly followed the gargles by chewing
peppermint and rose petals. I closed my
eyes and tried again

"We are fighting a war against a story,
against the history that is being written
by Saturn. We believed that silence was
our best weapon against the intrusion of
Saturn, that our silence would in turn
silence Saturn.

"But we have discovered an allergy to
lead, and learned that history cannot be
fought with sealed lips, that the only way
to stop Saturn is through our own voice."

That was the only rallying speech
I gave, but not much rallying was needed.
After years covered by lead and the
imposed quiet under open air, we were
ready to speak. We all went outside and
said all the things we had always wanted
to say, letting the words float. And those
who were too timid to use their immedi-
ate words wrote down what they would
say and then read it aloud. Others simply
pulled letters from their back pockets
and from underneath mattresses, or read
from underlined passages in worn and
dog-eared books.

EMF's army mobilized. Coordinated formations were at the battle front and reserves at the back, ready for the melee. The wind and sun at their back, following Sextus Julius Frontinus's *De re militari,* in which he advised to dazzle the enemy with rays and blind him with dust. Frontinus called on nature and then moved his cavalry forward as arrows shot through the air. When the Silures shot back, his archers lifted their shields above their heads, and those along the circumference kept their shields at their chests, marching forward in the tortoise formation. A tortoise with five hundred feet.

EMF's strategy was to envelop Saturn, to surround him, forcing him to concede territory. Saturn never wanted an all-out war, he did not want it to come to this, but he would fight back. He would retain his position and go on his own offensive and take all the territory if necessary. He would bring his full rage against these people who had consumed his thoughts and attention for so long and had been responsible for her leaving. Saturn had been distracted by Federico de la Fe and his town of flowers, and because of them he did not notice when she stood up from his bed and put on her green dress and walked away, walking to an apartment with pictures of pale men on the wall and crisper drawers filled with leafed lettuce neatly packaged in resealable bags. With Kennedy eyes staring at her from the portraits and the washed leaves in the refrigerator, she pulled up her dress and showed her dark full muff to a man who towered over two stacked Napoleons in full regalia. And when he whispered in her ear, he spoke beautifully, clearly, using words a lettuce picker could never pronounce.

SUBCOMANDANTE SANDRA

During our recruitment, as I knocked on strangers' doors, I came upon a woman who said she had known Saturn and had spent many nights lying next to him. But she said that was long ago.

"I knew him when he was very young, before he was Saturn. We were both young. I'm sorry, but I can't help you. I don't think I should even be talking to you," she said.

And as I walked away, the woman, who wore a green dress trimmed in white, called out.

"Can I ask you a question?"

"Yes," I responded.

"What does he look like now?"

"Saturn?"

"Yes, Saturn."

"I don't know—he only sees us. We never see him."

In the evening, as we met around the dominoes table, waiting for de la Fe, I told Froggy about the woman and what she had said.

Froggy shook his head in disbelief.

"That cannot be. If she was so close, in his bed, why didn't she cut his throat?"

SMILEY

For the first time since the ring of ash encircled El Monte, I watched as people stepped into town wanting neither flowers nor cockfights. They entered to witness the end of Saturn. Some came armed, holding handguns, not knowing that Saturn was impervious to bullets. Others came with flashbulbs and cameras, hoping to photograph the fallen Saturn.

In the evening, as more people crowded into El Monte, a black limousine pulled in, its tires rolling over the ash, the tracks of soot stopping in front of Apolonio's shop.

APOLONIO

Millionaires, butchers from the outskirts of the county, cattle ranchers holding fistfuls of alfalfa, two Hollywood starlets (both with cigarette holders), characters who had been absent for chapters and chapters, a cardinal and two altar boys, a tribe of lettuce pickers—by tire or shoe, they all descended on El Monte.

Some intended to speak and battle Saturn, but most came merely for the spectacle, entering the town as they would a stadium, awaiting entertainment, unaware that their mere presence, their chatter and thoughts, pushed Saturn further and further into a corner.

LETTUCE PICKERS

We followed her here, from her posh Hollywood home, past the flower fields, into El Monte. When her town car stopped we pegged it with heads of lettuce, yelling "Rita, vendida." We told her to go fuck her Hollywood white boys.

The chauffeur opened her door and she casually stepped out, kicking the lettuce to the side, signing autographs and blowing kisses, but none toward us. With a gentle flick of her wrist she ashed her cigarette and then looked up at the sky, searching for a sign of Saturn.

SATURN

Saturn was disciplined, always following Napoleon's prescribed diet and exercise routines: a hundred pushups on his fists before breakfast, followed by three eggs, unsalted, the whites fully cooked but the yolks left runny. And for lunch, three hundred sit-ups with three carpenter nails between his lips, sucking the iron from the metal and into his muscles. But most importantly, like Napoleon, he was careful to avoid anything that might remind him of lost love.

But when Sandra unknowingly knocked on the door of she whose name was once cited on the dedication page, Saturn violated the most important tenet of war: allowing love to enter his mind.

Instead of focusing on Federico de la Fe and EMF, Saturn pulled out photographs and old letters. He cleared his desk, shoved battle plans and maps to the side, and began drafting a love letter.

The EMF brigade moved forward, forcing Saturn against the page, but he just sat at his desk, writing to the woman he had promised never to bother again, impervious to the approaching sounds of the march.

FROGGY

We were forceful, imposing our presence where it had never been before. At first we were orderly, marching in perfect formation. But as we gained ground our forces scrambled, forgetting our plans and strategic arrangement. Instead our voices bloomed everywhere, like wild unfurrowed flowers. El Monte Flores were finally free to step wherever we wished, to think what we wanted, our story unobstructed, unexploited by Saturn.

And they were all here to witness our victory. Movie stars, the sacerdotal heads and laity, craftsmen in aprons, lettuce pickers, millionaires.

And it was here, in Monte, miles away from Hollywood, two continents and an ocean from the Vatican, and hundreds of years after Galileo had first observed the despotic nature of the ringed planet—it was here that Saturn would fall.

PELON

After weeks and weeks of thinking only of dirt and flowers, of the mineral composition of soil and the flow patterns of irrigation runoff, the crucial minutiae of agriculture—details that meant nothing, used to hide our true thoughts from Saturn—now it was these particulars that I could not get out of my head. "We are free, Pelon," Froggy said. "You may say and think whatever you want." But I forgot what the world was before—if the world is not about the diameter of piping and size of sprinkler heads, if the world is not about flowers, I don't know anything else.

They had ordered me to think only in one way, to look at everything as a catalog of inconsequential items, and now they say that I may look further, that I may see beyond the furrows and the working of the flower trade. But it is too late for that. I have lost no arm and suffered no shrapnel; my war wound is in the retina of my eye. The lingering affliction is my nearsightedness; I see only what is up close, and everything is magnified. And even here, in El Monte, I see no quiet days and trimmed lawns. Instead, I observe the individual crystalline masses of the dirt, a compound of sedimentary silt and igneous sand, blades of saint augustine grass with shallow roots penetrating only twenty-seven millimeters into the topsoil, the lawn browning and in need of aeration. This is what I see; there is no world beyond the till of the land and the planting of seeds.

THE TWO ALTAR BOYS

On this day, Tuesday June 14, in the year of the Holy Mother, we introduce his Eminence (and native son of Los Angeles) our cardinal and glory, christened and following the lead of the archangels, Cardinal Ryan Jeff Mahony.

On this day his Eminence sets foot in the City of El Monte, a city named after the hills it does not have.

Let this town be blessed

Be blessed by Mary, Mother of God

By our Lady of Lourdes

Our Lady of Fatima

Our Lady of Snow

Our Lady of Good Counsel

Our lady of Seven Sorrows

Our Lady of Walsingham

Our Lady, Refuge of Sinners

Our Lady of Thieves.

BABY NOSTRADAMUS

CAMEROON

To My Napoleon,

I found this postcard of your favorite corporal in the Louvre. Notice he's standing on a stool, funny. You were right, there is no dry wiping in Paris, they have bidets everywhere, but I have no one to wash away here.

Yours,

Cami

SATURN

The carpenter nails hung from Saturn's lips, the iron dissolved into his saliva. Thinking it was blood, Saturn spat into the sink and then returned to his desk to finish the letter. In the closing sentence, he wrote, "I have laid out a lawn for you. I water it every day and air it on Tuesdays, but I have yet to remove the burrs."

He signed and sealed the letter and then wrote the name of her new town on the envelope, a town with wide streets and sturdy oaks, with corner pharmacies that still sold ice cream served by soda jerks in paper hats. Her new town, where there were no elote men pushing their boiling pots full of corn or flower pickers resting in the shade with their necks and hands burned by sun and fertilizer.

But Saturn could also keep a neat lawn, green and with its edges sharp like those in postcards. There was no lamppost on the sidewalk; instead, he kept his porch light on, waiting for her.

CARDINAL MAHONY

The eyes of God are always upon us. And we cannot hide from His omniscience. So even if Saturn falls there is still a God above him.

Even before fig leaves and shame, He was there, watching over our first parents as they pointed at animals and plants, naming creatures and vegetables. He listened as Eve discovered the hiss on her tongue as she stroked scales and a rattling tail. And when He cast them out, their breath smelling of apple, He watched them walk from the green lawn of Eden and followed them into a land of droughts.

"I just want to make love to Julieta without anybody looking down on me," one of the EMF cholos said, unaware that such privacy could never exist.

JONATHAN MEAD

There is no Cameroon here, they do not recognize her name. "Cami," I say and they shake their heads. I describe her, talking of her as if it has only been days since I last saw her. Trying to imagine for myself what a lost daughter may look like. "She is a beautiful girl," I say. I want to say that she smells like honey, but somehow that is unkind.

The town is only rows of flowers and a water tower, stuccos with weather vanes all pointed in the direction of the church. But there is no trace of her here. I say her name and they shrug and point to a falling sky.

RITA

The roaring lion featured at the start of every MGM picture was trained with a lash and bits of meat by Charles Gay. At his lion farm he whipped and caged the wild feline, forcing her to perform circus tricks and growl into the camera on cue. After each roll of film, Charles would pull on the elastic of the faux-fur mane, fluffing the acrylic hair—the MGM executives never the wiser that their fierce alpha male was an outfitted lioness.

Ten years later, Charles sold her to a railcar zoo but kept her litter. While sleeping and dreaming of jungle theme parks and safari hats, the three cubs mauled his feet and arms. He survived, and it was he who told me that it is not elephants that never forget, but those we betray, those we hurt. Species that pass down their memories through generations, transferring their bitterness and resentment to their kin, never able to forgive, their arms always cocked with lettuce in hand. Unable to excuse a change of address or wardrobe. Telling their children and grandchildren that I am their sellout whore.

LITTLE MERCED

My father opened my bedroom window and brought in big Valencia oranges covered with cloves to freshen the air. On my lamp table he set down a bowl filled with mints and rose petals.

I held the orange to my nose, smelling its sweet citrus and spice and chewed the candy and flowers. I tried to do as the Baby Nostradamus had taught me: I closed my eyes, seeing only black and then trying to stretch the darkness. But fatigue and the stink must have over███████ I woke up, my father had ████████ bowl, topping it off over███████ petals and mints fell onto ████ looked out the window and my father was on his knees picking scraps of eggshells from the lawn and wiping yolk from the grass with our kitchen dish towels.

Again, I grabbed a handful from the bowl and put it in my mouth, slowly chewing and sucking the sweetness and smelling the scent of the cloved orange, trying to rid myself of the stink. But it was no use; I was only perfuming rotten fish. The smell of Lazarus was hanging onto me.

LITTLE OSO

I wrote down what I would say on a paper: I am Little Oso of El Monte Flores. I live on Maxson Road in a stucco that I painted and a roof that I shingled.

But that's all I could write. I didn't know what else to say. This is my home, this town of furrows and carnations, and I don't care where our flowers go, if they are sniffed by royalty or movie stars. Whatever happens beyond our borders is not my worry, it is only Monte and its sky that I care about.

APOLONIO

All Federico de la Fe wanted for himself and his daughter was to be left alone and in peace. To be left to live the quiet and complacent life of a flower town. And as the fall of Saturn approached, Federico de la Fe stepped away from the battle, remaining in his yard and tending to his daughter, bringing her mints and air fresheners. And when the stench seemed to subside he went outside to trim his lawn.

Twice a day he tested the softness: rolling the fragile eggs of dinner doves and balloons filled with water, and then, as a final test, kneeling and staining his own pants. He consulted with Pelon and pondered mowing and irrigation techniques that would reduce the friction and grass stains, ways to save Merced the labor of having to scrub her long and embroidered dress of contrition. Ways to make the trek easier on her knees.

A dress that was not white or of delicate material but made of tough fabric and set in earth tones. A dress that could be dragged and scuffed without easily unraveling. And when pelted with rotting greens and insults, the stains easily wiped from its fibers.

CAMEROON

Dear Salvador,

Barcelona is as I imagined. Full of Gypsies and street performers, but I'm sick of sangria and tourists. There are people with your accent here, and streets with your last name.

The boats leave every two days for Morocco. I am gone tomorrow. And there and gone again by the time you read this.

—Cami

215

SATURN

Saturn waited. He watered his grass. When she did not show, he spit the thinning carpenter nails from his lips and onto his yard. Five hours later, still no sign of her, he tossed two fistfuls of chestnuts onto the lawn, their prickly husks anchoring them to the soil. And two days later, when she had yet to arrive, he shattered six bottles and swept the glass shards into the grass. By the end of the week the lawn had become so treacherous that it penetrated the soles of his shoes, cutting his feet and soaking his socks with blood.

NATALIA & QUINONES

After four decades of winter we sold the hotel and headed home. We sold it to a man who carried a briefcase and planned to replace the bidets and install his-and-hers sinks and towel racks. He said he was going to tear the coal boilers from each restroom and install a centralized water heater controlled by an automatic thermometer. He also planned to make love easier, requiring identification only when guests brought out their checkbooks or approached the front desk to pick up a package.

The romantic age was over, and so we headed south, stopping here to watch a falling planet, to see the ravages of love. Perhaps, Napoleon was right all along— perhaps love causes more damage than good, cracking the sky and ruining the horizon.

SUBCOMANDANTE SANDRA

The end of Saturn was imminent. His role in the story had diminished. What was once a powerful planet was now shedding its mass, disintegrating into a trail of dust.

"All this time we wasted hiding under lead, shy of our own freedom and voice," I said to Froggy. "We should have fought from the beginning."

"But that was never de la Fe's way," Froggy answered.

Had it been up to de la Fe, we would still be walking around with our lips shut, thinking of ruffled petals, waiting for Saturn to flee from ennui.

But regardless of strategy, it was Federico de la Fe who had first led us against Saturn. Federico de la Fe had showed us that we were not free people, that we were enslaved and serving Saturn. Emancipation has many paths, some with more ruckus than others, but the quiet mediation of monks had failed us. We surrendered silence and opened our mouths, saying whatever we wished under open air.

After all these pages, as Saturn faded, it was our voices that directed the story, our collective might pressing Saturn into a corner.

No master pushed us forward or held us back. We were no longer obliged to serve anybody's expectations but our own. I could sit in my chair and do nothing. Glory or dénouement could come, and I didn't have to move.

CAMEROON

My Saturn,

There is no haze in the African sky, but the smell of smoke is everywhere. I stopped at the Tangier observatory, I wanted to see you, but the house astronomer said that there is no more Saturn. "Not even the rings are left," he said. Cameroon is still very far away, I will write when I get there.

Yours always,
Cami

LETTUCE PICKERS

She always wants the spotlight, forcing herself into stories that are not hers. The sky falling and she starts her dancing routine. She'll toss her cigarette holder in midair and catch it between her lips.

Same routine and she wants an ovation every time.

"Orson bought this for me," she'll say, and untwist her bracelet. But before Hollywood and fat white men it was we who watched her dance. We who laid out the paths of lettuce so she would not stain her sequined dress or scuff the bottom of her shoes.

Once she betrayed us, we stopped tearing the romaine leaves from their stock. Instead we dumped wheelbarrows of rotting salad on the headquarters of her fan club and tossed icebergs over the wall of her Hollywood home.

They splashed down in her pool, and in the morning when she went for her daily dip the butler had to remove the bobbing heads of lettuce. And when her movies premiered smears of green stained the screens.

JULIETA

I fled the town of El Deramadero, a town named after decay, where everything fell apart. A disease I thought I had left behind. And now in El Monte, sky came down in flakes, and the flower fields were trampled, spreading petals everywhere, sprinklers breaking, water soaking into our shoes.

Even the words of Little Merced smelled like rot. And our leader, Federico de la Fe, spent his days kneeling on his lawn, airing the soil with the tip of his carnation knife and rolling eggs across the grass.

But Froggy remained brave and confident. "Don't worry, Julieta. This is how war is won," he said, flakes of sky in his hair, mud on his shoes, smelling of incense.

"And after the war? What is left?" I asked.

"Reconstruction," Froggy said. "We sweep the streets, reseed the fields, and patch our roofs. We rebuild and live how we always wanted, with hammocks swinging from our backyards and cloth curtains hanging from our windows, only thin draperies between us and the world."

SMILEY

They trampled the flower fields and brushed off their aprons, leaving sawdust and trimmings of lard in the furrows, cigarette ashes and lettuce heads on the streets, the gray smoke from incense lamps lingering around the altar boys but leaving the stench of Rome where they stepped.

Their litter—newspapers, wrappers, postcards—all caught in the wind, floating over my skylight.

I stayed inside, watering the flowerpots and watching as Monte was slowly destroyed. Liberated from Saturn, from the order that for years had kept us in line, our narrative organized and mindful of the conventions of story. Now the order had been upset, lost in a melee of voices that for years wanted their freedom.

ELOTE MAN

I pushed my cart through the spectators, selling cobs of corn covered in butter and grated cheese. They kept looking up at the sky, anticipating the fall of Saturn.

But in the time I was there, selling corn to Hollywood starlets and millionaires, no Saturn fell. The crash heard in the flower fields was nothing but an old dinner dove tangled in his own wings. And in the late afternoon, with their necks still cocked to the sky, finally a small piece of Saturn fell: a blue flake floating down, resting on the soft lawn of Federico de la Fe.

SATURN

In his last days, Saturn spent his time tending to his bleeding feet and cleaning the rust-colored footprints that led from his bed to the bathtub.

BABY NOSTRADAMUS

APOLONIO

With the tip of his index finger Federico de la Fe lifted the flake of blue from his lawn and brushed it into the trash bin.

The fall of Saturn was not a violent rapture. It was a slow shedding. In the evening, as the sun colored the horizon pink, more flakes fell throughout El Monte.

Flakes which de la Fe brushed away from his lawn.

Flakes which I collected, sealed in jars, and cataloged in my Santeria books as the blue ashes of the planet Saturn.

LEGAL COUNCIL FOR THE RALPH AND ELISA LANDIN FOUNDATION

While Saturn's (Salvador Plascencia's) war against Federico de la Fe and the El Monte Flores (EMF) gang has been funded in part by the Ralph and Elisa Landin Foundation, the Foundation is not responsible for any of Saturn's actions.

The Foundation and its endowment are not liable for any loss or damage, whether it be incidental, direct, punitive, exemplary, or special, resulting from *The People of Paper*, the war on omniscient narration (a.k.a. the war against the commodification of sadness), or any involvement with this book. This is inclusive of all paper cuts, whether incurred on fingers or tongues.

CAMEROON

Sal,

I'm stuck in Morocco for a while. The bus drivers are on strike. They won't move their buses until dance halls extend their hours. "We want to dance until the early hours," they say. They sit all day so they want to dance all night.

In the market they sell honeybees in shoe boxes. I walk by and listen to them buzz.

In the day, I read and write letters. At night, I dance until closing time, sometimes with bus drivers.

I'm reading Jiri Grusa's *The Questionnaire*. Have you read it? Seems like a book you would like.

Yours,
Cami

MARCHING FRANCISCAN MONKS OF THE FIRST ORDER

Somewhere along the San Andreas we lost our brother; he disengaged from our formation and took his own path. A single set of footprints splintering from our centipede, walking west to feel the ocean breeze. On our return trip from the frozen plains of Alaska, as we headed toward the isthmus of the Americas to bless the mechanical locks and dams along its new man-made canal, we read our brother's letter scrawled against a cinderblock wall written in his own carnal ink. We photographed it and tucked it into the back pages of his posthumously released treatise on sadness and love, *The Book of Incandescent Light*. The photograph later became the official epilogue of the third and revised edition, which restored all of our brother's typos and misspellings and crossed-out graphs where he charted the thickness of his feet's calluses.

MECHANIC

In part ten, quatrain 67a, of the first French edition of Nostradamus's *Centuries*, printed on vellum in full folio size by Laurent de Murrell of Paris, Nostradamus foresaw a mechanical tortoise digging into the earth, compressing the tectonic plates, built by a once-naive mechanic who now lamented his preternatural understanding of machines, burning all blueprints of hydraulics and diagrams of gears and torque. The quatrain, which I translated sans rhyme, read:

X. 67A

As Saturn falls, the earth will be pressed together
by a metal reptile.
Man stained with grease and cut
by sprockets will wrench
The last of their mechanical kind,
Retiring to a life with beautiful wife and
Bunsen burners.

SATORU 'TIGER MASK' SAYAMA

Don Feliz handed me the prize money and a paper sack, stapled and certified by a notary's stamp, containing Santos's silver mask. The smell of potpourri was heavy, emanating from the bag and filling Don Feliz's office. In his last will and testament, Santos requested that he be buried like any other man, with his face bare and his Christian name on the tombstone, and that I be given his mask and papers.

My dear Satoru,
    If this has reached you it is because I have passed on and I am headed to a place where there is no ring or ropes. There is no point in taking Santos with me, so I leave this mask with you. It is with great sadness that I leave you, compañero. Of all the mats in the world that I tumbled on, it was always best with you.
    I console myself in my faith that Santos does not die, that he carries on.
    I trust that you will find a worthy protégé to carry the name and elude his holiness.
        Always, in life and death,
        Juan Meza

RALPH AND ELISA LANDIN

We came to see the war that we funded. We read the field reports; with our fingers we followed the path of Saturn over maps that illustrated the topography of land and the perilous terrain of love.
    But that was on paper. And if we had learned anything from this story it was to be cautious of paper—to be mindful of its fragile construction and sharp edges, but mostly to be cautious of what is written on it.

CHAPTER TWENTY-FIVE

● ● ●

CARDINAL MAHONY

The first time Pope John Paul II called Father Mahony, he was on the church roof scooping dog poop into a dustpan. Leviticus, the rectory dog, had been sent to the top of the church after biting the pudgy hands of two children. On the roof Leviticus guarded piles of broken porcelain that were once saints and eight seedling palms that would one day be burned to ash and spread on foreheads.

"Father Mahony?" the Pope asked.

"Yes?" Mahony answered.

"You have been called up to cardinal," the Pope said.

Two weeks later, on the same day that Leviticus jumped from the roof, dying on impact, a Swiss Vatican guard carrying a peacock feather and an inkwell knocked on Mahony's door.

"Sign here," the guard said, his breath heavy with chocolate. The guard then handed the newly ordained Cardinal Mahony a desk plaque that read "Thieves," which he was to carry whenever summoned to Rome.

On that warm spring day, the Swiss Guard escorted Cardinal Mahony from El Monte, the town of carnations and roses, to his new post deep in the desert's basin: the church of Our Lady of Thieves. Father Mahony did not pack; he took only the Easter robe he was wearing and the splatters of Leviticus's blood that had stained his shoes.

Twenty years later Cardinal Mahony returned to El Monte with his shoes shined and his cuffs stitched with gilded thread. He came to witness the fall of Saturn and to spread a paste of palm ash and holy water on the spot where his faithful canine friend had landed and folded into a mangle of flesh and bones. Cardinal Mahony had seen the sky collapse before, decades earlier, when he was still a student of history and had yet to discover theology. Part of the sky fell on his back, bruising his spine and crushing the carton of eggs he carried in his arms.

At the time he was one of those mournful students with such a memory that he remembered the first day he had ever scraped his knees—tripping on the sidewalk and tearing his only pair of dress pants—recalling even the sensation of skin against gravel. Mahony was always pained by the past; he cried when thinking about the introduction of gunpowder to the Americas and lay in bed for days thinking of the lost beauty of the dodo bird.

Despite Mahony's sensibilities, he flipped through his history books and bookmarked the engravings of Spanish ships approaching the continent. He stared at the masts and puffed sails, knowing that the ships would dock and pull horses and shackled men from beneath the deck, introducing slavery and the Spanish Conquista to the new world.

The first girl he ever kissed tasted like salt. She dried and chapped his lips, and the next day they swelled and bled as he spooned sugared cornmeal into his mouth. Mahony ran his hand through her hair, hair not soft and limp, slipping from his fingers, but slightly coarse, catching in the comb of his hand. Hair so beautiful to touch that it eroded his fingerprints and life lines, leaving smooth hands that baffled detectives and confused palm readers.

Her name was Ida, named after a flower grown only once in El Monte. She was the great-granddaughter of a man who had sailed on planks and bedsheet-sails from the island of Espaniola, fleeing smallpox and white men in shiny helmets. A man who spoke Castellano and Haitian French, versed in the Romance languages but forced to use his choppy English to court a woman who had twice been sold on the trading block before being emancipated by a man who carried love letters and dentist receipts in his stovepipe hat. They made curtains from the sails and settled in a state cut five times by a single river. In that river he laundered her dresses and washed his perfectly smooth hands, cupping the water, hoping to magnify the creases of his palm but seeing nothing but porcelain.

Mahony repeated history, leaving his fingerprints and life lines in Ida's hair. And so the irrevocable damage of slavery and colonization was lost fingerprints and falling in love with a girl descendent of these two histories. And it was she who had first broken heavens. Mahony was walking home when the sky unexpectedly fell on his back, soaking his shirt with the yolk of the eggs and spreading shards of sky and broken eggshells on the ground.

APOLONIO

From the day his mother was burned by the heat of the Virgin's halo, Apolonio was wary of church authorities. He never stepped on church lots, even during carnivals; when the bells tolled, he swabbed his ears after every call; and when the donation envelopes were slipped underneath his door he lifted them only while wearing latex gloves, careful not to leave his fingerprints. Apolonio knew the magic and alchemy practiced by saints and angels, but he was unsanctioned, illegitimate in the eyes of Rome, and as such he was always heedful, avoiding the path of any agent of the church.

But in those days when the shreds of Saturn were floating down, Apolonio, like everybody else in El Monte, kept his attention to the sky. While he stared up, holding the Baby Nostradamus in his arms, two altar boys walked into his shop, snapping pictures and taking notes. With the help of padded shoes, the altar boys floated across his floor. Had it not been for the slam of the door, Apolonio never would have turned to see them silently running away, disappearing into the church of Guadalupe and quickly resuming their duties, crossing the altar, holding the spill dish underneath the Eucharist, and quietly retrieving wine from underneath the priest's bedframe.

CAMEROON

Cameroon never reached the republic of her namesake. She stayed in

Tangier, drinking Moroccan mint tea and pressing the honeybees into her skin. Two days after the bus strike ended they found her body speckled with thorns and full of poison. The bus drivers wrapped her in scented sheets that dripped honey and then set her on the bench of a Ferguson bus headed for the blue cliffs of Asilah. Four drivers of sable blood, wearing linen touring caps, lifted her and tossed her into the sea. The fish were instantly drawn by the honey that had been spread between sheets, devouring the bedclothes and Cami. Her scraps and rags were chewed by the lingering scavengers.

The next morning the beach was crowded with sharks and schools of metanga fish, laid out on the sand, spitting up poison and honey.

CARDINAL MAHONY

Ida stayed in the sun all day.

Mahony only for an hour, but it was he who burned and peeled and was shamed by the pink of his skin.

"Ida," he said, rubbing aloe on his shoulders and arms, "can I tell you something?"

"Yes?"

"You are the first... the first girl I have ever kissed."

"The first black girl, you mean?"

"The first girl."

She blushed and smiled, confessing that he was the eleventh boy, but only the second she had tongued.

"And who was the first?"

She shrugged. An indifferent rise and fall of her shoulders. A shrug that caused the first fissure, a tiny pinhole that would eventually lead to the collapse of the sky.

Mahony was many years away from religion and adopting what became a lifelong low-sodium diet, but still he brought Ida treats and gifts. The presents, always in pairs, included: rock sugar and a statue of Mary holding the baby Jesus, three bars of milk chocolate and a hologram of the Archangel Michael, lemon drops and a mahogany crucifix.

The last gift Mahony gave Ida was a box of saints made from Bethlehem clay, an image of St. Martin de Porres on the lid blessing the peppermints that were held inside. He delivered it through her window, setting it on her desk amongst books of Darwin and the late letters of the disillusioned Erasmus. With his lucid imagination he envisioned the exact moment when Ida came upon his gifts. He would be home, five miles away, his nose deep in a history book, and hear the unwrapping of paper, and then imagine Ida holding candy in her hands and then hanging the frame he had given her or trying to guess what profession or hobby the saint watched over.

But that day, as he cradled the carton of eggs and walked across the flower fields, no wrapping paper rustled. Ida picked up the box from her desk and put it on her outer windowsill, returning the still-wrapped gift. And at the precise moment that the clay box of saints was set on the sill the sky broke and fell on Mahony. He lay there with the sky on his back, feeling egg yolks and whites on his stomach, but thinking it was blood that was soaking his shirt.

APOLONIO

The church officials came before nightfall, accompanied by a battalion of Swiss Vatican Guards. Some held spears, others pushed dollies, all of them at attention. The Cardinal knocked on the shop's door, his hand worn smooth by Ida's hair. Apolonio opened the door to a raised arsenal of sharpened spears.

They went through the shop, wheeling out statues of saints and cupboards heavy with ingredients and potions. Apolonio stood where the porcelain Mary Magdalen once sat. The patron saint of Hollywood actresses was wrapped in blankets and lifted into the cargo truck. Apolonio held the Baby Nostradamus, feeding him teething cookies and shading him from the view of the Swiss Guards and their sharp blades.

By morning the shop was empty and Apolonio was officially charged. Three hundred counts of heresy, sixty-four counts of sacrilege, and two fire code violations for the use of antiquated Bunsen burners. The most offensive of the confiscated artifacts was a parchment text bound in slabs of lead and containing cures for everything from bunions to stigmata sores.

No trial was held. Apolonio was excommunicated on the spot. He had voluntarily avoided contact with the church for years, but he was now officially prohibited from stepping on church grounds and forbidden from ever making the sign of the cross.

The last provision of his punishment was three small slits made on the tip of his tongue, assuring that any prayer uttered by Apolonio would leave his mouth earmarked and be promptly directed to purgatory, where prayers were never heard.

The church officials took everything, leaving only the counter and an old kite long forgotten behind crates and statues of saints. It was built from paper and shaven twigs, the kind easily mended with tissue and glue.

Apolonio repaired the kite, tying knots, fastening the paper sails, and attaching a roll of string. As the debris of Saturn came down, the Baby Nostradamus and Apolonio floated the kite, letting the wind pull it higher and higher into the sky.

CAMEROON

After receiving the news that she had been eaten by fish, the chambermaids entered. In her hotel room they found:

> One suitcase of clothes
>
> A stack of books, among them *The Book of Incandescent Light*, the legendary book of lost love
>
> Four shoeboxes, all filled with dead and torn bees, except for one filled with unsent postcards and letters

One letter, which Cameroon intended to mail from the Spanish coast, was ten pages long, with whole paragraphs crossed out, written in a cursive so angry that it broke through the paper. The letter barely held together, tearing when anyone tried to lift it. The letter was addressed to Saturn but referred to him by many different names: Salvador, Sal, Chava, and by other names, crude but deserved. The letter began:

> I have come across people, they say they know me. Know of me, they say. They began learning of me on page one hundred twenty-one, that's what they say. To them I'm honeybees and your cold-weather fuck. A clingy and desperate girl sitting on a bidet. They know the ways and coordinates of where we fucked. They know the feel of my pussy and yet they have never touched me. Not enough for you to fuck me, you must tell others. In your world of fiction and imagination you may fuck whomever you want; masturbate with your genius. But I'm not of paper. It is not decent, Sal. To fuck and then tell is one thing, but to write about it—to allow the telling

to never end...

The last page read:

> ...the people that I have encountered know of me, but know nothing about how unlearned and naive and desperate you were. How you had always fucked with your foreskin covering you, had not seen your own head until I pulled the skin and showed it to you. So Catholic and courteous with your missionary position; there's other ways to fuck, Sal. I had to show you that. Write about that, put that in your great American novel. Write about the day you burned yourself, believing fire took sadness away. I cleaned you and gauzed you. "You are so good and kind," you said to me, "maybe you should marry me." And it was I who had to say no.

CARDINAL MAHONY

Mahony lay with the whole weight of heaven on his back, the smell of rotting eggs beneath him, never understanding allusions to broken hearts because it was his back that ached.

He dreamt of soft clouds that would pad the weight, of apartheids where black girls could not hurt him, and of professions that could mend the sky.

APOLONIO

With no shop and his parchment confiscated by the church, Apolonio devoted his time to flying his paper kite and playing with the Baby Nostradamus. When airplanes tangled with his line and crashed into the fields, Apolonio complained to the crop duster company.

"Your planes are bringing down my kites."

The company apologized, promptly reimbursing him and promising to reroute the dusters.

CAMEROON

The People of Paper was pressed and published and soon out of print, a used-bookstore underseller. And there, among the odor of yellowing paper and the uncataloged mysteries and romances, Cameroon opened the novel and discovered she had been eaten by sharks. As she read, the tamed swarms of honeybees that buzzed above her quieted, landing and tucking in their wings, crawling over the spines and covers, over pages and bindings. Burrowing into chapters and then wandering through paragraphs, walking over this very sentence, obscuring this word, and then depositing honey in the spaces between.

She left the bookstore, leaving behind sticky and sweetened pages, two dollars for her copy, and a few honeybee carcasses, their thorns still attached. Bees that were smashed between the covers of books, trapped in a pool of sentences, and those that had feigned death simply to stay among shelves and papers. With her swarm above her she walked away, wondering why, in a novel, where many things are possible, her fate was such an unimaginative one. But she knew why. This was the fate of women who know too much, women who can upset the pride of Saturn. Because ultimately Saturn is a tyrant, commanding the story where he wants it to go. That is why they fight against him, why they hide under lead and try to push him to the margins. But Cameroon was just one, not a gang or an army—easily flicked from an African cliff.

CARDINAL MAHONY

Cardinal Mahony forsook history, wanting no memory. At the seminary the monks removed the shards of sky, dressed the wounds, and taught him how to love God above all else. With wine and wafers, they sat in the courtyard praying, Mahony joining them once he healed. He pressed his hands to show his devotion, hands so soft and smooth that they left no marks or prints. He adopted a regimen that included a menu of unsalted potatoes and greens and fifteen perimeters on his knees around the seminary grounds, never again thinking of Ida, or of the days before patched skies or the feel of her lips.

CHAPTER TWENTY-SIX

•

JONATHAN MEAD

Cameroon,

To find you, they said, go where the fruit trees are blooming and insects pollinating. So I sat in orchards and followed every worker bee back to its hive, but none of them ever led to you.

Twenty-three years ago, when we brought you home, the trees had shed all their foliage. We stopped the car, not knowing if we had parked on lawn or street. We got out and shuffled through dead leaves. I went ahead to open the door and your mother carried you, bundled but with your face uncovered so that you would feel the air and see the autumn sky. We had only been gone for two days. Two days of holding your mother's hand and telling her to relax and then to push. You finally arrived and she stayed awake long enough to hold you, before the nurses came and took you away. In the morning we lifted you from the crib, you had your first sponge bath, and around your wrist in blue ink they had written "Cameroon" on your ID bracelet.

And so we brought you home, rustling leaves as birds streaked above in V formations. On the side of the house, just below the eave of the roof, wasps floated with mud in their mouths, building their organ-pipe catacombs, and we rushed you inside. I came out and smoked the wasps and then scrapped their hanging nests from the wall, crumbling them back to dirt. I finished the job and came inside to see you, to see my new daughter.

It hid in my sleeves or somewhere in my collar, I don't know how, but there it was: its wings were tucked and it sharpened its mandibles against each other. Its stinger dragged across the comforter, as it crawled on the bed and then on your leg. Barely one day old and there were already insects. All those stingers you suffered. If only I had been more careful.

I swiped and caught it, crushing it, but not before it stung my palm, swelling my fingers fat and red. Slowly the inflammation went away, but not before nights of fever and dreams of swarms. I should have left then, but I loved you and wanted to be a real father, and so I tried, but I longed for the wasps' sting.

I drove you to the park, wasps in my pocket. We parked and you ran across the grass and into the sandbox. Three hours later you found me passed out on the car's bench seat. You were sunburned, and there was sand in your hair and stuck to the corners of your mouth. You were eating dirt while I was pressing stingers, and I knew then that I had to leave.

But I did not leave you for wasps. I was shamed by the dangers that I brought you. Shamed by your beauty, when I was so ugly. You will not believe me but I left because I did not want to hurt you, because I would do more harm by staying than by going.

Cami, whether we like it or not, our histories are of pollinating insects and feathered flight. The first day I met your mother the birds chirped and bees buzzed, but it was never love between us. I stayed only for you. Because I love you, Cami. There are no more insects. I have destroyed every nest, sprayed repellent all around my yard, and chopped down the fruit trees so there are no blossoms where they may gather. There have been no insects for five years but it's barely now that I feel whole again and worthy of seeing you. Worthy of asking for your forgiveness.

There was a sign, flocks of migrating birds flying south, not in their usual formations but in the shape of Cameroon. The country which you were named after, the land where everything came forth: the mud of

Adam, the rib of Eve, where thorned insects were first named and then expelled. Cameroon, you are everything and I was exiled but I want to return. I want you to let me return.

With love,
Your father,
Jonathan Mead
XOXO

CHAPTER TWENTY-SEVEN

SATURN

In the story of Samson it is the columns that supported him. The pits of his eyes had healed and his hair, shaved to the scalp, had sprouted back. His strength slowly returned as he leaned against the columns and steadied himself.

FROGGY

We weakened Saturn, steadily pressing, charging forward and overwhelming him with our numbers. We took control and spoke for ourselves whenever and wherever we wanted. I do not know the will of God, nor have I been pious. I have left Sundays uncelebrated, I have drunk outside of sacrament, I have lifted my knife to church authorities, and I have folded my body in ways that are profane. I am not noble in those ways. But in this war, against the tyranny, against the most despotic of planets, God is on our side.

The Lord says go and be free, act for evil or good but out of your own will. For we are not born righteous and we must be given a choice. It is an affront on God's kindness to limit us, to relegate us to strict columns and force us to act in one story and submit to the commands of a dictator. We may be meek to the God that is in heaven, but we will not be servile to a floating satellite made of dirt and gas.

CARDINAL MAHONY

It is not nuclear weapons or meteoroids that break the sky. It is always them. They who make us weary of what is above, driving us to celibate professions. They that we think of as the flakes of sky fall into the cup of our hands. We gather pieces in a box and send them to her. Let her see what she has done.

I have tried to act from the soul, looking to God, dedicating myself to years of reading and prayer so that I may ease this rancor. So that I may forgive Ida and the pain of shards on my back. I have been devout, obedient to holy laws, extending my lent well beyond its forty days, into a penitence of ten months—forgoing red meat, giving up even the simple comforts. Brushing my teeth with my fingers and, instead of quilted tissues, using squares of newsprint that I cut and set on the toilet tank. I have done everything in Scripture and still there is no escape from her. I have even broken professional protocol speaking to His Holiness John Paul II, discussing not the kingdom of God but the texture of hair and the chap of Ida's lips.

RITA

In the story of Samson it is a Philistine woman whom he loves.

A woman who never forgot where she came from: from men whose sex was always covered by skin, their foreskins always dangling like elephants' trunks.

And she chose her people and a bag of silver over her love of Samson, cutting his locks of hair with a borrowed razor and delivering him to his enemies. Samson was consecrated by God Almighty and defeated by the weakest of the sexes.

LITTLE MERCED

Froggy said that we had Saturn cornered, that he would fall onto Monte at any moment.

I told my father and he nodded.

"When you were not breathing anymore I wrote a letter to your mother," he said. "She has not yet replied, but I have laid out a lawn for her."

He told me about the lawn, listing the names of the different blades of grass, classified by thickness and edge.

Then he talked about the fertilizer, how he preferred to use rabbit pellets instead of cow or goat droppings, because they were less likely to stain textiles. He obsessed over the soil and the depth of the roots, occupying himself with the smallest details as if he was avoiding real thoughts and still trying to elude Saturn.

RAMON BARRETO

Some days it is the napkins that I pull from diners' dispensers; I crumple the paper towels in my fist and imagine that I am holding her hand. On Sundays it is the weekend edition that I spread on my mattress, the glossy ads I set by my pillow, and the newsprint I spread all the way to the foot of the bed. The cut has fully healed, leaving only a slight scar that runs to the tip of my tongue. I can no longer taste sugar, but nothing is bitter.

I pushed her away because she was not flesh. How could I make a life with pressed pulp? I spent hours at a time on the living room couch helping her unravel herself, getting up to throw away bundles of used paper into the trash bin.

QUINONES

Napoleon Bonaparte commissioned l'Arc de Triomphe to commemorate the conquests of his imperial armies. At the top of the monument—where the pigeons perch, cooing and tucking their beaks into each others' feathers—thirty shields were engraved into the masonry, each celebrating a major Napoleonic victory—Austerlitz, Borodino— but among the ornate shields there is one peculiar sculpture that the French Tourist Board has cut from every Paris factoid book. It is located at the southeast corner of the arc: the shield of Marie-Louise, a cracked tortoise shell with her name neatly etched at the base. It is best seen in the winter. In the summer, as tourists flock to the city of lights, the maintenance crew scrapes the pigeon droppings from around the Marie-Louise but purposely allows nesting debris and excrement to fill the grooves of the shell, obscuring Napoleon's sculpture to failed love.

APOLONIO

They took everything, my parchment, the porcelain saints, the drawers and jars of ingredients, every scrap of paper in the shop and house. They even took things that had nothing to do with being a curandero: my pillowcases and kitchen utensils, the bristles from my toothbrushes, and the soap holders from my bathtub. Things they said appeared on the list of unsanctioned items.

But the kite, which was also listed, forbidden because it may trespass heights that approach holiness—that they left behind. I performed minor repairs and then floated it into the sky, giving it enough line to reach as far as Saturn. But the falling flakes of sky accumulated on its sail, weighing it down.

SATURN

"Lord, forgive her that gouged my eyes and shaved my hair," Sampson said, unable to see but with his face pointed to the sky.

They brought him to the center of the temple, guided by a servant who led Samson by the hand.

"Put me where I can feel the columns," Samson said to the servant.

The Philistine leaders, in their cushioned chairs, and their subjects, seated in bleachers, all stared at the defeated Nazarite, laughing at his pitted eyes. They raised their cups of honeyed wine and thanked their god for delivering their enemy into their hands.

Samson, hearing their laughs and jeers, leaned into the columns, cracking the stone and cement joints, toppling the pillars and bringing the temple roof down upon his spine.

Under the wreckage, the whole town was crushed, the mighty Samson among them.

FROGGY

There was sky in the gutters, caught in our hair, and topping off furrows. Wipers cleared windshields and flakes clogged the vents and air filters. Julieta came outside to sweep the scraps from the porch, while sky gathered on tarps and flower baskets left out on the field.

I dragged a tarp to the scale, heavy as a day's worth of flowers, but the needle showed nothing, not budging above the zero.

I put some in my mouth; it tasted like communion, a softness that dissolved into nothing.

BEEKEEPER

I don't remember the year, but it was in the warmer days of the spring, the rains were mere mists, and the orchard was white with flowers.

I had packed twigs and leaves into the smoker. It was one of those old types without a compressed chamber or accordion pump—just a simple tin with a wooden handle clasped at the brim and nail holes punched into the can. I lit the leaves, waiting for the smoke to gather, and then walked toward the honey crates, but there were no bees buzzing or floating nearby. I propped open the crate and slid off the top plank. Inside, the hive frames were heavy with wax and honey. I cut six combs, all dripping with the sticky nectar, and dropped them into my bucket.

There was not a single worker bee crawling in the hives or hovering above the crate. Sometimes after a long winter, as the weather clears, the colony performs a cleansing flight, a giant cloud of bees pouring out of the honey crate. They flap their wings hard against the air, not returning until sunset, their bodies refreshed by crisp breezes. But sundown came and no bees returned. I went to check the crate again; I pulled away panel locks and frames of honey, until I reached the queen's cage. The wire mesh had been slit and no queen was inside.

I walked back to the house, carrying the extinguished smoker and a bucket of honeycombs. I opened the door and she was on the couch, covered in honeybees. I brushed the dead insects away. She was wearing only a tank top and panties and her whole body was pocked with stingers, her face freckled, barely breathing. Her hands were clasped together, but as I tried to lift her she unhinged them. In the basket of her hand, dragging her abdomen across the life lines of Cami's palm, was the queen. Her whole colony had died as they tried to protect her.

APOLONIO

The kite rose and fell, weighed down by the flakes, climbing again after shaking the sheddings.

And suddenly, when I expected its altitude to drop, it soared, its triangular shape disappearing into a mere dot.

It was a confetti sky, but EMF was still far from a victory celebration. Saturn was recovering. The glow of his rings was brightening and his axis rotation quickening. But EMF thought that they had overpowered Saturn and were waiting for him to tumble down. They awaited the Saturnian fall on the flower fields of El Monte, thinking of the legacy they would leave in astrology and war histories, EMF immortalized in the same pages as Voyager 2 and the Allied liberation troops. EMF, like the first spacecraft that circled around the ringed planet and the army that deposed Europe's most vicious dictator, was also bringing Saturn closer and overthrowing an unjust rule.

SUBCOMANDANTE SANDRA

The sky was ragged, steadily falling. A dry rain that crept into our shoes and the folds of our sleeves, sky clotting and accumulating on our shoulders. A steady downpour eventually giving way to scattered showers, then sprinkles, until nothing fell.

We thought that Saturn had fallen, that this was the end. Saturn buried underneath the blue.

CAMEROON

There are other creatures that are not bees, creatures that I do not miss. Like the shy snail between your legs—it leaves no honey, only a slimy trail of silk.

LITTLE MERCED

The rose petals and mint leaves began to work, but there was still a lingering stench that would not let me concentrate for long. My skills had dulled; in those rare moments when I was able to do as the Baby Nostradamus had taught me, I could lift only a small parasol for a short time. The shield was no longer sharp and angular, disappearigy drained.

RITA

It is Delilah who is the hero, the one who brings the brute down. Avenging the deaths of the thousands he killed. Standing up for the Philistine people and the tender skin of their cocks.

SMILEY

The sky was breaking, its pieces piling on my skylight like leaves.

"First the sky and then Saturn will crash down," Froggy said.

But there was no Saturn, just flakes covering everything, a coat of blue blanketing all of El Monte.

SATURN

Saturn remembered those days of sadness, when he trudged two miles through the snow for bread and milk and then returned with frozen feet, soot on his coat and boots, to a house littered with honeybees.

In the bathtub, while his toes thawed and Cameroon sat in the next room reading impossible books about capturing birds with pepper shakers and salt, Saturn dialed. She whose name is no longer cited in the dedication page would pick up and instantly hang up the receiver.

And when she would not pick up, Saturn talked into the answering machine: "It is me, Sal, me. Te extraño mucho." So that she would understand and she next door could not overhear. Cameroon would tap on the door and when he did not open, she slipped scrawled napkins beneath the door: "I need to pee." "I'm gonna throw your papers into the snow." "To catch a pelican: three tablespoons of salt on his tail."

Two weeks later, three utility bills, a catalog for snow shovels and boots, and a mimeographed letter from the incumbent mayor were stuffed into the mailbox. Saturn opened the phone bill:

9:15 PM Syracuse, NY Los Angeles, CA 238-5329
9:17 PM Syracuse, NY Los Angeles, CA 238-5329
9:21 PM Syracuse, NY Los Angeles, CA 238-5329
9:27 PM Syracuse, NY Los Angeles, CA 238-5329
9:30 PM Syracuse, NY Los Angeles, CA 238-5329

The record went on for pages and pages, with a three-hour rest in the hours of the early morning and then the calls resuming.

All his failed attempts at transcontinental communication were neatly itemized on perforated paper. Saturn did not crumple the bill; he carefully tore out the payment stub and wrote a check for the balance. His saliva was dry, but no longer bitter. He licked the stamp until it stuck and then walked the preaddressed envelope to the post office.

MECHANIC

There was one more mechanical tortoise to dismantle, and then the whole species would be extinct. I traveled up from La Quemadora, north on the interstate, all the way to El Monte. I left my metal detector in my workshop and instead inspected the ground for tracks, looking for the drag of its toes and claws.

I found its trail; I followed the groove the tail had dug into the asphalt and dirt, leading deep into a flower patch. As I came upon the tortoise, I saw it launch its front feet forward and hook its claws into the soil. Its locomotion was natural and fluid; somehow the spring jerk that I had not been able to solve had corrected itself.

It then anchored its back feet and drove its tail into the field. There was a sudden but slight jolt, producing the tiniest of earthquakes, compressing millimeters of dirt into rock, subtly diminishing the surface area of the continent.

MARCHING FRANCISCAN MONKS OF THE FIRST ORDER

The factory, where we turned mud into flesh and ribs, is to be forgotten, never to be mentioned. But there are days, as we march across the Americas, when we see our own handywork: old men pushing carts with tubs of boiling water and blanched corn and grandmothers with long scarves covering their mouths from the cold. It is then that we remember the factory, but we say nothing and march forward.

CARDINAL MAHONY

Many years later, Ida unknowingly entered my confessional, her breath smelling of salt and of the tapioca pudding she had for breakfast.

I thought she would say, "I once let the sky fall on a boy."

And I, who have been taught to forgive, would give her a light penance. Something that would take no more than a sitting. Ten Hail Marys and a dozen Our Fathers.

But she never mentioned the sky.

Instead, she spoke of a man who she loved but who refused to touch water. "I begged him to come into the tub with me, but he always refused," she said. But one day she lured him in, asking him if he truly loved her.

He followed her in, mounting her and then turning, shifting her on top. And that was when his body became heavy and limp and began losing its shape. He started to dissolve; when she tried to pull him out, her hands went right through, clutching only wet pulp.

She scooped him out by the handful, clumps of soggy paper that she piled at the foot of the sink—a mound that she desperately tried to shape into the man she loved.

Two days later the maids carried out the pulp, heavy and still dripping, leaving a moist bathrug and a trail of water.

RITA

There were two factions: those who launched rotting heads from the bleachers, rowdy and malcriados, spitting and cursing and sticking out their tongues between their fingers; and then there were the dignified representatives from the National Museum of Lettuce who brought me bouquets of washed red-leaf lettuce.

"Not all lettuce pickers are the same. Some of us love you and always have. We don't care if you sleep underneath the limbs and flesh of white men, or if the fruit of your plum trees is never sweet."

JULIETA

Froggy was confident that we would defeat Saturn.

"We have overrun him. There's no way he can make his way back."

I wanted to believe Froggy; I wanted the war to end, to give up the life of charts and schemes. But there was no way to know, no way to gauge Saturn's strength or position. Saturn could be just coiling back, amassing gravitational energy, readying itself for its thrust.

SATURN

Saturn dumped two truckloads of rotting lettuce in her apartment pool and wrote a letter to the National Museum of Lettuce.

"I wrote to them and told them never to let you in, that you would only betray them," Saturn says to her.

"If I'm so horrible why won't you just leave me alone?"

Saturn does not say: Because you are not, because I still remember the sourness of you, the parted halves of lime you left on the kitchen counter. "Brush your teeth," you would say, knowing the dangers of citric acid as your teeth had already began to corrode.

The days we spent on the floor in apartments with no beds, making our own from faded blankets and handed-down sheets. The hot afternoons when the car radiator overheated but still we'd drive wherever you wanted. The color of the El Monte sky when you and I were still underneath it, when it was still elastic and not brittle.

The day you confessed, "I am made of paper," but I had known all along. I was always careful, never folding the foreskin back, going down but never for too long.

Instead he says:

"Because there is no escaping you. Four years of war just so that you may look in my direction. A whole war for you. To prove that I too am a colonizer, I too am powerful in those ways. I can stand on my tippy toes, I can curl my tongue and talk that perfect untainted English, I can wipe out whole cultures, whole towns of imaginary flower people. I can do that too."

But Saturn was not Cortez; he did not want to trek across the land and stab flags into the dirt and nail royal crests into walls and oaks. Saturn would end the war, tumble all the columns, even if it meant his own destruction. He was tired of the martial life, tired of wars spurred by lost love. Saturn was a giant, a titan among planets, but he was also a little man who stepped on a stool to open the top kitchen cupboards. Who stood on crates and imagined kissing her. But that is all war commanders are: little men with broken hearts.

SMILEY

At first it was only the potted flowers that were affected, their petals burned by too-close proximity to Saturn.

Saturn was not falling as Froggy had predicted. Its mass was increasing, expanding, and the heat and glow of its rings accelerated the growth of the flowers—from seed to bloom in less than a week. But as the flowers budded, they revealed loose, burned petals that fell from the stem and broke into a sandy grit.

I estimated the distance of Saturn by the grade of ash. I held up a flower every three minutes, letting the petals break into the black powder. I compared the different burn residues; the ash was progressively finer. Saturn was definitely approaching, but it was not in a free fall. Saturn was moving on his own energy.

MECHANICAL TORTOISE

0001010010010101010101010
1010110011010101010010011
0001010101010101010001010
1010010011111001001010101
0101010101010100101010101
0010101010101011001011010
0110100010000100010111111
10101001110101010

MECHANIC

I took out my crowbar and swung it over my shoulder. I aimed for the head of the mechanical tortoise and then let the iron drop. I hit it right on the beak, then again on the crown of the head—two solid blows before it tucked in its legs and head. I jammed the bar into the front end of the shell and then leaned in, using my whole weight to pop out the head. I maintained the leverage until I was able to wedge the head with the blocks of lumber I carried in my tool sack. It was the strongest of my mechanical tortoises. When I was finally done my whole body was sore; my crowbar was bent at its handle and its chisel worn down to a knob.

The mistakes of my youthful exuberance, as the Elder Nostradamus had predicted, have finally been rectified.

LITTLE MERCED

There was a new presence where it had never been b█████████ my father lifting m███████████ a man who wo███████████ hrough his ey███████████ that could ███████████ ns that h█

In ███████████ tch from the ███████████ ght me a bag of roa███████████ sked for limes to squeeze ████ the bag.

My father stayed on his lawn, laying on his back and staring up at sky.

Nothing was falling anymore. A flock of Oaxacan songbirds streaked through the sky and a crop duster circled around Apolonio's kite.

CARDINAL MAHONY

I gave her a pithy penance. One Angelos and three Ave Marias.

"He was only paper," I said, trying to console her. We are of meat, we are who matter, but I did not tell her this.

She left the confessional and I followed closely behind. But I was afraid to catch her, because it was one of those days where the sky seemed fragile and my fingerprints and lifelines had finally resurfaced.

APOLONIO

In stars it is known as a supernova, their mass expanding and expanding and then suddenly disintegrating. In planets it appears as a healthy growth, a sign of its strength and orbital stability, increasing weight to anchor itself to its solar system. Often the growth stabilizes and the planet remains. Other times it explodes, leaving only a trail of space dust spread across its orbit.

RALPH AND ELISA LANDIN

We must regretfully inform you that we are withdrawing our support for the war.

Several items have been brought to our attention.

Falsified wedding certificates and nests of honeycombs are not behaviors the Landin Foundation wishes to promote. They are unbecoming of the character we wish to encourage.

IDA

From pulp you are and to pulp you shall return.

Saturn began to regain his strength, each day growing stronger, writing her letters in which he told her that the lawn was now covered with nails and broken glass.

He told her that her skin was so rough that to her it would feel like crawling through the freshly plucked down of young ducks.

She only replied once, a phone call. She said, "I don't deserve this. I have forgiven myself. What I did to you was not so bad. It happens."

And Saturn nodded and hung up the receiver and then dusted the lamp tables and emptied the ashtrays, dumping matchsticks into the trash bin, the spent lighters and burnt butter knives settling at the bottom. And from the ceiling corners, where cobwebs and beehives hung, Saturn knocked down the honeycombs with the broom stick. Larvae were curled in the wax chambers but no more bees floated around the house.

Cameroon had gone long ago. She left her snow boots in the pantry, below the cans of beans and next to the bunched grocery bags and crumpled aluminum cans. She said she was going to a place without snowfall, where she would not slip on sidewalks or burn her nose against the cold breeze. Where there were no desperate boys slipping into her bed and calling her names that were not hers.

Saturn walked into the kitchen. He pulled the stool from the corner, climbed its single step, and then reached for the top cupboard. He paused, pondering war, forgetting to bring down the crock pot. Instead he thought of all the great commanders. All of them standing with their chests forward, their boots padded with two inches of newspaper and their pockets stuffed with unsent love letters. And indeed they were all little men.

But sometimes they stepped down from their vanity stools and rose above their short stature. They forgot the divisive allegiances of country and race and forgave petty feuds and the trespasses of others. They removed their hands from inside their waistcoats. The ache from what she did is still there underneath his lapel, but the pain is warm now, a pleasant fever that is a part of him. As he walks he unbuttons his cape and then removes his emperor's hat. He moves forward, unconcerned with his own demise, wanting only to save the falling sky and restore the quiet that was there before.

APOLONIO

It was never the Baby Nostradamus's war, but still he tried to fight back, to preserve some of the page while EMF regrouped. But as the day wore on, the Baby Nostradamus tired, no longer able to push Saturn back. He touched the palm of my hand:

"It is Saturn that wins the war."

And that was the first and only time the Baby Nostradamus ever told me anything. He often lifted his hand to touch my face and pat my head, but he never again warned me of what was to come.

BEEKEEPER

Virgil, the great Roman poet, kept two crates of honeybees. He called the insects his birds of Muses. "Let a bee touch an infant's lips and she will speak in verse," he said.

Golden bees adorned the sangrail, where the blood of our Lord was once held, and holy kings commanded that their caskets be filled with honey and their graves with a mound of bees.

Napoleon Bonaparte ruled half the world from his throne while wearing a cape embroidered with honeycombs and bees. And the Kennedys used only pure beeswax to seal their inauguration invitations.

It is not an insect of shame but one of noble lineage. Look closely at the portraits of royalty from Rome to the American Camelot, and you will notice at the very least a freckle, sometimes three dots, or, if the sleeve is pulled back, a full constellation.

CAMEROON

Saturn had spread his papers on the hotel bed. I brought in snow from the sidewalk, carried it up the elevator, and crumbled the snowball over his head. "A snow flurry," he said. We laughed and wrestled, tangling in a formation diagrammed and photocopied in puzzle books, solved only after two MacArthur grants but never publicly disclosed, fearing the solution would demystify love.

We laid on sheets stiff with industrial starch, touching each others' faces. He put his finger between my lips.

"Cami, I would not mind if we could do this again tomorrow," he said, and then kissed me. But that was before the sharks, before the beekeepers returned, when he was calling me by the name that is my name.

CARDINAL MAHONY

The overarching lesson of seminary was that our hands could be pure, and that through prayer and meditation we could touch the sky.

But there were much quicker methods. Easier ways of touching sky—feeling its weight and jagged edges—and of acquiring hands so pure that they would be confused with those of church saints.

So when the theology students came I told them about airplanes, and then about the greatest holiness, found in the touch of a girl's tangled hair.

SATURN

Not even the Baby Nostradamus could stop him. The sadness still circulated through Saturn, clogging capillaries and inflaming his lymph nodes, his liver never able to filter the melancholy, but his body had adapted. At times debilitated by the thought of her, but still able to summon enough strength to press against the columns. Saturn's weight leaned against the structure. At first there was only a single crack at the base of the column. He thought of her, of her perfidy, and then of the others throughout the story: Delilah, Merced, Ida. The lone crack splintered into a web of fractures, buckling the structure and crumbling it to rubble. Once the first support was down the others were easily tipped, all the columns falling, giving Saturn full control of the story.

Once again able to wander wherever he wished, he saw Sandra inside her house. The doors were shut and the curtains drawn, but still Saturn could see her on her bed folded in a position first chronicled in the Book of Job. Her eyes swollen with the coming tears as she remembered what it was like to make love to Froggy.

Froggy was three blocks away, walking back to his stucco, cutting across the wilting and ashing flower fields. His mouth was dry from spitting out grit instead of the wet pink cud of chewed petals. Froggy lost the war, there were no more turtle shells to hide under and he was too tired to think of things that were not thoughts. Saturn entered his mind, finding the dejected psyche of a war commander who blamed himself for a poorly coordinated offensive. Froggy's stomach burned with the regret of having not attacked earlier when Saturn had initially retreated, when Saturn was so sad that he thought only of Liz. Before his sadness became rage and before lead leaked into the water and air.

Julieta sat in the kitchen surrounded by spackled walls, plaster covering the holes where the scutes of lead were once hinged. She waited for Froggy. He entered with his head hanging. Julieta wiped the ash from the corners of his mouth and then brushed the flakes of sky from his hair.

"Froggy, you are still my comandante," she said, knowing that the war had been lost.

On the tiled floor, fully aware that Saturn was watching, he kissed Julieta and then hiked up her dress, pulling down her panties and then turning her over, entering her the way Job had once entered his wife, before she had left and the boils had ravaged Job's body.

"This is what you want," Froggy said in a low voice, making sure that Julieta could not hear, "to watch me while I make love, while I sleep, and when I sit on the toilet. This is what you wanted..." And Froggy went on talking to himself.

Smiley was naked, looking up through the skylight as Saturn quickly passed over him, and instead Saturn focused on the kite that hung in the sky, following the string down to the hand that held it. The tug and pull of the line had chafed and burned Apolonio's hand, bringing him the pleasure Federico de la Fe often found in fire. The crop dusters circled and Apolonio lowered the kite, letting it rise once again when the planes landed. The Baby Nostradamus was safely strapped to Apolonio, exhausted from trying to hold the columns. He fell in and out of his nap, too weak to raise his shield of black, and for once Saturn was able to infiltrate into the Baby Nostradamus's consciousness.

The Baby Nostradamus was too tired to push Saturn out. Saturn had grown stronger, eclipsing the strength of Jupiter, and was cited in *Astronomy Today* as the most resentful and unforgiving of the planets and also as one of the saddest, second only to tiny Pluto. The journal wrongly speculated that Saturn was doomed to exile from the solar system.

But through the Baby Nostradamus Saturn saw his future and knew that he would remain; he would keep his orbit and even gain satellites. An old Froggy pointed his telescope into the galaxy, looking into the viewfinder with scorn, carefully tracking Saturn's phases on graph paper.

His EMF tattoo had faded into a faint bruise. And his hair, once dark as tar, had matured into silver and white. Julieta was with him, but her diseases of decay had returned, eroding her molars and wasting the cartilage of her knees. But still she knelt in her garden, plucking weeds and watering her flowers, tending to the plot of soil. The flower plantation had wilted and its furrows had eroded long ago. Julieta's garden was all that remained. The crop dusters had grown into a fleet of passenger planes flying under damaged and patched skies, shattered and torn by war and lost love and by the sharp blades of carnation knives.

The planes landed on an airstrip paved where flowers and sprinkler systems once grew. And at tower control, built on the exact spot where the weigh station used to stand, a small bleep on the radar screen puzzled traffic controllers. The next week the Federal Aviation Administration banned all kites and metallic balloons from the sky. When the ordinance was announced, Apolonio reeled in his kite and punched two holes through its sail and cut the tail. The Baby Nostradamus was still strapped to his back, but he had grown and when he stretched his prophetic feet—leaving prints of the future—it was the Baby Nostradamus who carried Apolonio. His steps were clumsy and he often fell, pinning Apolonio beneath him, falls that banged the Baby Nostradamus's head so hard that they hurt the future, shuffling chronologies. Predicting inventions that had long been in use and retelling a history of anachronisms: Dark Ages with electric lampposts and a Hellenist era ruled by the Kennedys of Massachusetts.

Sandra was not there to help Apolonio and the Baby Nostradamus stand up; she had left El Monte long ago. She had driven her truck to a town that had real hills but where the dirt was black and metallic, and as she disappeared into its valley she was thinking of Froggy and then was never seen again.

But word still came from her each spring. When the flowers bloomed in her new town, an envelope gilded in lead and written in metallic ink was delivered to the El Monte post office. The mailman quietly alerted Froggy about the arrival and Froggy excused himself, telling Julieta that he was going out to buy plant food; instead he walked to the post office and signed for the letter.

Each year Sandra's handwriting became smaller, her *i*'s nearly invisible in her late letters, but her sentences grew, stretching to the edge of the page. Froggy returned empty-handed with the letter folded in his back pocket and his carnation knife dulled by the lead envelope. But he never revealed what the letters said; it was his small way of triumphing over Saturn.

And one spring, the wettest on California record, no letter came, and in mourning Froggy spread tar across the letters of his neck and chewed all the flowers from the garden.

And then there was her, whose name was once cited on the dedication page and a hundred times over whispered into the ears of women who were not her. She lived five miles northwest of El Monte in a town that claimed to be the city of roses. She sat with ▄▄ on their painted porch swing. He was of meat, his skin wrinkled at the eyes and brow, but still she said, "▄▄, all these years and I still love you," and she touched his face with her paper hands.

Their tender moment was interrupted by their grandchildren, who came running up the lawn. The youngest, a girl of eight years, tripped and fell, but the grass did not stain her dress. She stood and walked up the steps and then sat between her grandmother and grandfather. Her name was Elizabeth, like her grandmother, and she carried an illustrated book of the galaxy. She opened the book to where the solar system spread over two pages; and there was Saturn with his rings glowing. Liz touched the page, telling her granddaughter the name of each planet.

"This is Mercury," she said, "and this is Venus..."

Finally touching Saturn, bringing a happiness that had not been felt for pages and pages.

"And this is Saturn."

Saturn concentrated on the future, staring at her finger and the way it seemed to hover the longest over the ringed planet, and then looked at her face, wondering what it would be like to touch her Gypsy hair again, to wake in her bed and taste her paper lips and write love letters complete with graphs and charts on her paper skin as she slept, so she would wake and say, "You wrote all this for me?" and Saturn would simply nod.

He thought about all these things, what it would be to make her coffee and build her bookshelves and to fight over things like lint traps and morning television shows.

And while Saturn thought about all these things, preoccupied with a future that would never be, no matter his strength, Little Merced helped Federico de la Fe button his Pendleton shirt and pack his bag. Together they walked out of their stucco, through the softest of all lawns, and Little Merced, who still stunk of dead fish, raised her parasol, shading her and her father. They walked south and off the page, leaving no footprints that Saturn could track. There would be no sequel to the sadness.

ACKNOWLEDGMENTS

La Familia: Mama y Papa, whose sacrifices and hard work made everything possible. My lil' sis, Betty, who is a better sister than I am brother. Los Abuelos de la Tortuga and Juchitlan, who started the story. Las Tías and Tíos, who kept them going.

A debt to my hometown and the Monte mob—the whole gang, but especially to the Durfee Junior High crew: Sergio "the beast" Cabrera, Tony Villalobos, Mario Ortiz, Herlim Li, who's been like a brother, the Frank Wrighters: Freddy Zamora, Peter "Boo" Gallardo, and Mindy Hung. And of course the futbol bola: Chupacabras F.C. and Monte United.

A bit south and to the east in Whittier: Michael Garabedian, Sarah Tillman, and Matthew Stuart. All three indispensable in ways that they would not imagine.

East and into cold weather: Christian TeBordo, Adam Levin, my big sis Cheryl Strayed, who taught me much more than pretty sentences, Christopher Boucher, and Chris Kennedy.

Los Maestros, in varying geographies: Mr. Santiago, Tim O'Rourke, Les Howard, David Paddy, Arthur Flowers, George Saunders, and Mary Caponegro.

Under sunny skies and palm trees: my two platonic crushes Marija Cetinic and Bridget Hoida; and on 6th and Main, Ali Mazarei and Allan Mason.

In the bay: Eli Horowitz, whose keen insight and margin scribbles transformed this mess of a novel into something much shinier.

Much gratitude to the Paul and Daisy Soros Foundation for New Americans for its generous support. It should be noted that the foundation never recanted its support and that without its kindness the completion of this book would not have been possible.

And to those that may not be named.

ABOUT THE AUTHOR

Salvador Plascencia was born in Guadalajara, Mexico, and now lives in Los Angeles. He is a graduate of Whittier College and holds an MFA from Syracuse University. *The People of Paper* is his first novel.